PATRICK LEE

The
Breach

HARPER

An Imprint of HarperCollinsPublishers

HARPER

An Imprint of HarperCollins*Publishers*
10 East 53rd Street
New York, New York 10022-5299

Copyright © 2010 by Patrick Lee
Excerpt from *Ghost Country* copyright © 2010 by Patrick Lee
ISBN 978-0-06-158445-9

First Harper paperback printing: January 2010
First Harper special printing: August 2009

HarperCollins ® and Harper ® are registered trademarks of Harper-Collins Publishers.

Printed in the United States of America

Visit Harper paperbacks on the World Wide Web at
www.harpercollins.com

10   9   8   7

So what the hell had happened here?

What else was normal in Paige's world? What capabilities did her enemies have? What were they up against?

A sound broke the moment. The last sound he wanted to hear. Rotors. This was it, then. Two minutes from now, he and Paige would be dragged from the building, onto the aircraft, and then they'd be winding through the valleys at low level, probably on nobody's radar. Maybe these people would have drugs and instruments to keep Paige alive for a while, then wake her up for a new marathon of agony.

Unless he killed her first.

There might just be time. Could he make that choice? Logic, hard and clear, told him he'd regret it sorely if he didn't.

With the indecision came hatred, more bitter than he'd felt in years. Hatred of these people for pushing him to the edge of this decision.

And then the chopper exploded.

By Patrick Lee

THE BREACH

Coming Soon

GHOST COUNTRY

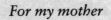

For my mother

Acknowledgments

The following people I can't thank enough, but here goes. Janet Reid, the hardest-working agent in the business, who may have taken that "city that never sleeps" thing literally when she moved to New York. My editor at Harper-Collins, Sarah Durand, who saw what this story needed to be, and made all the difference in guiding it through the transition.

Thank you to Emily Krump and all the very cool people at HarperCollins, for more hard work than I can shake an acknowledgements page at.

PART I

BLACKBIRD

CHAPTER ONE

O n the first anniversary of his release from prison, Travis Chase woke at four in the morning to bright sunlight framing his window blinds. He put his backpack in his Explorer, left Fairbanks on State Route 2, and an hour later was on the hard-packed gravel of the Dalton Highway, running north toward the Arctic Circle and the Brooks Range beyond. From the crests of the highest hills, he could see the road and the pipeline snaking ahead for miles, over lesser ridges and through valleys blazing with pink fireweed.

The trip was not a celebration. Far from it. It was a deliberation on everything that mattered: where he stood, and where he would go from here.

The console showed an outside temperature of fifty-nine degrees. Travis lowered the windows and let the moist air rush through the vehicle. The height of summer here smelled like springtime back in Minneapolis, the scent of damp grass just freed from snow cover.

He reached Coldfoot at ten o'clock and stopped

for lunch. The town, with a few buildings and a population of less than twenty, survived entirely on commerce from travelers on the Dalton. Mostly truckers bound for the oil field at Prudhoe Bay, 250 miles north. Coldfoot was the last glimpse of humanity along the highway, before the elevation divide and the long, downslope run to the sea.

Travis wouldn't be going that far. The mountains he'd come for were right here. To the west of town, Gates of the Arctic National Park followed the range in a two-hundred-mile arc to the southwest. There were no roads leading in—no foot trails, even. All hiking in the Brooks Range was back-country, though various websites and published guides detailed the most trusted and trafficked routes. Travis had studied them all, then plotted his own course to avoid them.

He left the Explorer at the depot, filled his water pouches, strapped on his pack and was on his way before eleven. By the time he stopped for dinner—a freeze-dried packet of brown rice he cooked over his tiny propane burner—he'd reached the top of the first ridge, two thousand feet above town. To the south, the last seventy miles of the morning's journey receded toward infinity—back toward the world, and the places between which he had to choose.

Alaska or Minnesota?

There was pressure to go back home, of course. Pressure from everyone he knew there. He'd only been out of prison a month when he'd bought his one-way ticket to Fairbanks; some of his relatives hadn't even gotten the chance to see him. What future did he see for himself up north, two thousand miles from his family?

What future did he see among them? Even to the few who could understand and forgive what he'd done, he would always be the brother who'd spent half of his twenties and all of his thirties in prison. Twenty years from now, in the eyes of the next generation, he would still be that guy. That uncle. You could only get so free.

He pushed on to the next ridge before making camp for the night. What passed for night, anyway: a few hours of cooling twilight as the sun dipped through the haze toward, but not quite to, the northern horizon. He staked his tent into the soft earth beside a snowfield that planed away for miles across the upper face of the ridge, and sat outside for an hour waiting for sleep to settle over him.

Maybe five miles to the west—distance was tricky up here—a stony ridge rose higher than the foothills he'd crossed so far. In the long light he thought he saw shadows flitting on the face of the rock. He took out his binoculars, steadied them on his knees, and scanned the ridge for over a minute before he saw them: Dall sheep, twenty or more, moving with spooky ease across a nearly vertical granite face. Lambs no more than two months old followed their mothers with sure-footed skill. Travis watched until they vanished behind a fold of the cliff wall.

At last feeling a calming heaviness in his limbs,

he climbed into his tent and sleeping bag, and faded away to the rustle of wind over the short grass.

He woke with a quickened pulse, aware that something had startled him, but unable to tell what, exactly.

The sunlight through the tent fabric was stronger. His watch showed that it was just past three in the morning. He blinked, trying to fully wake up, and then the treble range of a thunderclap crashed across the ridgeline. Seconds later the bass wave shook the ground, seeming to radiate directly from the mountain beneath him.

Relaxing, he sank into his bag again, and rubbed his eyes. Silent lightning flashed, brighter on the west face of the tent than elsewhere. He measured the seconds on his watch and counted thirty-five before the accompanying thunder reached him; the storm was seven miles away.

Sleep began to draw him down again, even as the storm intensified. He found a strange comfort in the sound of it, a lullaby suited to this hard and unforgiving place. Within minutes the lightning and thunder were much closer, and almost continuous.

Just before he slipped over the edge of consciousness, he heard something in the storm that made him open his eyes again. He turned an ear to the west. What had it been? It really hadn't sounded like thunder at all. It'd been more like a scream, though not human or even animal. More than anything, it'd reminded him of the rending of sheet metal in the prison drill shop. Well, that was it,

then. Just his own ghosts troubling him at the brink
of sleep. They were persistent, but he'd learned to
ignore them.

He closed his eyes again and drifted off.

Three nights later, Travis set up camp thirty-six
miles from Coldfoot, though the wandering route
he'd taken, displayed on his GPS unit, added up to
just over forty-nine. He ate his heated pouch of en-
chilada soup—all these freeze-dried meals tasted
more like the pouches they came in than what was
written on them—on the rim of a steep-walled
valley some six hundred feet deep. Its floor, broad
and flat, extended relatively straight toward the
northwest for what had to be three miles.

A cloud bank churned through the valley like a
smoky river, swirling around outcroppings of rock
and pooling in the deepest places. Directly beneath
Travis, the valley floor was completely obscured,
though for a few moments when the sun's lateral
rays shone straight along its length, he saw the
sparkle of something underneath the fog. Water,
or maybe ice.

He slept easily, waking only twice, not to thunder but to the howling of wolves. He had no idea
how far away they might be, though at times they
seemed no more distant than a quarter of a mile.
He'd read that wolf packs randomized the volume
of their howling in order to confuse prey—and
other wolves—as to their distance. It worked on
humans, too.

At six in the morning he woke, opened the tent

flap and sat up into crisp air, colder than it'd been the night before. The visible horizon extended farther than it had at any time during the trip.

Alaska or Minnesota?

He'd come here to answer that question. He'd failed, so far.

The pros and cons of each place cycled through his mind of their own accord. Home was family, friends. For all the judgment they could never hide, they would always be more accepting of his past than strangers would. Home was his brother, Jeff, offering to let him in on the software business he was starting out of his house, and show him the ropes from the beginning.

Home was also a place full of ghosts, every street in the old neighborhood sagging under the weight of troubled memories.

Alaska was this. This perfect emptiness that made no claim to understand his character one way or the other, and no effort to push him back into old grooves. In his move to Fairbanks he'd brought along nothing. Not even himself, it sometimes seemed. He wouldn't have believed it even a year before, in his first days of freedom, but up here he sometimes went a whole day without thinking about prison, or what he'd done to put himself there. Up here, sometimes, he just wasn't that guy anymore. And damned if that sensation wasn't getting stronger by the month.

All of that would end, the hour he set foot in his old world again.

For that reason, if for no other, he thought he knew which way he was leaning.

He unzipped his bag, pulled on his pants and boots, and swung his feet out onto the ground. The grass, soft the night before, now crunched beneath his treads. He stood and stretched, then knelt and took from his backpack his propane burner and metal cup. A moment later the blue flame was hissing beneath the water for his coffee. Waiting for it, he wandered to the drop-off overlooking the valley, its depths now revealed in the crystal air.

He stopped.

For a moment he could only stare, too disoriented even to blink.

On the valley floor lay the wreck of a Boeing 747.

CHAPTER TWO

Travis packed everything within ninety seconds, including the tent. He set off along the valley's rim at a sprint.

How could it be here?

How could it be here without choppers hovering over it, and a hundred rescue specialists armed with acetylene torches and schematics cutting carefully into the fuselage in a dozen places?

How could it be here alone?

The valley wall below his campsite had been too steep to descend, but half a mile northwest he could see a concavity where it shallowed to something like a forty-degree incline. Still steep as hell. He'd have to be careful to avoid going ass over pack all the way down, breaking every limb in the process. A lot of help he'd be to survivors then, if there were any.

As for help, he was it, at least for now. He had no means to call anyone. The cell phone in his pack had become useless forty miles out of Fairbanks, and his CB—the preferred mode of communication on the Dalton Highway—was thirty-six miles away, in the parking lot of the Brooks Lodge and Fuel Depot.

As he made his way along the precipice, his eyes hardly strayed from the impossible vision below.

The pilots had tried to land—that much was clear. The wreck lay pointing down the length of the valley as if it were a runway. Behind where it had come to rest, deep furrows were gouged into the earth for more than three hundred yards. Halfway along this scarred path lay the starboard wing, sheared from the plane by a stony pillar that had weathered the impact just fine. At the torn wing stub jutting from the fuselage, where fuel and scraping metal must have converged, only blind luck had prevented an inferno: the remainder of the plane's long skid had taken place across a snowfield that covered the valley floor.

The rest of the craft was intact, more or less. The tail fin had snapped and lay draped on the port-side stabilizer like a broken limb held on by skin alone. The fuselage had buckled in three places, wiring and insulation curling from foot-wide vertical ruptures. Through these openings Travis could see only darkness inside the plane, though at this distance even a brightly lit interior would have shown him nothing.

He saw no movement in or around the wreck, and no sign that there'd been any. Nobody had dragged supplies out of the plane and set up shelter in the open. Had they simply sheltered in the fuselage? Were they too injured to move at all?

Distance and perspective made it pointless to

look for footprints. The snowfield, glazed by the temperature drop, was almost blinding to look at, and from six hundred feet above it offered no contrast. There was no way to tell if anyone had left the wreck to hike out in search of help.

Help. That notion brought him back to the situation's most confusing aspect. How did a 747 crash without anyone coming to its aid for—how long? Jesus, how long had this thing been here?

Three days. The metal shriek in the thunderstorm came back to him with clarity. He'd heard the damn thing crash.

Three days, and nobody had found the wreckage. Nobody had even come looking—at no point during his hike had he heard the drone of a search plane or the rattle of helicopter rotors. He couldn't square it. This wasn't a single-prop Cessna that had taken off without a flight plan and disappeared. Airliners had redundant communication systems: high-powered radio, two-way satellite, and probably a couple other kinds he didn't even know about. Even if all of those instruments had failed, the tower at Fairbanks International would have logged the plane's last known position. There should have been an army looking for it within the hour.

Travis reached the inlet in the valley wall, a grassy funnel that extended to the flat bottom below. The slope was more severe than he'd supposed, but there was nothing kinder for miles in either direction. Tackling it in a straight line to the bottom would be suicide, even here, but a sidelong transit looked feasible. He stepped onto the grade and found its surface to be as obliging as he could have hoped for: soft enough to allow traction without yielding in a muddy slide. He found that if he leaned into the hillside and braced a hand on the grass, he could make good progress without risking his balance.

Fifteen minutes later, sprinting hell-bent alongside one of the gouges in the valley floor—up close, the torn furrow was deep and wide enough for a Humvee to drive in—he passed the starboard wing, flung like a broken piece of a toy against the formation that had severed it.

He crossed onto the snowfield and was immediately enveloped by the smell of jet fuel. The snow was saturated with it. Every depression his boots made in the surface instantly pooled with the pink liquid.

The airliner was less than a football field ahead now, pointed away down the valley and rotated a few degrees counterclockwise, so that its left side—with the wing intact—was more visible than the right.

So far, no tracks in the snow.

Ahead, the tail loomed over the valley floor, four stories above Travis's head, even with its fin broken. The aircraft lay canted to the left by the weight of the port-side wing, both engines of which were submerged in the deep snow. He passed the tail and stopped ten yards shy of the wing, between the twin ruts carved by the engines' passing.

All three of the fuselage ruptures he'd seen from

his campsite were on this side of the plane. The nearest, just steps away, was wide enough to admit him. Even from here, the darkness beyond the tear was featureless. The windows were even less help: tilted downward, they offered only a reflection of the snow.

Travis inhaled deeply and shouted, "Is anyone there?"

His echo came back in distinct bounces. There was no other reply.

He went to the opening, tested the strength of the metal on both sides of it, and pulled himself into the plane.

It wasn't an airliner.

CHAPTER THREE

Row upon row of instrument stations filled the space Travis had entered, a claustrophobic version of NASA's mission control that extended from the tail of the plane to a bulkhead thirty feet forward of his position. Swivel chairs were bolted to the floor at each terminal; everything else in the room lay in ruins, heaped against the left wall, the low end of the tilt.

The smell of fuel, still intense, gave way to something fresher. Familiar, too. In the close darkness, speared by shafts of window glare that only made seeing harder, he identified the scent just a breath before he saw its source.

Blood. Pooled beneath the tumble of debris. Pooled beneath his feet.

His stomach constricted; he turned to the rupture in the wall, thrust his head outside for fresh air and got a lungful of fuel vapor. It helped. Forcing control, his breathing shallow, he pulled back inside.

He held up a hand against the glare and scrutinized the disarray for what he knew must be there.

He saw them immediately.

A dozen bodies lay among the debris.

Atop the debris, actually. Which was strange.

He moved closer, saw the reason for it, and felt ice in his stomach where the nausea had just been. They hadn't died in the crash. Each victim had taken two bullets to the temple, tightly clustered.

Travis went still and listened for movement aboard the wreck. Logic told him the killer, or killers, couldn't possibly still be aboard. The plane had been down for three days. The killings had probably happened soon after. There would be no reason for the shooters to stay with the aircraft, and every reason to get away from it.

He listened for another ten seconds anyway, and heard nothing but wind scouring the valley and moaning in the cracks along the fuselage. A hymn for the dead.

He returned his eyes to them. They wore uniforms: black pants and crisp blue shirts, not necessarily military, but a long way from casual. The clothing was devoid of insignia or indication of rank. Even their nationality could only be narrowed by degrees: nine of the dead were white, three black. Seven male, five female. Their ages were hard to tell because of the bloating, but Travis guessed they ranged from thirty to fifty.

Now an obvious aspect of the plane's exterior occurred to him, one he'd overlooked amid the clamor of more pressing observations: the outside of the aircraft was completely blank. He hadn't seen even a tail number.

What was this thing?

He'd watched enough middle-of-the-night programming on the Discovery Channel to know the government maintained special aircraft for dire situations—flying backups, in case command hubs like the Pentagon were taken out in a first strike. "Doomsday planes," they were called. Billions of tax dollars, which, God willing, would remain wasted forever.

But if this was a doomsday plane, wasn't it that much more improbable that no one had found it?

Well, someone *had* found it, hadn't they?

Travis rose and swept another gaze across the executed bodies and the machines they'd manned.

A thousand questions. No answers.

No need for any, either.

This was none of his business, and there was no helping these people. That was it, then. Time to go. Time to head back to Coldfoot and tell the good folks at the burger shop he'd had a nice, uneventful hike.

He returned to the tear in the outer wall, glancing forward as he went, his now adjusted eyes taking in the space beyond the door in the forward bulkhead. A corridor lay there, stretching a hundred feet toward the nose of the plane, windows on one side and doors on the other.

He'd already slipped his head and one shoulder out of the plane by the time his mind processed what he'd just seen in the hallway.

He shut his eyes hard, though not because of the glare from the snowfield. For maybe ten seconds he hesitated, willing his body to keep moving, to put the corpses and the plane and the whole fucking valley behind him. One quick drop to the snow would seal the decision. His legs would take over from there.

Instead he withdrew his head into the plane again, and turned to face the corridor.

A punctuated blood trail, nearly invisible on the black floor of the equipment room, led onto the beige hallway carpet and stretched fifty feet farther to a doorway on the right, where it turned in. Bloody handprints flanked a heavier trail in the middle. Not drag marks. Crawl marks.

Travis went to the threshold of the corridor. Four doors opened off the right wall, facing the Plexiglas-covered windows on the other side. The blood trail went in at the third. A fifth door capped the far end of the hall, probably leading to the stairwell, then the upper deck and the cockpit.

The bloodstains in the carpet were brown, long since dried; the pooled blood in the room behind him had only remained viscous because there were gallons of it. If the attack had followed on the heels of the crash, then the wounded survivor had been dying in that room up the hall for three long days. No chance of survival.

But it would take only a minute to be sure. Travis stepped into the corridor.

The first doorway was haloed by a constellation of bullet holes, which seemed to have been made from both inside and outside the room, at chest and head level.

Travis came abreast of the open doorway. Two dead men lay against the far wall, downed behind an executive desk they'd upended for cover. Wearing crew cuts, black suits and ties, they looked like Secret Service agents—or, Travis thought, just about any high-level security personnel. They'd been dropped with shots to the chest and neck, then executed for good measure like the victims in the aft section.

Unlike the aft victims, however, these two had been armed. And still were.

It'd been a very long time since Travis had held a gun, and he'd been well out of the loop on modern firearms during his extended stay with the Minnesota Corrections Department, but he easily recognized the M16 variants that lay beside the dead men.

He crossed to the nearest of the weapons and lifted it. The translucent magazine still held about half of what Travis guessed was a thirty-round capacity. Leaning the rifle against the desk, he inspected the second weapon's clip, found it nearly full, and ejected it. In the coat pockets of the two dead men he found another full magazine each. They had nothing else on them, including identification. Pocketing the ammunition, he took the rifle in hand and proceeded to the next room along the hall.

What he found there gave him a longer pause than the bodies had.

Centered in the space was a three-foot-wide cube of solid steel, cut in half across its waist and hinged. At the moment it lay open; two heavy-duty chainfalls hanging from I-beam rails on the ceiling had been needed to get it that way. Carved into the exposed inner face of each half of the cube, right in the middle, was a square depression perhaps four by four inches across and two deep. If the cube were closed, those twin spaces would form a single cavity at its core, large enough to hold a softball, and surrounded in every direction by more than a foot of steel.

Whatever had required this much protection was gone.

On the side of the cube was a metal plate with simple black lettering:

BREACH ENTITY 0247—"WHISPER"
CLASS-A PROTOCOLS APPLY
SPECIAL INSTRUCTION FOR THIS ENTITY—
NO PERSON SHALL
REMAIN WITHIN FIVE (5) FEET
OF EXPOSED ENTITY FOR LONGER THAN
TWO (2) CONSECUTIVE MINUTES.

Something about the steel around the core space of the cube caught Travis's eye. He stepped in for a closer look, but almost immediately wished he hadn't. In both halves of the cube, the metal directly around the central cavity was discolored to a dirty blue. The grain of the steel itself had been warped there, pushed outward as if by some unimaginably powerful and patient force.

His mind suddenly full of the frantic rattle of a Geiger counter in the red, Travis retreated from the room. He realized only once he reached the hall that he'd been holding his breath.

He turned in the corridor—not toward the third room but back the way he'd come from. The bright crack in the fuselage wall was just twenty paces away. If he stared at it much longer, he'd find himself slipping through it.

Then, angry at himself, he pivoted and made for the third doorway. This was going to be simple:

He'd find the victim dead and cold.

He'd wipe his prints from the M16.

He'd leave the plane and put three mountains between it and himself, and then he'd brew his goddamned coffee like he'd set out to do.

He was certain of all that until he walked through the third doorway, and then he was certain of nothing.

The victim was dead and cold. But this was not going to be simple.

CHAPTER FOUR

Travis had experienced the surreal before:
moments as impossible to accept as they
were to deny. What he found inside the third
room took him back to one of those, the feeling
channeling the past like an obscure scent not en-
countered in years. Sterile courtroom. Strobing
fluorescent lights reflected on the narrow windows, all closed except one. Through the open
window, the sound of a girl laughing, somewhere
down the block in another reality far from this
room and this judge and this sentence. He'd expected it, of course, and deserved much worse,
but the gut punch of the moment had swayed him
anyway: twenty-five years old, and he would be in
his forties the next time he saw a night sky.

Here was a moment as difficult to grasp.

Here was the First Lady of the United States,
dead with her eyes open, looking right through
him, seated against the wall with a bloody notebook page in her hand.

Ellen Garner. Beautiful even now. Her features,
always pale and delicate, had hardly been altered

by the loss of her blood, which had soaked into the carpet around her. A single bullet had punctured her abdomen.

Beside her lay something that looked like an early-model car phone, a bulky handset connected by a black spiral cord to a suitcase. It could only be a satellite unit. Dried bloody fingerprints told the story: Mrs. Garner had crawled here from the tail just to get this thing, had taken it from its wall cabinet, found it damaged, and exposed its wires and boards in a wasted attempt to fix it.

Travis set the M16 aside and went to her. He knelt and gently took the paper from her fingertips, which death had long since stiffened, and read:

I hope that someone from Tangent finds this. If you are anyone else, do not contact local authorities. Go to a phone as quickly as you can, dial 112–289–0713. Ignore the consulting firm recording and enter 42551 at any time. A human will answer. Tell him/her that Box Kite is down at 67.4065 north, 151.5031 west. All dead except for two captives, taken by seven hostiles. Hostiles have almost certainly encamped within a few miles of this location—Tangent will know why, and will know what to do.

Two blank lines followed, and then the text continued. Here the writing was faint, wandering up and down over the light blue lines, written by a much weaker hand.

I know we are down somewhere remote. Have to assume now it is so remote, will not be found for days, and whoever finds this will be days from phone. Crash happened at 3:05 a.m. local time 26 June. If you find me more than two days after, if telephone is very far away, then ignore above message. Not enough time to call Tangent.

Hostiles are torturing our two people for info within close range of this crash, they will not leave area until they have broken them. (Not a guess, there is a reason they can't leave before then.) Do not know how long our people will withstand them before breaking. Days I think, but I don't know.

I am failing quickly—no way I can detail what is at stake. It affects you, whoever is reading this. It affects everyone. It's bad. I understand that you won't think you can do this, but I am asking you to kill these people.

Arms locker at aft wall of upper cabin, combo 021602. M16 rifles inside, can do full auto. Kill everyone. Most important to kill our people, captives, even if you fail to kill all hostiles. Kill captives first. I am sorry to ask this.

Another gap, and then a last passage, this portion so faint that Travis had to tilt the page toward the light.

PS—If you kill them all don't go near the thing they have taken, three-inch sphere, dark blue, just get away and call Tangent.

Travis read the full page over again. By the time he'd finished, he felt a chill his heavy coat couldn't keep out. He noticed a second slip of paper just visible in the pocket of Mrs. Garner's shirt. He withdrew it and unfolded it. There were only a few lines.

Richard,

I'm fading in and out a lot, and when I'm out, I'm back in the dorms, back in Room 712 under that quilt with you, watching the snow over the law quad. Lucky life, spent with the only one I ever loved.

Ellen

Feeling like a trespasser, Travis carefully refolded the note and returned it to her pocket, exactly as it had been.

He stood, and saw for the first time the ground outside the starboard windows, above where Ellen sat. Here at last were the footprints. And ATV tracks. Though they terminated at the edge of the snowfield, forty yards away, there was little doubt which way they led.

CHAPTER FIVE

Paige Campbell stared up at the pines and tried to slip into dream lucidity. She'd managed it twice so far, for maybe a minute each time—not much, all things considered, a few crumbs of peace, but oh Christ, they were worth it. Even as something to look forward to, they helped.

She wouldn't need them to look forward to, of course, if she could just move her head a few inches. Raise it up from the tabletop, then bring it down again as hard as she could, crack open the back of her skull and rupture something, anything. Three or four solid whacks, before the rat-faced man could stop her, and then she'd be gone.

Why was that asking too much? Why was it a pipe dream just to want the chance to die?

Because the rat-faced man was good at his job; that was why. Because her head was strapped fast to the wood, like every other part of her. Even her tongue had been clamped to her teeth, to keep her from biting through it and choking on her own blood.

So instead she tried for dream lucidity. It was

magic when it worked. All at once no pain, no straps, no clearing in the freezing daylight that never ended. The dream places were familiar, safe. The first one had been the reading nook in her living room. She hadn't read anything there in the dream; she'd just walked through the space, barefoot on the stone tiles, and run her hand over the soft fabric of the chair.

The second place had been the beach at Carmel, pushing her fingers down into the sand, past the baked surface to where it was cool. She hadn't been there in years, but the memory of it came back in high definition now.

The opportunities to slip away were rare. It was only possible when the drug started to wear off, in the last five or ten minutes before they injected her again. If she wasn't careful they'd catch on, and start injecting her sooner. That meant closing her eyes was a no-no, as much as it would have eased the way into dreamland. She'd just have to get there with them open, but that was fine. She'd done it both times.

One trick was to stare at the pines instead of the sky. The light was less intense that way, maybe half the effect of letting her eyelids fall shut.

This time around, though, none of it was working. Too many distractions. The rat-faced man and one of the others were arguing just a few feet away, jabbering machine-gun fast in their language. Once upon a time Paige had loved the sound of that language, had considered minoring in it, going abroad for two semesters to immerse herself in it, and had moped for months when her academic path had swung her away from that option. Now, she thought, if she had a big red button in front of her that would magically tear the tongue out of every man, woman, and child on the planet who spoke it, she'd break her hand on that button.

If her hand wasn't strapped to a fucking table.

The argument ended, and here came the rat-faced man's footsteps again. Here came the needle again. No dreamland this time.

Here came the tears, too, even before the injection and the resumption of the pain. She hated that she couldn't stop herself, hated having ceded that much control to these people.

Her body jerked when the needle touched the skin beside her navel. Then it was inside her, and though the effect would take several minutes to set in, she could feel the drug itself blooming cold and sharp across her stomach.

The pines blurred and swam, her body shaking hard now and jarring the tears. The baffle across her mouth—there to rein in her screams, which might carry unusually far in these mountains—did not prevent her from hearing her own voice, pleading no, over and over like a mantra. She couldn't stop that, either.

Now came the rattle of the crank under the table, the surface pitching over sideways until it was almost vertical, her body no longer resting on it but held by the straps.

Looking sideways now instead of up.

Looking right into her father's eyes.

His own straps held him immobile against the base of the nearest pine, his head trapped between the blocks of the casing that kept him from looking anywhere but straight at her.

Her tears spilled out sideways. His remained pooled in his eyes.

Then the rat-faced man moved out of view behind her, and got ready to work on her, the same way he'd done it each time. She could never see for herself what he was doing, but her father's expression reflected what it must look like better than any mirror could have.

She could picture it, of course. It couldn't have been more obvious what was happening to her. The very first time—something like three days ago now, just after the rat-faced man had strapped her down—he'd opened her upper arm with a scalpel and parted her triceps wide with a wedge clamp. He'd avoided damaging the artery, of course; it wouldn't do to let death rescue her that easily. His prize had been the radial nerve, thick as a pencil once he'd freed it from its lubricated sheath beside the bone. After that, he'd been able to access it immediately each time.

He was about to do that now, making a big show of his preparations. She was sure it was part of the torture, the psychological aspect of it, all the cues to whet her anticipation of the pain: the zipper of his tool bag opening slowly, the clucking sound of his tongue, like he was sad to have to be doing this, and then the sigh.

Now her father's eyes moved, because the rat-faced man was looking at him before beginning.

"What kind of daddy you being, then?" the rat-faced man said, his English broken, lyrical. "How you expect you look yourself in the mirror after this? How you let your little girl get hurt this long?"

Then the high-pitched laugh, rapid-fire, like a squirrel chittering.

Her father's eyes hardened and looked away from the man, meeting hers again, his tears over-running now.

This was supposed to be part of the torture too, obviously: making them lock eyes while he hurt her. Maybe it worked on some people, but they'd miscalculated sorely in this case. Her father's eyes were all that made this bearable for her.

Of course, the point of the eye contact wasn't its effect on her. The eye contact was for him. He was the one they were trying to break.

Was it working? Was it breaking him?

No, not a chance of that. Why had she gone through all of this, if he was only going to submit in the end?

More to the point, he was just stronger than that. Of that much Paige was certain. Her father knew the stakes, which were bigger than this clearing and anything that might be done to them in it. Telling these people how to switch on the Whisper was simply not on the list of options. End of debate.

Blinking through her tears, she tried to look strong, tried to send him assurance. It was all okay. Really, it was okay, even now when she was shaking like this, and so fucking scared, even as she could hear the rat-faced man rummaging in his bag and bringing out the tool, her tears intensifying because any second it was coming, even now, she had to send him the will to bear watching this, because giving them what they wanted was so much worse—

The tool snapped to life with its grating hum, and a second later its teeth closed around the exposed nerve, and the image of her father shattered like a reflection on broken water as she screamed.

Travis lay very still on the rock shelf and tried to recall the mind-set of a killer. It was far back along the corridor of years, where he'd meant to leave it forever.

Until now.

Through his binoculars he watched the little guy with the string mustache move the instrument back and forth inside the young woman's arm. Even through the muffling attachment she had across her mouth, Travis could hear her screams. His perch was perhaps a hundred fifty yards from the encampment, and seventy feet above.

Seven hostiles. Two captives.

The surreal fabric of the situation still enveloped Travis, as it had since the moment he'd found Mrs. Garner. Who the hell were these people? What was all of this about?

Even when he focused past the disconnect, and forced himself to take stock of the circumstances he was up against, questions remained. Why had the hostiles chosen to remain here? How could they consider themselves safe less than three miles from the wreck of a 747 that had carried the First Lady of the United States? Not to mention whatever had been in the steel container. Why stay near the crash for even a single hour, much less three days? Mrs. Garner had said in her note that there was a reason for that, but hadn't expanded upon it.

Well, the plane hadn't been found by any of the authorities who must be looking for it, including, presumably, the president. Somehow these guys had pulled that off—their confidence in their safety must stem from that. They hadn't even posted a lookout. For now, it was enough to know that Mrs. Garner had been right: these guys were not expecting trouble.

He could get them all from here. Easily. Skill was simply not a variable from this range and elevation, and with these weapons—he'd brought five M16s, their selectors set to full-auto. Anyone who could douse a flower bed with a garden hose could kill all nine people in that encampment from this spot, probably before firing the first two rifles dry. Certainly by the fifth.

Yes, he could do that. He could do that right now and have it done with.

But he wasn't going to.

In truth, he hadn't squared with that part of Ellen Garner's message, whatever the unmentioned stakes might be, but if even a scrap of the idea had lingered in his mind, it had vanished the moment he'd trained his binoculars upon the young woman on the torture table.

He wasn't going to kill her. He'd accrued enough of that brand of guilt for one lifetime.

But he was going to kill.

He continued watching String Mustache enjoy his work, while the young woman's body spasmed in the binds, and he found the killer's mind-set coming back to him easily.

He could do this.

He just needed to get closer.

His footsteps are the only sound in the night, and they don't carry far.

For this time of year in Minneapolis, the day has been warm and wet, but in the past hour—the hour before midnight—a chill has moved in on the city, stirring wraiths of fog into the graveyard quiet of Cedar Street.

This deep in the neighborhood, there are no streetlights. Some of those who carve out their lives here prefer it that way. Tonight, so does Travis Chase. It is dark enough that he presents neither shadow nor silhouette, and his shoes make only faint ticks on the broken pavement. The only things in the night sharp enough to sense his presence are those things wilder than himself—even as he thinks this, a dog chain rattles softly on a porch, somewhere in the fog to his left—but his business on Cedar Street at this hour doesn't concern such things. His approach will not be detected by anyone that matters.

The .32 is in his pocket, loaded with hollowpoints.

Ahead of him the fog thins, and he sees the house. Emily Price's house. The only light comes from the big living-room window, casting its shape out into the mist.

He can picture the two of them inside, maybe sitting on the couch, holding each other close and saying little or nothing. When he thinks of that, Travis's shame burns.

He has no idea what will happen when he knocks on the door.

CHAPTER SIX

Travis saw within minutes what it would take. A lot could go wrong, but he thought the advantage was his, even against these numbers.

On the far side of the encampment, fifty feet beyond, the pines were dense. More than heavy enough to conceal him. He could reach that spot undetected if he traveled far enough along the valley on this side, low among the rocks, before crossing over and coming back.

Fifty feet was close, and with surprise on his side he might do well to just start shooting. The first shot would be a free kill, maybe even the second. Then it'd be him against five, and confusion on their part might give him the edge for another kill or two, if he was fast enough.

But the ifs would stack up quickly then. Those left standing would reach cover. If even two of them found safe positions from which to return fire, he'd be in trouble. Most likely he'd be dead.

Surprise wouldn't be enough. He needed misdirection. He needed them looking exactly away from where he'd be firing from. He needed them looking at the place where he lay right now.

The idea came to him quickly, probably because he had so little material to work with.

He leaned one of the M16s against a waist-high fallen rock, and took from his backpack one of the nylon bags that held a single change of his clothes. He dumped the clothes back into the pack, and hung the empty bag—nearly weightless now—by its drawstrings from the M16's trigger.

Then he set a full water pouch atop the rock, and made a pinprick hole in it with his knife. What came out wasn't even a fine stream, but just a ceaseless drip, which he positioned to fall directly into the nylon bag. Designed to keep water out, the bag would keep it in just as well. When it held enough, and weighed enough, this gun would fire its entire clip into the sky.

Peter Campbell was going to break.

He kept his eyes locked on Paige's as she cried, while the stringy little shit with the whiskers continued probing inside her arm with the nerve actuator. From time to time she would narrow her eyes and manage the slightest shake of her head within the strap, her message unmistakable: don't.

But he would. Had to. He'd been in denial about it for hours, though he'd only just now begun to recognize it.

These people had simply won. Help was not coming—would not be coming for days and days, if even then. Drummond had seen to that.

Drummond. He'd broken, hadn't he? And under what pressure? Nothing like what these past three days had been. As Peter understood it, the man had gotten a call from his wife, crying somewhere with a gun to her head. Almost anyone in the world would have caved to that, but Tangent operators were supposed to be stronger. That was one of the key attributes they were selected for, and Peter would have bet his life on Stuart Drummond's integrity. In fact, he had. And he'd lost.

It was little solace that everyone else had trusted Drummond too—trusted him supremely. Who else would have been tapped to fly a plane carrying some of Tangent's highest-ranking people, along with the most dangerous object ever to come out of the Breach? But the flight—coming from Tokyo and bound for Wind Creek, in Wyoming, where the object would have been secured forever—had made an unscheduled course change somewhere over the Aleutians. Drummond had murdered the rest of the flight crew, then depressurized the plane without releasing the oxygen masks. Finally he'd taken the jumbo jet down to pelican height—somewhere in there, overriding the damn safeties to keep the interior pressure equivalent to high altitude—and gone north into Alaska below radar.

Peter and the others had revived to the metal screams of the aircraft coming to rest God knew where, rejuvenating air at last flooding the plane through the broken fuselage.

Even as they'd heard the ATV engines closing in from outside, Drummond's voice had come over the comm, so hysterical he could barely speak. Peter had made out fragments of the apology and the story of Drummond's abducted wife, and then he'd caught one final phrase before the man killed himself.

The final phrase—*Ink Burst*—had unnerved him more than the gunshot that ended the transmission.

Just like that, he'd understood that hope was lost. Ink Burst—a technology derived from another Breach object, albeit a relatively benign and manageable one—was a defensive measure designed to hide a crashed aircraft from satellites. Even visual satellites. It pulled a variety of clever tricks to fool them; one involved broadcasting an omnidirectional signal that caused spy birds to ignore the live crash site and substitute their own archived shots. The effective radius was something like five miles from the crash site, to cover any possible debris field. Currently every satellite platform in the world was vulnerable to it, though DARPA had a system ready to launch in November that was immune—after all, you never knew when your own toys would be used against you.

That precaution would come a few months late, as it turned out.

The whiskered man made a sudden adjustment to the nerve actuator's power, and Paige's body convulsed, a new flood of tears brimming in her eyes. He did that every few minutes to break up the pattern, keep her from getting used to any one strain of agony. This round would go on for another hour and a half, and then they'd crank the table flat again and let her rest an hour, as the drug lost its edge. The resting hour had nothing to do with kindness; it was simply the whiskered man's understanding of how far he could push her and still keep her alive. The drug must be one of a dozen shock-inhibiting agents Peter knew of.

It was time to break.

He no longer cared what consequences would befall the world as a result. His world had shrunk until it no longer contained even himself. There was only Paige.

He could end her pain right now; in twenty words he could tell them where the Whisper's key was hidden on the plane. An inch-long strip of something like clear cellophane, the key was the easiest thing in the world to hide, and among all the components of a 747, even a team of Boeing engineers could spend months searching for it, if they didn't know where to look. Peter could give these people its location, and once they'd found it and verified that it was valid, they'd put a bullet in Paige's temple, and his own.

Chirping laughter broke from the group encircling the campfire. That the arrogant fuckers had built a fire at all had made it abundantly clear to him, three days earlier, that this place would not be found in time. For the first twelve hours he'd clung to the hope that Ellen had survived. He and the others in the equipment room had forced her to hide in a mainframe cabinet; she'd protested, unwilling to be spared the others' fate, and had given in only as the ATVs had stopped outside the plane. If she'd lived, she could have waited until the attackers left and then called for help.

But the hostiles, after executing everyone but Paige and him, had fired magazine after magazine into the equipment room, shredding every piece of machinery. He'd watched four shots pierce the compartment where Ellen lay hidden. There was close to zero chance she'd survived.

By the end of the first day, when Paige had already endured eight cycles of the torture, Peter's resolve had withered to a thread, and all that had kept it from breaking had been the angry insistence in his daughter's eyes, promising to hate him if he gave in.

All these impossible hours later, her strength was still intact.

But his was dead and gone.

It was time.

In the pines at the edge of the campsite, Travis set two of the spare M16s on the ground. Another he kept slung on his shoulder, and the last he held in his hands.

Fifty feet away, String Mustache was still about his business. From this angle Travis could see the face of the other captive, an older man tied to a tree near the young woman. Travis wondered if a look of greater anguish had ever existed in the world.

Ten feet from String Mustache, four of the other men were gathered around a fire, carefully tended to burn clean without visible smoke. It was more or less a bed of embers that they continually fed sticks to. One of the men was cooking a lump of meat over it. These four seemed intent on keeping their attention off of the torture, their conversation— Travis couldn't pin down the language—serving as their own white noise to mask the woman's muffled screams.

The remaining two hostiles were seated facing the torture table as if it were a matinee screen.

Travis crouched, tensed to move. It would happen any time now. He'd made the trip from the overlook in twenty minutes, hoping like hell with every step that he hadn't misjudged the speed of the water drip, or the resistance force of the rifle's trigger.

Now it didn't matter. He was ready.

He thought he'd take the four at the campfire first. He might get them in one burst, depending on how much they separated when they turned away. After that he'd switch from full-auto to single shot—his thumb already rested on the selector—and be more precise with the other three, who were closer to the captives. By that time his rush would put him inside the camp, firing almost point-blank.

Breathing steady. Hands dry. Any second now.

And then the older man tied to the tree said, "Stop."

CHAPTER SEVEN

S tring Mustache switched off the thing in his hand, though he kept it inside the woman's arm. With the buzzing stopped, the only sound in the clearing was her soft crying, and the occasional pop of something in the fire.

Travis couldn't see her eyes, but the man facing her—it had to be her father—looked more wretched than ever. He whispered what looked like, "I'm sorry," and then, "I love you," repeating the latter at least three times as his eyes ran over.

Finally he turned to her tormentor.

"Tell," String Mustache said.

The bound man spoke, his voice wasted and all but dead. "The forward-most lavatory—bathroom— right behind the cockpit. Remove the fan cover in the ceiling, reach above and to the right. It's there."

String Mustache had his back to Travis, but Travis could picture the man's eyes narrowing, calculating. Then he turned and spoke in his own language to two of the men at the fire. They got to their feet and went quickly to the ATVs that were parked at the edge of the encampment. Their own rifles slung on their shoulders, they mounted two of the four machines and raced away along the valley floor, in the direction of the crash site.

String Mustache watched them go, then turned to the father, who was still whispering something to the young woman on the table.

"Hope what you told me is true," String Mustache said in his rough English. "I keep going until I know."

Then he switched the handheld device back on, and the woman and her father screamed at the same time.

The two remaining at the fire averted their eyes. The two that comprised the peanut gallery smiled. Travis was just processing his own reaction—rage, beyond what he'd already felt—when automatic rifle fire shredded the air above the camp.

String Mustache dropped his device and threw himself flat—no rifle anywhere near his reach. The other four did as Travis had hoped: they took cover, and they got it exactly backward. He broke from the pines as the masking roar of the staged M16 continued. Fifty feet from the encampment, now forty, thirty. The four armed hostiles crouched behind their trees, looking the other way, backs exposed to him like hay bale targets.

String Mustache was still on the ground, with neither cover nor weapon in hand—his hands, in fact, were covering his ears.

Twenty feet. Travis arrested his forward speed, his feet sliding on the loose soil, and shouldered his rifle. He thumbed the selector switch to single shot—the targets were too widely spaced for a sweep—and brought it up to sight on the leftmost of the armed men.

In that moment the staged gun on the ledge ran dry, the instant silence far more jarring than the gunfire itself had been.

Travis pulled the trigger. His shot took the first hostile dead center in the back, and though he couldn't see the exit wound in the man's chest, the eruption of blood onto the tree was almost absurd. Like the guy had swallowed a grenade.

The others were already turning. Fast. Travis swung the barrel toward the second man and squeezed, the shot catching him through the side of the rib cage and propelling most of its contents out the far side. Following through on the gun's sideways momentum, Travis fired again a quarter second later, the shot going wide of the third man and only slicing open his shoulder.

By now the last two armed hostiles were fully facing him, their weapons coming up smoothly.

What came next, Travis could only think of as autopilot. He'd felt it before, at times when his survival had balanced on a pivot-point made of seconds, or half seconds. His body just seemed to make its own call.

His knees bent. He dropped fast, just as both of the weapons facing him roared. In the same instant that he felt the baked-air trails of bullets passing his face, his thumb flicked the selector switch back to full auto, and then he was firing.

The autofire didn't exactly knock the two men backward—that only seemed to happen in movies—but instead knocked the life from their bodies. Punctured across their upper torsos, they simply dropped, the left of the two crumpling so tidily in place that he cracked his head on his own knee before flopping sideways.

Travis felt the weapon fire empty even as he remembered String Mustache. Turning now, already letting go of the rifle and shrugging the second one from his shoulder, he saw him.

The man was no longer cowering. He was standing. Still not holding a rifle, but drawing a 9mm from inside his coat. He wasn't even looking at Travis. His eyes were on the man tied to the tree, and his pistol was coming up.

The young woman screamed, so much louder than before that the sound baffle strapped to her face seemed not to affect it.

Travis got his left hand on the spare M16's barrel guard. Twisting his body, swinging up the stock, his right hand finding the grip and the trigger well—

String Mustache put his pistol to the bound man's head and fired. The woman's scream doubled.

A half second later, as the man pivoted to execute the young woman as well, Travis's M16 barked, already set to full auto. Three shots caught String Mustache across the face before the recoil pushed the weapon off target. Travis stopped firing, watched the torturer fall, his 9mm tumbling away over the dirt and pine needles.

Travis swept his gaze across the bodies of the first four hostiles to be sure they were dead. They were dead.

He slung the rifle and went to the woman on the table, taking his knife from his pocket as he went. She startled when she saw him, and he realized she had witnessed almost none of what had just happened—just her father's death and then String Mustache's.

The mechanics of the crank table were obvious enough. Travis took hold of the metal handle and turned it until the surface lay flat. He carefully lifted the strap of the sound baffle, cut it, and pulled the thing away.

She wasn't screaming anymore. She lay there hyperventilating instead.

The straps holding her body were sturdy, but his knife got through them without any trouble. Her hands went to her face; her legs folded up to her chest as she rolled on her side. She felt for something inside her mouth and pulled it out. A rubber clamp of some kind.

Her upper right arm looked as bad as anything Travis had ever seen, but she paid no attention to it now.

Thinking to give her some privacy, Travis turned and walked to the edge of the camp, cocking an ear to listen for the ATVs. He could hear the engines, very distant now and still receding; no way could the riders have heard the gunfire over the roar of those machines up close. They'd left maybe ninety seconds ago. They were probably halfway to the crash now.

"Who are you?" The young woman's voice was broken and faint.

Travis turned, and was surprised to find her sitting up on the table. Her body still shuddered with sobs, but she showed remarkable control, all things considered. She looked to be in her late twenties. Dark hair. Large, dark eyes. He found himself thinking she must be beautiful on anything but the worst day of her life.

"Travis," he said, suddenly lacking a better answer. She seemed to be waiting for more. "I'm just a guy. I found the plane, found Mrs. Garner."

"She lived?"

"Long enough to leave instructions."

Before she could ask about that, movement between them drew their attention sharply.

String Mustache was alive, trying to turn himself over in the dirt. Though a good chunk of the man's face had been cleaved away by one of the bullets, Travis now saw that the other two had glanced on the hard cheekbones and skull. He unslung the M16 and was an instant from finishing him when the woman spoke.

"No." The word came out rough, halfway between whisper and growl.

Then she surprised Travis by pivoting and putting her feet on the ground, and standing—shaky for a moment, but standing all the same.

With her undamaged left arm she took Travis's knife from where he'd set it on the table, and dropped hard with one knee onto String Mustache's back, pressing him flat to the ground. She put the blade, edge-up, under his armpit and pulled savagely. Travis heard a sound like heavy elastic parting, and the man screamed. The arm quivered, uncontrolled. She did the same to the other arm, then turned a hundred eighty degrees and slit both of his hamstrings behind the knees. His screams ebbed to a low moan, gurgling blood in his throat.

The woman stood, put the knife aside, then stooped and gathered a fistful of String Mustache's back collar.

Had Travis actually wanted to stop her, he wasn't sure he'd have had time. She lifted String Mustache's upper body, dragged him ten feet across the needles and loose soil, and dropped him facedown into the white-hot embers of the campfire. He screamed and thrashed, but could only command his limbs to jerk about; all control had literally been severed. He managed to contract his back muscles and raise his face for a few seconds, but then the young woman put her foot on the back of his head and pressed him deep into the coals again. She kept the foot there until his hair caught fire. By that time he'd stopped moving and screaming. She watched him for another ten seconds; then she picked up a rifle dropped by one of the hostiles, thumbed it to auto without even looking at it, and fired a burst into the back of String Mustache's head.

She dropped the gun and turned back to Travis,

and for a moment he wasn't sure her eyes were even human. Then they fixed on her father, dead against the base of the tree, and all doubt about her humanity evaporated.

She crossed to the pine and sank beside his bound corpse, pulling herself against him, her face pressed to his despite the blood. She cried again, silently.

Travis went back to the edge of the camp and listened to the distant ATV engines. Thirty seconds later they stopped.

CHAPTER EIGHT

Travis expected to have to gently pry the young woman from her grieving. They needed to get out of the encampment and find positions from which to kill the other two hostiles when they returned.

But she sat with her father only a few minutes before standing, taking Travis's knife again and cutting the dead man free. She set him carefully flat on the ground, then looked around, troubled.

Travis understood. "Where do you want to take him?"

Her gaze settled on the dense stand of pines where he'd hidden earlier. "There."

Travis knelt and lifted the man, and carried him to the trees. He maneuvered the body among the boughs and laid it under the deepest cover, then waited silently as the woman stood looking down at it.

"We need to get out of here fast," she said after a moment. "As soon as we kill the two that left on the quads."

"There are more besides them?" Travis said.

"A lot more." She nodded toward the camp. "These guys were calling in on a satellite phone every hour. When their people don't hear from them, they'll know there was trouble. They'll send reinforcements with a helicopter."

The woman took a hard breath, gave her father a last look, then turned away, back toward the encampment. As she did, Travis got another look at her right arm. The set of clamps the torturer had used to pry apart her triceps were still in place, keeping the skin and muscle wedged open at least an inch. Heavy black clots filled the cavity, along with what could only be infected tissue.

Seeing him stare, Paige turned her arm and saw the opening herself. Travis knew by her reaction that she was looking at it for the first time. She took it well.

"I wouldn't pull those clamps out without a doctor close by," Travis said. "You don't want to trap those infections inside your arm, away from the air."

"I don't think I'll be in a doctor's care anytime soon," she said, but made no move to detach the clamps.

She stepped out of the pines and moved into the camp. Travis followed.

"Can you use their satellite phone to call for help?" he said. "Get the military in here, or whoever your people can send?"

She shook her head. "These guys had to use a

code to make outgoing calls. If I were more of a tech, maybe I could get around it, but I'm not. How far from a town are we?"

"On foot, fifty miles." He looked at the remaining two quads parked nearby. "We could cover two thirds of it on one of those, taking the long way around a few ridges. Then there's a river, and no way across but log bridges and rocks. We'd have to ditch the quad and walk from there, maybe a full day to reach Coldfoot."

She considered that, looking more concerned than hopeful. Her eyes went past him to the open valley and the succession of mountain ridges beyond, as if the landscape were an executioner's scaffold. Travis imagined a full day's walk over the mostly exposed terrain, being hunted by armed pursuers in a helicopter. The young woman's expression suggested similar thoughts.

"This is going to get bad," she said. She stared a moment longer, then looked at Travis. "My name's Paige. Thank you for saving my life."

The riders were coming back. The engines had started up a minute earlier, and now the two ATVs were just visible past the curve of the valley, maybe a mile away yet.

Travis kept his M16 steady against a pine trunk. Paige held her own rifle at the next tree over, left-handed—clearly not her natural choice—and braced across a branch. Her damaged arm hung at her side.

In the silence of the clearing, the distant hum

of the engines was no more than an insect buzz. The wind through the boughs was louder. So was Paige's breathing, each intake more a gasp than a breath.

Travis wondered at the kind of resolve someone would need to even be standing after all she'd just gone through. Then he wondered at the stakes required to fuel that resolve.

"You're worried about a lot more than just your own survival," Travis said.

"Yes," Paige said, her eyes staying on the gun sights.

"I want to know what all this is," he said. "I saw the steel container on the plane. And there were details in the First Lady's note, but not enough. I'm going to help you get to Coldfoot, regardless, but if I'm going to risk getting killed over something, I want to know what it is. I don't think that's asking too much."

She looked up, met his gaze evenly.

"What's Tangent?" Travis said. "What the hell is a Breach entity?"

Her eyes stayed on his a moment longer, as the drone of the incoming engines rose. Then she lowered her face to the rifle stock again, eyes down the barrel. Travis looked down his own sights. The riders were still a thousand yards out, just now resolving into distinct shapes. There was no danger of them spotting Travis or Paige where they stood, against the darker backdrop of the camp and the tree cover.

"Tangent is an organization," Paige said. "Our

entire purpose revolves around the Breach. Guarding it. Controlling it. And the Breach is . . . very hard to describe."

"I'm more open-minded today than I was yesterday," Travis said.

Several more seconds passed as Paige considered what to say next. Travis could see the gleam of sunlight off the chrome handlebars of the ATVs.

"Have you ever heard something described as the strangest thing in the world?" Paige said. "A two-headed snake, a potato chip that looks like George Washington, something like that?"

"Sure," Travis said.

"Even in strict scientific terms, with no hyperbole, the Breach is the strangest thing in the world." She thought for a moment, then went on. "It's a source. A technology source. We get things from it. I know that's vague, but I can't say it more clearly. Not just because it'd be an act of treason, but because you'd never believe me unless you were standing right in front of it, seeing it for yourself."

Travis saw her draw the rifle tightly into her shoulder, her left eye narrowing down the sight line. The riders were still well over five hundred yards out, too far for guaranteed kill shots. Travis was about to suggest that when they came into range, he take the left rider and Paige take the right, when her rifle cracked, a mini thunderclap in the stillness. The left rider jerked—Travis saw blood in the center of his chest—and pitched sideways, pulling the handlebars so tightly to the right that the machine jackknifed, flipped and threw him like a crash-test dummy. Which, by that point, he essentially was. Before he landed, Paige fired again, and the second rider's head vanished above the jaw. He stayed on his quad for another five seconds, then tipped straight backward and fell off. The machine rolled thirty yards farther, throttling down to idle, and then just sat there growling.

Travis turned to her, saw her staring at the kills, her eyes hard and—if he was reading them right—unsatisfied with her work.

"I'm better with a scope," she said.

She leaned the rifle against the tree, turned, and went to a pile of the hostiles' gear in the middle of the camp. Within a few seconds she'd pushed aside their belongings—among them a little dirt-crusted shovel—to reveal a steel plate on the ground, eighteen by eighteen inches and half an inch thick. She lifted it with her good arm and let it fall flat on its other side, exposing beneath it a leg-wide hole in the dirt. Its bottom was too deep for Travis to see from his angle.

What caught his eye first was a disturbance to the plate's underside: dark blue corrosion, and a just-visible bulge where the metal had spanned the hole in the ground. Exposure damage, caused by whatever lay unseen at the bottom.

"Any piece of technology we get from the Breach is called an entity," Paige said. "This one is designated Whisper, and it's dangerous as hell. The man who sent these contractors wants control of it. If he succeeds . . ." She paused, looked at Travis, then shook off whatever she was thinking, and knelt over the hole. "He can't succeed. It's that simple."

She reached deep into the hole, almost to her shoulder, and lifted out a fist-sized object, perfectly round, its surface a dark, iridescent blue Travis was sure he'd never seen before.

The object from the hinged steel cube aboard the 747.

For a moment Paige gazed at it with a mix of revulsion and fear, as if it were a spent fuel rod saturating her bones with lethal rads. Then she narrowed her eyes and seemed to focus past the irrational feeling.

Travis sensed that whatever danger this thing posed wasn't as simple as any physical risk from holding it. Not directly, anyway.

He lifted his gaze from the thing and met Paige's eyes.

"Are you saying the Breach is a lab?" he said. "Some place where we build things like this?"

She shook her head. "It's not a lab. And we didn't build this thing."

"*We* as in Americans?" Travis said.

"*We* as in people."

She held his stare a few seconds longer, then stooped and picked up the shovel from the hostiles' gear.

Travis continued staring at her, replaying her last sentence in all its gravity.

Standing, Paige said, "Do me a favor. The thing the other two went to retrieve from the plane looks like an inch of clear tape. It's very important. It's the key that switches the Whisper on. They'll have it with them now. Get it, while I bury this where their backup won't find it."

"We're not bringing it with us?" Travis said.

"We'd never make it. The Whisper's too dangerous without containment. But we can bring the key. All that matters now is keeping these people from recovering both, and contacting Tangent as soon as we can."

With that she turned away, Whisper and shovel in hand, and left the clearing through the trees on the far side.

Travis watched after her a moment, listening to her footsteps recede across the forest floor. Then he headed toward the distant ATVs. He'd gone only a few paces from the camp when he heard the hostiles' satellite phone begin ringing behind him.

An hour later they were two valleys away, racing north through one leg of the long and snaking course he'd quickly mapped. Paige was seated in front of him on the quad, boxed in by his arms as he held the handlebars. She'd grown steadily weaker as they'd prepared to leave—the result, she said, of the interrogator's drug wearing off. That and three days of zero sleep catching up. Travis couldn't see her eyes now, but at times her body went slack and leaned back against him before she jostled awake again.

However long it took the hostiles' backup to reach the camp, it wouldn't be long afterward before they noticed a quad missing. At that point, a glance at a map would leave no doubt as to the direction their prey had gone. Coldfoot was the only way out, and there were only so many paths by which to reach it.

Travis kept the ATV on hard ground that took no imprint from the tires, and did his best to avoid the snowfields.

CHAPTER NINE

Darkness over LaGuardia. Dawn at the horizon, cherry red like a heated wire. Karl watched the world come to life, the hotel room dark around him. His reflection in the windowpane, side lit by the bathroom light, stared back with its visible eye blue and cold.

Twenty-five minutes to takeoff. He had all the time in the world. Nobody would make him wait in line.

Not when he was wearing the suit.

It lay in two halves on the chair beside him. He felt for the bottom half, found it, sat on the bed and pulled it over his jeans until he felt the built-in feet, like the feet of a child's pajamas, snug tightly around his shoes. He found the shoulder straps and secured them. He reached for the chair again, felt for the suit's top half, and slipped it on as he stood. He smoothed its long hem, which overlapped the waist of the bottom half by a foot or more. The material, so unlike anything else he'd ever worn, was hard to get used to, even after all his experience with it. It felt like spandex in a way, matching every dimension of his six-foot frame, but at the same time it seemed almost relaxed. At least, *relaxed* was the closest term he had for it. It was also breathable like the screen of a tent, and nearly weightless. On a previous occasion he'd worn it for more than forty-eight hours straight without any discomfort, even from the portions that covered his hands and head. Though he'd never asked his employers about it—not that they knew any better than him how the thing worked, considering where it had come from—he felt sure that the suit's perfect fit resulted from some narrow intelligence of the material itself. Even now he felt the suit taking the shape of his body until he could hardly tell he was wearing it. It would not be surprising, of course, to learn that the suit had intelligence built into it. It would also not be its most impressive attribute. Not by a long shot.

Karl checked the peephole, saw that the hallway was clear, and left the room. He passed by the elevator bank, opting for the stairwell—elevators were a no-no, of course. Five flights down, he put his face to the little window in the door that accessed the lobby. It was empty except for two girls at the front desk, thirty feet away.

Walking out in front of them was not ideal, but protocol allowed it given that there was no easier option. He pushed the door open and stepped out. As he had expected, both girls glanced up at the opening door, expressions casual and then perplexed, trading looks now. As Karl passed directly in front of them, their eyes stayed on the door, falling shut far behind him with a light thud.

"Um . . . okay," the older girl said.

The other shook her head and went back to her half-finished sudoku puzzle.

Karl could leave by the main exit, right in front of them, but because he had another choice this time—it would take less than a minute to reach the back door, around the corner and down the hall—protocol demanded that he take it. Really, the rules governing the use of the suit boiled down to three words: don't fuck around.

He reached the rear exit and, quite alone, shoved it open and strode into the chilly New York morning.

Traffic on the Grand Central Parkway was heavy enough to merit caution, even at this hour. He waited for his chance, then sprinted across all five eastbound lanes at once. A moment later he'd crossed the other half, scaled the fence, and was out on the open sweep of LaGuardia, the terminals and airliners silhouetted against the red eastern sky like an alien fortress.

He walked across Runway Four, two access roads, and rounded the Central Terminal Building to the nearest entrance to Concourse D.

Outside the sliding door, he waited; its electric eye could no more see him than could the sleepy rent-a-cop standing a few feet to the side. No matter—caution would have demanded that he wait for someone else to trigger the door anyway. Airports were no places to start getting overconfident. No places to fuck around.

He waited only thirty seconds before a weary-looking businessman got out of a cab and lumbered through the entrance. He followed the man inside, broke left and made his way past the sparse lines of early travelers at the baggage check. From here on in, everything was easy. The security checkpoint, a farce even without the suit, was reduced to something like a kindergarten obstacle course. He stepped onto the raised barrier that boxed in the metal detector lanes on the left, and simply walked past the entire charade, stepping back down to the floor twenty feet beyond.

The concourse itself would have presented a challenge had it been busier. Crowds, even moderate ones, were a logistical nightmare; people would walk right into him if he wasn't careful. At this hour, however, the wide, open passageway was mostly empty, save for the clot around Gate D7 far ahead, his destination.

When he reached it, he paused for a long while, studying the layout of the crowd. Where to stand? Not here, certainly. People would be coming and going in both directions, and the movements of those already camped here would be unpredictable. Worse, two little kids were chasing each other around, their mother, absorbed in a paperback, giving them only an occasional half-assed admonition to sit down.

The prime spot was obvious: right beside the jetway door, beyond the attendant's stand. Karl skirted the crowd at a comfortable distance, ducked the stanchion barrier, and took his place. It wouldn't be long; the 737 was already docked outside. Beyond it, the city skyline jutted into the still dim morning like a row of teeth.

The attendant went to his microphone. "Ladies and gentlemen, Cayman Airways flight 935, non-stop service to Georgetown on Grand Cayman, is now boarding rows one through five. Rows one through five."

Another attendant opened the door, and the moment she stepped away from it, Karl moved past her and into the cool air of the jetway, moving fast now to stay well ahead of the first passengers. He paused briefly at the door to the plane, where a stewardess blocked the way. She glanced through him down the jetway, saw nobody coming just yet, and ducked back in to speak to one of her coworkers. Karl slid past her and went to the back of the plane.

On a 737, depending on its configuration, the best place to ride out the flight was almost always the aft concession storage. The tiny room was empty for much of the flight, and even when a crew member came in to take or return a cart, evasion was a simple matter of ducking into the nook beside the ice bin.

Getting off the plane, of course, would be even easier than getting on.

Karl sat at the edge of the shade, five feet from the naked girl sunning herself by the pool.

By far the most interesting aspect of wearing the suit was the ability to study people when they thought they were alone. Until the first time he'd found himself in that position, it had never occurred to him what a unique perspective it could be. Ordinarily, you could never be with someone who was alone, simply by definition. You could set up a hidden camera, but it wasn't the same as being there.

Nobody ever showed outward signs of anxiety when by themselves. No one ever fidgeted, or blushed, or moved awkwardly. What a strange thing to find: everybody was cool when there was no one around to judge them.

The girl was twenty-three and heartbreakingly beautiful. Olive skin. No tan lines. Deep brown eyes and sun-faded hair. She was five-foot-two and probably not a hundred pounds soaking wet. Five minutes ago she had in fact been soaking wet. Karl had watched her remove her clothes and dive into the pool. Now the Caribbean sun had almost completely dried her. He watched the last little collection of moisture droplets evaporate from her skin in the dry heat.

Her name was Lauren Cook. Karl had learned that fact along with everything else he'd learned about her father, Ellis Cook.

Lauren had the house to herself at the moment, all fifteen thousand square feet of it, overlooking Bodden Bay and the wide, blue Caribbean to the south. There were security personnel, of course, manning the entrances and ready to storm the place at the first cry for help. They were American, and professional; Karl had taken a close look at each of them and concluded that they were ex-something impressive, a hell of a lot more impressive than cops. The house's fortifications were rounded out with thermal cameras and motion detectors, all of which might as well have been hollow decoys where Karl was concerned.

A yellow cabbage butterfly landed on Lauren's thigh. She flinched and waved her hand at it, then saw what it was and smiled, watching it corkscrew away. It flew behind Karl and, by chance, dragged Lauren's line of sight directly to meet his eyes for just a heartbeat. He felt a chill pass through him, meeting her innocent gaze. Then she sank back into her lounger and closed her eyes again.

Beyond her, the two-story house more than filled Karl's frame of vision, extending seventy feet both to his left and right. Several of the second floor windows were open above the balcony, which was easy to climb to. Karl had already done so, had already walked the rooms of the house, inspected cabinets and drawers in Ellis's bedroom, and formed his plan. It was very straightforward, no room for mistakes. Don't fuck around.

A few minutes later Lauren rose, gathered her clothes and went inside, locking the patio door behind her. Karl went to the poolside rail and gazed down at the manicured lawns, and the yachts riding at anchor in the harbor beyond. He felt bad for the girl; she didn't deserve what was coming. Though he had yet to see her interact with another soul, she had kind features and was probably a nice kid.

Well, it wasn't a nice world.

* * *

Twilight over the bay. Haze had rolled in during the afternoon, and now the horizon was a blur between pink water and purple sky. Only the brightest stars shone through.

Karl watched Ellis enter the bedroom. The man walked past all three sets of balcony doors, wide open to the sea, without shooting so much as a glance through them. Why live here, then, Karl wondered.

Ellis went to his computer, switched it on, and paced while it powered up.

At the back corner of the desk were two framed photos: Lauren, and Ellis's wife. Karl had seen no evidence of the wife's presence in this house. The information provided by his superiors had indicated trouble in the marriage.

Karl reached deep inside the overlap of the suit and took hold of what he'd found in Ellis's nightstand.

Icons bloomed on the computer screen.

Ellis sat in his chair.

Karl drew the chrome-plated .45, put it to Ellis's temple and fired.

Immediately came shouts from security outside the house. Screams, too, from Lauren's room. Seconds left to finish the job.

Karl lifted Ellis's hand, wrapped the man's fingers around the pistol grip, and fired again, this time into the framed photo of Mrs. Cook. Powder burns now assured, he let both the hand and the pistol fall free. Not two seconds later the bedroom door broke in, almost off its hinges, and four security men were in the room, MP5s shouldered and covering all angles.

"Room clear."

Two broke formation, one to the master bath and another to the enormous closet.

"Bathroom clear."

"Closet clear."

Karl chose the broadest stretch of the wall, far out of the way, and simply stood. Outside in the hallway, other security men were holding Lauren back as she screamed and demanded answers. The men in the room spoke over headsets with other teams outside, locking down the grounds, though a certain calm had descended in their eyes. They could see what had happened.

Watching from the perimeter of the chaos, Karl felt his cell phone vibrate. He was expected to answer under all but the most unforgiving circumstances. These qualified.

Ten minutes later, in the lull between the security response and the arrival of local police, Karl went to the balcony, slipped over the rail and dropped to the patio. He saw two security officers just inside the living room—one of them a woman—sitting with Lauren, holding on to her and speaking softly.

He went to the far end of the patio, where a six-foot drop put him on a gentle slope to the beach.

A quarter mile up the shore road he found an empty bench, and sat. He took out his cell phone and, as expected, found a text message.

RETURN TO AIRPORT, NUL CURRENT JOB IF
NECESSARY. TAKE UNITED 820 TO CHICAGO,
THEN UNITED 71 TO FAIRBANKS, AK. WEAPONS/
INSTRUCTIONS WILL BE WAITING IN YELLOW
LAND ROVER W/GREENPEACE STICKER, LONG-
TERM PARKING D. THIS WILL BE DIRECT AG-
GRESSION AGAINST TANGENT PERSONNEL.

CHAPTER TEN

E ven after the sound of the helicopter faded, Travis watched the ridgeline through the cedar boughs for ten minutes. The way ahead, visible from this rise, stood bare and shadowless for more than two miles. Getting caught in the open would be suicide.

The going had been as rough as he'd expected. Five times now, in just over twelve hours, the chopper had come hunting the valleys for them, making slow and methodical passes or simply stopping to hover for minutes on end. Concealment had been sparse but always reachable within the short warning time provided by the incoming rotors, echoing among the peaks.

They'd reached these cedars by the breadth of a wish, Travis setting Paige deep beneath the branches and pulling his own limbs under just as the aircraft rounded the nearest bend in the valley.

Now the silence felt sturdy again. As sturdy as it was going to get, at least.

Paige had drifted off—had barely been awake to begin with, in fact, even when the drumbeat of the blades had passed within a hundred feet. She was in bad shape and getting worse by the hour. The skin around the fissure in her upper arm had grown angry red, and the infected tissue inside appeared to have tripled its presence since Travis had first seen it. Most frightening of all, the veins visible in her forearm had distended and darkened, at least some aspect of the infection spreading that far. And that was only where he could see it. Where else was it branching to?

His first-aid kit might as well have been a make-believe set for a toddler playing nurse. It had nothing that could deal with this injury, though he'd tried the spray can of bactine anyway, with her assent. The only clear result had been searing pain, which she'd tried her best to hide from him. She'd failed—you could only blink away so many tears.

By the time they'd ditched the ATV in the river—after skirting the bank for miles to find a stretch of rapids foamy enough to conceal it—Paige was running a high temperature and unable to stay conscious for any real amount of time. So Travis had dumped his eighty-pound backpack into the rapids as well—keeping only the smallest water pouch—and carried her.

It was harder than he'd supposed it would be. She weighed maybe forty pounds more than the pack, and she hadn't been designed by North Face to distribute the load to his frame. Uphill distances became leg-press workouts. Downhill was worse, every step compressing his ankle and threatening to roll it over into a sprain. Which, in a roundabout way, he realized, would amount to a fatal injury. For both of them.

It helped to consider what Paige had gone through these past three days. All his discomfort was a shin-bump against a coffee table by comparison.

He lifted her carefully now from beneath the cedar. Her eyes opened for a second but didn't focus on him. He wanted to believe that her catatonia was mostly a result of the drug and the sleep deprivation, but had to accept that the infection's role was considerable, and growing. Her forehead beaded like a windshield in rain.

He left the cedar stand and got moving, pushing the pace faster now than at any time before. The open space ahead was the physical distillation of anxiety itself. He imagined that this was how agoraphobics felt in shopping malls. Like prey.

There was no reason to think the chopper might be friendly. Had Paige's people somehow located the wreck, they'd have shown up in greater numbers: fighters overhead, and multiple helicopters offloading personnel along every ridge for miles. It would have been the confident presence of a force on its home soil.

This lone chopper was more like a prowler in someone's house.

Ahead, the valley curved gradually, revealing that the open space continued farther than he'd seen at first. He'd hiked this route on his way in, but couldn't recall the specific layout of tree cover.

He recognized the high, rocky crest on which he'd seen the Dall sheep, his first night in the park.

At that time he'd been a few miles east of it, on the Coldfoot side; he was far west of it now, still deep in the range. Adding up the rough distances, and considering his speed—slower than he'd traveled with just the pack, despite the urgency pushing him now—he put Coldfoot at least another twenty hours away.

He wouldn't sleep, of course. Paige would live or die based on how soon she received treatment for the infection. Hours would count.

As he walked, he thought of what she'd told him in the clearing.

Tangent. The Breach. The Whisper.

He had in his pocket the piece of clear plastic he'd retrieved from the dead ATV riders. The Whisper's key. What exactly would the Whisper do, when its key was applied? Paige's words came back to him:

We didn't build this thing.

We as in people.

The implications were hard to get his mind around, and not because he didn't believe her. Just the opposite.

Paige interrupted his thoughts, murmuring something in her sleep. No words—just a scared sound, miserable and pleading. It lasted only a few seconds, and then she was quiet again, though Travis felt the tension in her muscles linger, and saw her eyes flitting back and forth behind their closed lids. He wondered how long it would be before she could dream anything other than nightmares.

"You're safe," he said quietly. "They're gone."

He didn't expect it to work, but it did. She relaxed almost at once, into what passed for dreamless sleep.

Mostly, he tried not to look at her.

Tried not to notice her eyelashes, or the way her bangs fell on her forehead, or the nearly invisible traces of long-lost freckles across the bridge of her nose. Tried not to think of how, in spite of his muscles burning as if battery acid were flowing through them instead of blood, this was the best he'd felt in a decade and a half.

She was something. No escaping it.

In a way, she was everything. Everything that his future would never contain. A year out of prison, he hadn't even humored the idea of dating again. He'd spent fifteen years learning not to think about what he was missing. He'd gotten pretty good at it, too, and his freedom had brought little reason to change that perspective. His body might not be constrained behind razor-wire borders any longer, but his chances with a woman like Paige sure as hell were.

It wasn't that he'd be alone forever. There were ways to take the edge off his past, and he was working on them. He'd been doing construction in Fairbanks for most of the year he'd been there, on a contractor's crew. Working hard at it, and working smart, paying attention to the business side of the job. And saving his money. He'd be in a position to head up his own crew before too long, starting with medium-sized projects, mostly additions.

If he played it right, he'd be putting up new homes on spec within five years, and eventually—maybe another five years after that—the homes would be high-end. Somewhere along that arc, with a solid career to speak for him and with prison far enough behind, he'd find someone who'd give him a chance.

But not someone like Paige. Not even close. And that was fine, as long as he didn't think about it.

So he tried not to look at her.

But mostly he failed.

The open span, which turned out to be over three miles long, terminated at a grove of alders where three smaller valleys converged from high above. He'd gone a quarter mile beyond the grove, into more open space, when he heard the chopper again. No chance of getting back to the alders in time. He tried for them anyway.

He was a hundred yards shy, moving faster than good judgment counseled on the rough ground, with the rotors like drumsticks on sheet metal and the chopper seconds from breaking into view, when he took the misstep he'd been dreading.

He saw it a tenth of a second before his foot touched down, time enough to recognize the mistake but not redeem it. The bare patch of dirt, no larger than a dinner plate, was dark and moistened, either by snow runoff or a spring somewhere beneath it. All the dirt on this slope was moist, but grass roots held it firm—where there was grass. Travis had simply taken his eyes from the ground a half second too long, watching the ridgeline for the chopper.

His foot hit the soft earth and slid sideways as if on ice.

For a second—his balance gone, his body pivoting without any pretense of control—he simply knew it was over. They would sprawl. The chopper would be on them before he could even pick himself up, much less Paige. And just for a challenge, here was a jagged boulder in his path, perfectly placed for him to crack his head against when he fell.

Somewhere in the churn of his thoughts rose the impression of driving on ice. Spinning out. Turning into it instead of against. Stupid—but all he had. He pitched his shoulders forcefully counterclockwise, the direction of the spin, and found himself standing still so suddenly that it was almost disorienting.

The rotors were drumming against his skull now. Any second.

A single hope had tempered his anxiety during all the time spent in the open: the men in the chopper had no idea who had killed their friends at the camp. They'd be forced to assume a hidden survivor from the jet had arrived, or that the captives themselves had somehow taken the upper hand. Either way, they would expect the fugitives to be dressed for room temperature inside a 747—not an Alaskan hike.

The boulder, just above knee-height, was only a step away. He turned and backed against it, sitting roughly and keeping Paige in his arms, her legs now draping across his lap. She was already wearing his heavy coat, minus a sleeve to let the wound breathe. He let that arm—her right—press against him, out of sight to anyone high above.

Then he pulled her face to his, close enough to create the illusion that was their only chance for survival: that they were an ordinary couple hiking in the back country, caught in the middle of a kiss.

At that instant the chopper broke into the clear above the nearest ridge, angling north at a good clip. Then it stopped. The pilot had seen them. Travis had only a peripheral sense of the thing; Paige's face took up most of his vision.

The clatter of the blades intensified as the aircraft fixed on them and moved in.

Travis shut his eyes—they'd be visible from the chopper's height—and tried to make the kiss look real. One hand holding the back of her head, the other around her waist. His mouth pressed against hers. The turbines settled in directly overhead, screaming and pounding and lashing their hair against their faces hard enough to sting.

All of which provided enough sensation to wake Paige.

Travis felt her body flinch. He opened his eyes and found hers staring right back at him, wide and startled, from less than an inch away. This was it. This would blow it. She'd pull away, and a few seconds later, machine-gun fire would herald the last seconds of their lives.

Then her eyes changed, and she understood. She

pulled him closer, her free arm coming up, her fingers in his hair. And now she was really kissing him, her mouth parting, so warm and intense that for the most fleeting moment it was all Travis could focus on. No thunder of turbines, no rotorwash, just her kiss, as desperate as her need to keep breathing. For that moment, it almost didn't matter that it was fake.

It occurred to him only in passing that they should probably wave at the helicopter, as almost anyone would, but by then he heard the engine change pitch, and a moment later the aircraft was moving away up the valley and taking its downblast with it.

She continued kissing him for another ten seconds, until the chopper was far away, and then they separated, eyes still locked on each other's, six inches apart.

"Good thinking," she said, whispering because it was all she had the strength for.

He managed a nod, suddenly hard up for dialogue.

She turned to stare after the helicopter, but had hardly moved when her breath caught and she nearly passed out from a wave of pain. She'd accidentally pressed her damaged arm into his side, so lightly Travis had barely felt it.

She regained her composure and slowly brought the arm out in front of her. She saw the purpled veins spiderwebbing her forearm, more than a foot from the infection's source, and for the first time since he'd met her, Travis saw fear in her eyes.

"How far from town now?" she said.

"Just a few hours," he lied. "Close your eyes again and we'll be there."

For a long moment he thought she would do just that. She leaned into him, her forehead against his cheek. He was about to stand when she spoke again.

"Remember this. From the place where they tortured me, go in the opposite direction from the crash site, and at fifty steps find the biggest tree around. You can't miss it. The Whisper is on the far side, buried two feet down. I scattered needles to hide the ground I disturbed."

"You don't need me to know that," Travis said. "You're going to report it yourself."

He waited for her reply, but none came. After a moment her breath against his neck fell into a steady rhythm, slow and even.

VERSE II
AN OCTOBER NIGHT IN 1992

Through the sheer curtain across the living-room window, Travis sees that he was close to right: they are seated, holding each other, though they've squeezed into one of the big recliners instead of the couch.

He knocks, and sees the man's shape turn. A moment later Travis sees his face through the little window in the door as he approaches across the laundry room. The man's eyes are blood red from crying. Behind him, the dining-room table is covered with flowers and somber cards.

The man does not even look through the door before opening it—he expects someone else, anyone else—and when he finds himself face to face with Travis, he flinches angrily. His eyes narrow. A tear spills from the left one.

Looking into those eyes, Travis expects the man to turn from the door, stride into the next room, return with his shotgun and open fire. If it happens, Travis will not try to run. He knows he deserves it, for the misery he has brought to these people.

But Emily Price's father does not turn away. Behind him in the house, her mother calls out to ask who's there, her voice stretched and ruined by her own tears.

She gets no answer.

Mr. Price holds his glare on Travis and says, "What do you want, Detective?"

Travis hears the contempt behind the last word. He knows he deserves that, too.

"What have the police told you?" Travis says.

The man's eyes harden. "Why don't you go ask them? They trust you, right?"

Travis says nothing. He waits for the answer.

"They're not going to charge anyone," Mr. Price says at last. Hate and despair and torment become a unified whole in his voice.

"Why not?"

"No evidence. They didn't even find her body. Just her car. But they said there was so much—" The man falters. For a moment he seems incapable of saying more. Then: "There was enough blood, her blood, that a girl her size couldn't have sur—"

His voice gives out then, of its own accord. He looks down. His lower lip shakes.

Through the tremors, Mr. Price says, "She didn't do anything to them. This is all you. It started with you."

Travis manages a nod. He steps closer and speaks softly. "It's going to end with me."

Mr. Price looks up at him.

"I wasn't here tonight," Travis says. "Can you agree to that, Mr. Price?"

Emily's father only stares. Seconds pass. He knows what Travis is saying. He knows what he means to do. For a moment he actually considers his response, as if there's any real choice. But then, because Emily was his only daughter, because she took her first awkward steps into his arms, because when she was a teenager she used to fall asleep resting against his shoulder on the couch during The Tonight Show, *and because three times today he's gone into her bedroom and pressed her pillow to his face to breathe in whatever fading trace is left of her there, he nods.*

"Okay," Travis says.

Mr. Price closes the door, and Travis turns away, back into the night and the fog, and his hand goes unconsciously to the .32.

CHAPTER ELEVEN

Travis ran the last thousand yards to the highway. His knee joints felt like they were riding on glass chips instead of cartilage. Through the front windows of the Brooks Lodge and Fuel Depot he saw half a dozen patrons, maybe the regulars watching a baseball game on the TV above the serving counter. It was eight o'clock at night, the sunlight slanting long and red from the northwest.

He stopped at the road, a hundred feet from the restaurant. Paige was stirring in his arms, jostled by the run but unable to regain consciousness. Her breathing had developed a rattle in the past two hours. Sometimes she took a deep breath and sounded like she was choking for a second before getting past it.

Travis studied the patrons as well as he could at this distance. They looked harmless enough—to the extent he could judge it.

There was every reason to expect trouble from Paige's enemies here, the one place where their arrival could have been predicted—and predicted well in advance. The only advantage the town offered was its limited size: there was simply no place where the enemy could have set up a stakeout without attracting attention. No sprawling parking lots to conceal a van. No residential side streets, either. The one place in town where a person might sit for a few hours without drawing looks was the restaurant in the lodge, but if the hostiles' reinforcements were anything like the ones Travis had seen at the camp—foreign nationals armed with halting English—then blending in that way would be off the table as well.

Granted, they probably had the connections to send someone who didn't stick out so much, and they'd had a day and a half now to do it, but even at that, Coldfoot was just not a place where outsiders lingered. Truckers heading north to Prudhoe Bay might stop for a meal, and the occasional van full of tourists might spend the night, but nobody hung around. Coldfoot was a stop on a long road that went to exactly one place. It was nobody's endpoint.

No, if there were watchers here, they were in concealment high above town. Travis swept his eyes over the encircling ridges; there were so many pine and alder groves it wasn't worth scrutinizing any one in particular. Either they were there, or they weren't. If they were, then trouble would arrive long before help, and it would simply have to be dealt with. The 9mm pistol from the hostiles' camp, the only weapon he'd brought along, felt reassuring in his back waistband, his shirt draped loosely over it.

He crossed the highway and jogged the last distance over the gravel lot, past his own Explorer, two Jeeps, and a yellow Land Rover. When he was thirty feet from the building, a big guy in a John Deere hat inside saw him coming, looked confused for a second, and then ran to shove the door open and meet him.

"What happened?" the man shouted.

Behind him, the others had forgotten the ball game and were on their feet, staring through the windows as Travis ran up.

He had the abridged version of the story well rehearsed, and the stress in his delivery would simply be genuine.

"I found her in a valley west of here," he said, hearing his own voice for the first time in twenty hours and finding it convincingly ragged. No doubt his appearance matched it.

The big guy held the door aside as Travis stepped through, and the gathered patrons reacted as one to the sight of Paige's arm; it couldn't have been much worse if he'd brought a corpse into their midst. A blonde woman who'd come from behind the counter—Molly, according to her shirt—choked down most of a scream, stepping back and knocking over a wire newspaper stand.

Then everyone was talking, a short woman with her hand on her mouth, her eyes going from Paige to Travis and narrowing, maybe judging, the big guy in the hat coming around from the door now, reacting hard at the sight of the clamps, asking what in the holy fuck they were—

"This is how I found her," Travis said over them all. "She hasn't spoken, I don't know who the hell did this. I don't know anything, just call it in, okay? How fast can the cops and paramedics get up here?"

That last bit was for the locals' benefit only—he had no intention of waiting around for police or anyone else, or entrusting her to their protection even if they somehow arrived before whoever Tangent sent.

But it worked. Any suspicion aimed at him vanished. Molly was already rounding the counter, picking up the phone and dialing something longer than 9–1–1.

"Gonna be five, six hours for the cops," the big man said. "There's no highway patrol on the Dalton. Medevac chopper out of Fairbanks, figure ninety minutes at least. Had a trucker come in here having a heart attack, couple years ago, took that long for them to make the flight."

Molly, waiting for the call to connect, shouldered the phone and scooped a key from a pegboard. She tossed it to the big guy and said, "Three's clean, he can set her in there."

The man led Travis through the back exit of the room, into a short hallway lined with doors.

Room Three was simple and clean, lateral sunlight casting a coppery glow on the bedspread. Travis set Paige carefully atop the cover, taking the most precaution with her arm; letting anything press against the wound might traumatize her. As it was, the change of position triggered another of the deep breaths that seemed to nearly choke her.

The guy in the hat stood just inside the door.

Travis watched Paige's breathing return to normal and then said quietly, "Do you have any weapons here?"

In the corner of his eye he saw the John Deere hat turn toward him.

"The camp I found her in," Travis said, keeping his eyes on Paige, "there were different kinds of boot prints, three at least, none of them hers. No telling where those people are now, but if they were to show up here . . ."

"Christ . . ." the man whispered.

"The cops are six hours away, like you said," Travis continued. "Anyone familiar with this area probably knows that too. If you've got a gun, be ready with it. You and anyone you trust, if you have more."

The guy nodded, then went to the window and stared out, the brim of his hat touching the glass as he scanned the ridges to the west.

Travis felt bad lying to him, but the truth was simply not workable, and it would have been far worse to stay silent, given the risk he'd just brought upon this place. That part, he felt the worst about. But what choice had there been?

The man in the hat turned back to him. "Yeah, let's not fuck around," he said, and made for the hallway.

"Can I call out on this?" Travis said.

The guy stopped in the doorway and looked at

the phone on the nightstand Travis had indicated. "Dial nine first," he said, and left.

Travis pushed the door most of the way shut, took the First Lady's note from his pocket and began to punch in the number she'd provided. As he finished dialing, he heard the door creak, and saw it swing slowly open again under its own weight. The phone cord kept him from reaching it now; no matter.

The call rang once and then a lively recording began. "Thank you for calling Laketon Associates, your consulting solution for dynamic—"

He entered 4–2–5–5–1. The line clicked, and within less than a second a woman spoke.

"Key term," she said flatly, more a demand than a question.

Travis blanked. "I don't know it."

"Who is this?"

Matching her lack of banter, Travis said, "I'm a civilian. I found your plane. Everyone's dead except Paige Campbell."

Things happened very quickly then: a rapid exchange of voices somewhere, then muffled clicks as other extensions opened.

A man: "Where are you calling from?"

Travis thought they probably already knew that. "Coldfoot, Alaska," he said. "The crash site is thirty-six miles west of here—"

"Stop," the man said. "Your line's not secure. Give us direct answers and don't elaborate—"

"They're dead," Travis said. Exhaustion and stress had made it easy to get pissed. "You have one survivor, and if you want to keep her, you better send a goddamn cargo jet full of paratroopers up here, and make sure one of them's a surgeon. She might last another hour, and I could be really fucking wrong about that."

Silence for three seconds—either they weren't used to being spoken to that way, or they were writing it down. Then somewhere in the background of the call, he heard a woman say, "Move on it, go," and he felt better.

"Please answer this question with a yes or no only," the man said. "Are there hostile elements that can reach you within the next hour?"

"Yes."

"Again yes or no, can you estimate the number of possible aggressors?"

"No. But they have something you should know about."

"Go ahead."

"A helicopter. It's not an attack chopper, I doubt it's any threat to another aircraft, but whoever's coming here should be aware of it."

"Good," the man said. Sounding more human, he continued. "Don't say anything about your own defenses on this line. Be as prepared as you can manage, and wait for our people. I'm going to connect you to a surgeon who'll ask you to describe Miss Campbell's condition. Do that quickly and then set about your preparations."

The conversation with the doctor took three minutes. He didn't sound optimistic.

Travis finished, hung up, and pulled a chair from

the corner to the bedside. He sat beside Paige and stared. She sounded terrible—worse now than when he'd stopped at the edge of the highway. Her good arm lay facing him; he took hold of her hand in both of his, and closed his eyes. Through the open door he could hear the baseball game on television.

The floor creaked in the hall. He opened his eyes and turned to the doorway. No one there. The creak came again, farther away now, moving toward the front of the lodge.

He'd just turned back to Paige when he heard a pneumatic snap, like a pellet gun firing, and a woman screamed in the front room. The snapping sound came in rapid succession then, and the front of the lodge filled with screams of fear—and pain, clearly. Travis rose fast from the chair, shoved it aside and spun to face the doorway, the 9mm out of his waistband, up to level.

In the instant it took him to do that, the screams from the restaurant were reduced to just one: a man crying and saying "Please," over and over. With a final snap, there was only the sound of the ball game.

Travis waited, the gun steady, keeping himself between Paige and the open door.

The hallway floor creaked again.

CHAPTER TWELVE

The strangest thing about wearing the suit was holding something. A silenced USP Mark 23, in this case. Its bobbing motion, hovering before Karl as he walked, seemed to him very much like the movement of a floating thing. Floating on nothing.

The open door was ten feet ahead on the left.

This would be tricky.

The woman—the only Tangent operator here, and maybe the only one who knew anything—was about a dozen breaths from the grave by the sound of her. He'd gotten a nice long gaze at her arm a few minutes earlier, inside the room while the guy—whoever he was—had called her people.

A random hiker, the man seemed to be.

Karl's orders had been clear but also flexible, given the number of unknown variables in the situation. His superiors had known that Paige Campbell was unaccounted for, would arrive in Coldfoot if she arrived anywhere at all, and that she had hidden the Whisper somewhere near the site of her torture. She could not have taken it with her; nobody on foot could carry a heavy enough containment system to protect against it. She could only have concealed it near the place where, by means entirely unknown, her seven captors had suddenly ended up dead and she'd ended up free.

That mystery wasn't Karl's concern. It was enough that she was here now. She and her new friend. The relevant question was whether, after enduring three days of torture without breaking, Paige had been willing to trust a stranger with her secrets. Did this man know where she'd hidden the Whisper? Equally important: did either of them have the key now?

He quietly raised the upper half of the suit and holstered the weapon, making it vanish. With nothing to give him away, he moved forward, shifting his weight carefully to minimize the floor's creaking. It creaked anyway. Well, better old wood than carpet. Technological marvel though the suit was, it couldn't hide the depressions his feet made in a soft surface—

He nearly gasped aloud, having come abreast of the doorway to find himself staring into the bore of a Beretta, not two feet away in the hiker's hand. He flinched and, recovering just enough to keep from taking a hard step, moved a foot to the side, out of the weapon's line of fire.

Where the fuck had it come from? The guy had made no mention of it earlier, when he asked the fat-ass in the tractor hat about guns.

Calming, Karl stared at the hiker. The pistol was steady in the guy's hand, all things considered. In the eyes there was fear but not panic. Had anyone visible stepped into the doorway, this guy wouldn't have hesitated to kill. That wasn't quite what Karl had expected from a random civilian. Well, some people had more of the devil in them than others.

He took a step toward the man. By providence the floor directly at the threshold kept its silence. His next step—also quiet—put him where he needed to be. His left hand went to the Beretta's barrel, not touching it yet, but encircling it. His right he drew back, tensed.

Travis waited. Whoever was out there could only be feet away. He considered opening fire through the wall. He could put a shot every six inches until the clip ran dry. But if he used every bullet and missed anyway—if the killer dropped too low or was farther down the hall than he sounded—then it would all be over.

Silence now. Ten seconds at least. It was worse than the creaking.

Then he felt the gun in his hand jerk impossibly downward, as if drawn by a supermagnet in the floor—but before he could even process the sensation, pain exploded below his ear, his vision flaring white. Then black.

What had happened? Awareness came back slowly. He was lying on his chest, face to the floor, ankles bound together. His hands too, behind him—the bind felt like duct tape. Another loop surrounded his head, covering his eyes.

He was still in the room with Paige. Her breathing was worse; how much time had gone by?

Now he remembered the baffling movement of his gun, and the blow to his head from nowhere. Had it really happened that way, or was he remembering it wrong because he'd been knocked out?

A man spoke, the voice deep and without emotion. "Tell me where she hid it."

Travis considered the options, each so bleak he almost didn't care to choose. If he said he didn't know, and if the guy believed him, he'd turn his attention on Paige instead. Could she even be woken at this point? Maybe, with enough pain. This guy would have no qualms about administering it. On the other hand, if Travis said he knew where the thing was buried, the guy might decide Paige was of no use and kill her immediately. Really, almost every outcome he could imagine ended with both of them dead inside of an hour.

Except one—the worst one, and probably the most likely. Without a doubt, this guy had the means to contact the team in the valley. They could be here with the helicopter in twenty minutes, grab him and Paige and be far away before help arrived.

When *would* help arrive? How long had he been unconscious? If he could stall for time, maybe it would only be a little longer. He and Paige wouldn't survive, of course—the guy would kill them before fleeing, no question of that—but at least they'd only be dead. The lesser evil by a wide margin. Holding up the show by even ten minutes might make that possible.

"It was fun killing your friends," Travis said.

The man didn't respond.

"The little guy with the cattle prod, especially," he continued. "Then again, technically, I didn't kill him. He managed to survive. Briefly. Should've seen what happened to him then."

"I hear it was fitting," the voice said.

"No, it would have been fitting if he could have smoldered alive for three days."

"Where's the Whisper hidden? Did she bury it? She couldn't have carried it far without heavy containment, which she didn't have."

"We played catch with it for a while, then we got bored, decided to head back to town. It's probably just lying wherever we left it."

The floor strained. When the man spoke again, he was closer. "Sarcasm doesn't come naturally to a man in your predicament. It sounds like a contrivance to me, which means it has a purpose—and for now, that tells me all I need to know."

Then he lifted something—it was heavy and plastic, from the sound it made against the wall— and left the room. He was only a few steps into the hall when Travis heard the digital tones of a phone number being punched into a keypad.

* * *

"He knows where it is," Karl said. "And he has the key in his pocket. For now I've left it there, to keep him confident."

Karl was standing outside the front of the restaurant, far from the hiker's hearing range. He explained his plan into the phone. When he finished, the man on the other end of the call remained silent, considering it.

The breeze had picked up since earlier, coursing down from the north through the gap where the highway transited the range. The sun, also farther north, shone blood red along the gravel ribbon.

"If your idea doesn't work," the man on the phone said, "then what you're suggesting will be a terrible sacrifice." His voice sounded hollow over the satellite connection.

"If it does work, it's worth it," Karl said. "Regardless, it's the only way to get what you want now."

More silence. Karl knew to let it play out. As he waited, he turned and stared off to the south. The hiker had guessed correctly about one thing: Tangent would send help by way of the Air Force, probably a C–17 Globemaster coming out of Elmendorf with its ass on fire, a couple Special Tactics teams ready to bail off the ramp. Elmendorf was in Anchorage, four hundred miles south, give or take. If the C–17 had lifted off within ten minutes of the call—a near certainty—it would be here within the hour. But because the hiker had told Tangent about the helicopter, Karl knew there was something else coming from Elmendorf, moving a hell of a lot faster than a cargo jet. Maybe three times as fast.

The man on the line finally spoke. "All right. Do it. When do you want the helicopter?"

Karl did the math. Even accounting for some unpredictability, the timing should be good enough.

"Go ahead and call them now," Karl said. "Tell them to take off right away."

CHAPTER THIRTEEN

A lone with the sound of Paige trying to hold on, Travis found his mind returning to the attack that had knocked him unconscious. He didn't think he was misremembering it now. The details were clear. The gun in his hand had suddenly pulled itself down—but not just down. Down and forward. There'd even been a twist in the motion.

As if a human hand had grabbed it.

Then, half a second later had come the blow to the side of his head, from someone who must have been standing out of sight behind him.

But how? Travis had been in this small room from the moment the big guy in the John Deere hat had led him to it. There'd been nobody here. There was no closet to hide in, and the window had been closed. How had the attacker gotten behind him, unless he'd been hiding under the bed?

Even in that case, Travis knew there was some deeper flaw in the picture. Something more fundamental. But for the longest moment he couldn't put his finger on it.

Then he remembered.

The sunlight—coming from the northwest, almost straight into the room through the window. While he'd stood there with the gun leveled at the doorway, his own shadow had been projected on the wall just inside the room, hard and sharp as a picture on a movie screen. Anyone behind him—anyone within five feet of him in any direction—would have been shown there as well. He could not possibly have missed it.

So what the hell had happened here?

In his mind he saw Paige in the clearing again, holding the Whisper, telling him humans hadn't created it. Saying it like it was the most normal thing in the world. The most normal thing in *her* world, anyway.

What else was normal in Paige's world? What capabilities did her enemies have? What the fuck were they up against here?

A sound broke the moment. The last sound he wanted to hear. Rotors. This was it, then. Two minutes from now, he and Paige would be dragged from the building, onto the aircraft, and then they'd be winding through the valleys at low level, probably on nobody's radar. Maybe these people would have drugs and instruments to keep Paige alive for a while, and wake her up for a new marathon of agony.

Unless he killed her first.

There might just be time. If he contorted his body the right way, he thought he could get himself seated upright against the wall, and be standing without much trouble. His ankles were bound, but he could reach the bed in a couple jumps. Then just smother her with his shoulder. As weak as her breathing was, it would be simple.

He could make those moves. Could he make that choice? Jesus, could he do that to her? Logic, hard and clear, told him he'd regret it sorely if he didn't.

The necessary time was slipping away now, the rotors coming in loud, like a clock ticking off the seconds at hyper speed.

With the indecision came hatred, more bitter than he'd felt in years. Hatred of these fucking people for pushing him to the edge of this decision.

And then the chopper exploded.

A concussion wave shook the building, and in the wake of its bass came the most beautiful silence Travis had ever heard. Five seconds later a fighter screamed overhead, its own shockwave rattling the window. He heard the engines whine through some kind of power adjustment, and then the roar, instead of fading into the distance, seemed to even out. The jet was circling.

Obviously it couldn't save them from the man who was already here. Any second his footsteps would come pounding down the hall from wherever he'd gone; a quick detour to murder them before fleeing. But the worst possibility had been cancelled out. Travis had that to be thankful for while he waited to die.

Half a minute passed. No footsteps. He felt hope sliding back in, whether or not he trusted it yet.

Then instead of footsteps he heard voices, people shouting. Coldfoot's remaining residents, probably fewer than ten, had emerged from their homes and were calling one another outside to see the spectacle. He heard a woman call Molly's name, approaching the lodge, and then she screamed, and a moment later other voices rose around her, and the front door of the building swung in.

Travis yelled for them.

They came to him cautiously; it was a minute or more before they'd entered the room, sat him up and removed his blindfold and bindings.

Through the window, framed like a portrait, the steep ridge across the highway was strewn with the burning remains of the helicopter.

"Who did this?" the old man who'd released him asked. "Where'd they go?"

"I don't know," Travis said. "Any of the victims up front have guns on them?"

The man nodded, his curiosity deepening. "Molly and Lloyd both," he said. He glanced at Paige and then returned his eyes to Travis. "You gonna tell me what's happening here?"

"The military's coming," Travis said. "Maybe they can tell us both. Just get the guns and tell everyone to keep their eyes open until help arrives."

The man accepted that and left the room.

Looking at his own shadow on the wall, solitary as it'd been before, Travis wondered if that last advice even mattered.

CHAPTER FOURTEEN

Forty minutes later a cargo jet rumbled in out of the south and, from three thousand feet up, offloaded two dozen paratroopers. Travis went to the window—he was unwilling to leave Paige alone in the room—and watched them circle down in tight columns, landing within fifty yards of the building. They were dressed in black, their uniforms bulked out with body armor, their weapons slung on their shoulders as they touched down. By the time the last of them landed, the first had already taken positions around the lodge.

Four of them stood out. One, maybe ten years older than the rest, pointed and gave orders, his sharpness and efficiency apparent even from beyond hearing range.

The last three needed no orders. They were surgeons. They made straight for the building, waved in by the locals, and Travis called them to the room as soon as they entered. They carried packs and duffels loaded with all the equipment a modern ER would have, plugging in two power strips to create enough outlets for the monitors, lights, and other machinery they arranged around the bed. Travis got out of their way and watched them take command of the situation. The specifics of their technical speech went by him, but the meaning came through clearly. They could save her.

Moments later the commander came in the front door of the lodge, carrying a satellite phone like the one Ellen Garner had tried to repair. He was speaking to someone on it already, and as his eyes found Travis in the hall, he said, "I'm here with him now."

He strode to Travis, but instead of handing him the phone, he paused, listening to the caller. "Of course," he said. He looked past Travis into the room. "Dr. Carro, status."

The oldest of the surgeons, Carro, answered without looking up from his work. "She's stable."

The commander relayed the message into the phone, then said, "Yes, sir," and handed the unit to Travis. As he did, for just a moment his eyes held the same curiosity as the old man who'd unbound Travis earlier. Then he walked away down the hall.

"Hello," Travis said.

The reply came from the man he'd spoken to when he'd called Tangent earlier.

"We have a more secure connection now," the man said, "but we're still going to be careful about what you say on your end. Those first responders are military; they're not cleared for what we'll be talking about."

"Okay."

"First, thank you for intervening on behalf of Miss Campbell. We owe you a great deal. The following questions, I'll ask you to answer with a simple yes or no. Did you see an object the size of a cue ball, dark blue—"

"Yes."

"Is it in the possession of the people who were holding Miss Campbell?"

"Not exactly," Travis said.

"Did she hide it somewhere?"

"Yes. I can tell you where—"

"No," the man said. "Don't do that. Just confirm for me whether it's hidden near the encampment where you rescued her."

"Yes," Travis said.

"All right. The F–15 pilot verified that there's nobody left at that site. The hostiles must've all been aboard the chopper when it was hit. So here's how this is going to work. We have two Black Hawks coming to you, a little over an hour away. The pilots and crew aren't military; they're our people, and they're cleared for this. One of the choppers will evacuate Miss Campbell. The other will take you to the camp in the valley, where you'll show our people the Whisper's location. They'll have the means to contain it for transport. Once it's secured, you'll receive further instruction from them."

"Okay," Travis said.

"Do you have any questions?"

Travis was on the point of describing the strange attack in Room Three, but found himself unable to frame it in any way that made sense. He hadn't even done that in his own thoughts yet.

"None," Travis said.

The man thanked him again and hung up.

Fuck.

It was all Karl could do to keep the curse to himself. The easy version of the plan had nearly worked.

From the open door of the fourth room off the hall, ten feet from where the hiker had stood with the satellite phone, Karl had watched the conversation.

He'd been in this room since just before the helicopter's demise, after using the sound of its rotors to mask his return down the creaking hallway. The room had proven a fine place from which to listen to the hiker's phone call, though Karl had been prepared to follow him elsewhere if necessary.

It really should have worked.

With the chopper down in flames, and the fighter pilot's word that the valley was clear of hostiles, Karl had been certain Tangent would ask the hiker where the damn thing was hidden. He'd even started to tell them, before they'd stopped him.

That knowledge would have ended the game. Karl would have easily taken the key back from the hiker—probably by way of a silent kill in the hallway while the doctors were preoccupied—and left the building. He'd stowed his own satellite phone in the drain trench beside the highway, three hundred yards south. A quick jog, and he could have sent his superiors the location of the hidden Whisper more than an hour ahead of Tangent's arrival at the site.

It would have been more than enough time. His people had already dispatched another chopper from their own staging point; it was screaming along the Brooks Range at this moment, below radar, toward the valley where the 747 lay in ruins and the Whisper lay hidden. The F–15 had long since turned for home, having spent its fuel inefficiently in the mad scream to reach Coldfoot.

One spoken sentence, and every tumbler would have clicked into place.

Fuck.

Karl waited for the hiker to wander back to the open doorway of the makeshift emergency room. The noise from equipment and voices inside provided ample sound cover. Karl moved past the man, down the hall and out the front door.

By the time he reached his phone, the lodge and the soldiers around it were distant specks, inaudible over the wind. He dialed and waited.

"Tell the chopper to land five miles west of the site and wait there," he said when it was answered. "It's going to be complicated."

CHAPTER FIFTEEN

By the time the Black Hawks arrived, the wind out of the north had hardened. Travis put his back to it and watched them come in, their shadows rippling over the landscape far behind them. They were still a mile out when Dr. Carro came to the door of the lodge and waved him back inside.

"She's asking for you," Carro said.

He followed Carro back to the room and found Paige with her eyes open, though unable to focus. He took her hand, and she dragged her gaze to meet his, like a child pulling a heavy weight. He wondered if this was all she wanted: just to see a face she knew, if only barely. Then she spoke, her voice so weak Travis had to lean close.

"If you have to wake it up," she said, "then do it. It's worth it, if there's no other choice. But let go of it as fast as you can."

The doctors traded looks, and Carro said, "Confusion is normal for someone under this much sedation. She'll be fine after—"

"I know I'm on ten milligrams per minute of propofol," Paige whispered. "Please shut up and let me speak."

Carro shut up.

Paige fixed her eyes more firmly on Travis and said, "I know Tangent is coming. I know everything seems safe. But we never assume. We can't afford to. If things go bad . . . if you have to use the Whisper . . . press the key against it to wake it up."

She faded for a few seconds, then drew a deep breath and said, "Just let go of it as soon as you can. If you wait too long, it won't let you."

Then her eyes closed, and her breathing stabilized.

Outside, the Black Hawks came in low over the building. Travis heard pebbles from the gravel parking lot scatter against the front of the restaurant. Then, through the window on the north wall, he saw both aircraft set down on the grass expanse outside. He held Paige's hand a few seconds longer, then left the room.

By the time he reached the front of the lodge, a man had disembarked from the nearer chopper. One of the soldiers on guard cocked an ear at something the man shouted, then pointed at Travis as he stepped from the building.

Travis had expected the Tangent operatives to ask exactly one question, and otherwise not speak to him. Instead, the man shook his hand, identified himself as Shaw, and thanked him with the same gravity as the man on the phone.

Shaw was outfitted the way Travis imagined Navy SEALs would be. His rifle, modified to the nines, drew looks from the nearest soldiers.

"We're ready right now, sir," Shaw said, indicating the open door to the Black Hawk's troop bay.

Travis followed him to it. It crossed his mind that, even a few days earlier, climbing into a military chopper full of commandos would've qualified as a strange thing. He pulled himself in and took a seat on a padded bench at the rear wall. Shaw climbed in beside him. In addition to the pilots, there were six men in the Black Hawk, all equipped for the end of the world. The turbines revved, and a moment later the chopper was high above the lodge and turning west, tinted shafts of sunlight swinging through the interior like spotlight beams. Travis looked over his shoulder through one of the small windows, and saw the surgeons bringing Paige out on a stretcher. He kept his eyes on her until the first ridgeline swept below the aircraft, blocking his view.

Facing forward again, he saw a squat metal shape in the center of the floor: a cobbled-together and much smaller version of the steel box that had contained the Whisper aboard the 747.

Outside, ridges and valleys that had taken hours to cross on foot slipped by like sections of sidewalk.

The encampment had seen heavy traffic since Travis had left it. Staring down from the circling Black Hawk, its starboard door now wide open as the men scrutinized the valley for movement, he saw a broad patch of disturbed ground that had served as the hostiles' landing pad. Skids had dented the surface in all directions, and the comings and goings of the hostiles had turned the grass there to bare earth.

Satisfied that the valley was clean, the pilot set down on the torn earth, the clearest place in sight. As soon as the wheels touched, the men exited from both sides of the chopper. Travis was the last one out, glancing forward along the fuselage as he stepped from the door.

Something made him stop.

He knew the feeling, though he hadn't felt it in years.

A supplier he'd known had called it getting your whiskers flicked. A kind of intuition maybe only criminals—or bad cops—could feel, sharpened by years of doing things they couldn't afford to be caught doing. The slightest thing might trigger it: multiple cars tapping their brakes on the same stretch of road for no apparent reason, hinting at a police presence just out of sight.

As Travis stared forward along the side of the Black Hawk, something flicked his whiskers. Hard.

But he couldn't place it. He swept his eyes around, and for some reason he kept coming back to the front right wheel, extending down and away from the side of the fuselage on a foot-long strut. There was nothing wrong with it, as far as he could tell. The tire and strut both seemed fine.

Shaw saw him looking. "What is it?"

Travis had no answer for him, and shook off the sensation. He hadn't slept in over thirty hours—unless he counted the few minutes he'd been unconscious after getting knocked out—and had spent the last two of them wandering around a mass-murder scene. A little jumpiness should be expected.

"It's nothing," Travis said, and nodded ahead through the trees. "What you're looking for isn't far. Fifty steps past their camp, buried near the biggest tree in sight."

He took another glance at the wheel, then passed through the group of men to take the lead—

—and stopped again.

He turned back to the Black Hawk.

In the soft dirt on either side of the wheel was a footprint, each one facing outward—the prints a man would make if he were sitting right on the tire with his back against the side of the chopper, maybe holding onto the gun mount above it for balance.

Travis stared at it, part of him expecting the footprints to shift before his eyes. Then he became aware of Shaw standing beside him.

"Tell us," Shaw said. "I don't care if you think it's stupid. Tell us what you're thinking, right now."

The guy sounded more than just serious. He sounded scared.

"Look at the prints beside the wheel," Travis said.

Something like a second passed—enough time

for Travis to imagine these men laughing when he was compelled to explain himself.

A second later, he understood that he was very wrong in that impression.

Shaw flinched—Travis was sure he saw it, though the movement was swallowed up by the blur that came next, as the man snapped his rifle up and opened fire, putting a burst of half a dozen shots through the side of the Black Hawk, a foot above the tire.

The bullets punched through the metal. No blood. No screams.

"Eyes open for a weapon, all sides!" Shaw yelled; already he was sprinting over the disturbed ground toward the chopper. The men around Travis shouldered their rifles, each choosing a direction. They did it instantly and without discussion, as if they'd drilled for this sort of thing. Travis suddenly felt sure they had. Even the pilots, also out of the chopper, had drawn sidearms and were scrutinizing the sparse trees around them.

Shaw vaulted into the Black Hawk's troop bay and swept his rifle back and forth inside, in large but efficient strokes. He didn't so much aim with it as feel with it, like a blind man whose life depended on finding his quarry. Travis's eyes easily picked out the handholds the enemy could have used to pull himself into the chopper without touching the ground.

Shaw found nothing.

He returned to the door. His gaze fell to the

dirt before it, and went cold. Travis saw why: the ground leading from the troop bay was saturated with their own footprints—so many they overlapped—leading off of the bare earth onto the grass. The enemy's path could be any of them.

One of the men whispered, "Fuck . . ."

That single word, so drenched with fear while coming from someone so hardened, told Travis all he needed to know about the trouble they were in.

He had a second to think about that, and then the pilot took a bullet to the head. There was no sound of a gunshot—just the impact, like a heavy oak panel being split, and then the man was down, already gone. The others were shouting, training weapons and eyes in all directions. Travis saw Shaw jump from the chopper and run to his men, screaming for them to be quiet, and he saw the co-pilot staring around, scared shitless, as a terrible understanding came to him, and even as Travis made the connection himself, the man took the second shot right over his left eye, the entry wound facing Travis so directly that the bullet must have passed right over his shoulder, and now Shaw was looking at him and shouting, "Which way?" and Travis threw his arm out to point behind himself, and in the next instant the world was nothing but machine-gun fire.

They fanned out. Travis got behind them and watched the red tracer rounds carve a wedge of space against the valley wall sixty yards north.

Shaw screamed for them to get more space among

themselves. He'd just finished saying it when a bullet hit his throat and came out the back of his neck, making a fist-sized crater. He dropped, his eyes wide and his hands pawing at his collar.

The men broke formation, running and firing at the same time. One of them stooped, grabbed Shaw's rifle and threw it at Travis; he just managed to get his hands up and catch it.

Then he was running with them—the half that had split in this direction. Running for the encampment, and then through it, his mind only now getting around to what his body had already decided.

The tree stood out like an obelisk, easily twice the width of any other nearby. He pulled up short and swung past it, kicking aside the carpet of needles to expose the gouged surface where Paige had refilled the hole.

Somewhere a man screamed and went down hard as he ran. He lay crying for help, but after only a few seconds Travis heard him gargle as his windpipe filled with blood.

Travis dropped the rifle, fell to his knees beside the hole and attacked the dirt with his bare hands. It was soft, having been torn up and replaced only a day and a half earlier, but the going was—

Not fast enough. No way was it fast enough.

Because the killer knew it was buried here. Travis had given this location out loud, right outside the helicopter.

He heard another head shot, twenty feet to his

left, and turned to see a body still plunging forward with its running momentum, but with the top of its skull missing. The shoulder hooked a tree trunk and the body twisted around it, falling in a tangle at the roots.

Travis dug faster, his ears suddenly keening with the rush of blood through his carotid arteries—why could he hear that now?

Then he understood: the shooting had stopped.

He quit digging and looked up.

They were all dead.

CHAPTER SIXTEEN

H is hands went to Shaw's rifle again and lifted it. They were caked with clay; he could barely get his finger into the trigger well.

In the silence, only a soft breeze moved. The boughs of the smallest saplings rose and fell with it.

What had Shaw yelled? *Eyes open for a weapon.* Would the killer's gun be visible?

Travis swept his gaze left to right, slowly, trying not to focus on any one thing. With no other sound or movement among the trees, maybe he'd see something.

Then he did see something—but not in front of him.

At the bottom edge of his vision: a shimmer of blue. Against all instinct to keep his eyes on his surroundings, Travis looked down. His last handful of dirt had exposed a dime-sized portion of the Whisper's surface. The color swam across the face of the sphere. It looked like a little world, all ocean, all in twilight at the same time, somehow.

Something stirred in the trees.

He snapped his gaze up but saw no sign of movement. He couldn't even be sure which way the sound had come from. He pivoted, still kneeling, but saw nothing on any side.

The killer was being careful, now that it was just the two of them, but there was no question of how this would end. The question was how many seconds of his life remained.

If you have to wake it up . . .

He took no hope from the idea. Whatever the Whisper did, how could it possibly help him in this situation? This was far beyond any danger Paige could have foreseen.

Ten seconds? Did he have even that much time left? Ten seconds on his knees in the dirt, wondering if he'd feel it when the bullet fragmented in his head?

It wasn't much to lose.

He dropped his free hand from the rifle's barrel guard, drew the cellophane key from his pocket and plunged it into the hole, mashing it against the Whisper as he pulled it free of the dirt.

Light flared from the thing, searing blue, so brilliant that even over the pulse of his own fear a new thought dominated: *it was a star, somehow he was holding the heart of a star—*

Then that thought was gone as well, like a scrap of paper in jet exhaust, and his mind filled with a voice more beautiful than the blue light, and he realized he knew it, though he hadn't heard it in years: Emily Price, when she was seventeen and he was seventeen; Emily's voice in the humid dark of the tree house in her parents' yard, the night she'd told him it all felt right, that the moment was right—

But she wasn't saying any of that now.

"*Behind you,*" she said, "*two feet left of the double pine. He's drawing. Go. GO.*"

Travis spun, the rifle coming around in his right hand, stopping just before the twin pine that came up in a V from its roots, fifteen feet away.

He heard a man gasp—surprise laced with anger—and in the same moment he saw the impossible: a silenced pistol slipping into view as if from a fold of nothingness.

Travis fired.

The heavy rifle gutted the air, the cyclic recoil maybe three times harder than the M16's had been, pushing him off target almost immediately— but it didn't matter. Even over the blast-chatter of the rifle he heard the killer scream, and the pistol went sideways, end over end in a pitched arc. A second later the lowest bough of the double pine bent violently downward; it seemed to pin itself to the ground.

Travis let go of the trigger. Silence. Then he heard the man crying and fighting to breathe.

Travis looked at the sphere in his hand. The blue light was strobing now, the rhythm matching his own accelerated pulse.

Emily's voice cooed in his head, and he heard her giggle.

"*Gave him a hurts donut, didn't you? Gave him a whole box of them with sprinkles and cherry filling.*"

Travis felt his logic slipping. He understood that the voice wasn't Emily at all, that this thing had nothing to do with her, but even that understanding began to fade—by the second—as he held the thing. He felt the clarity of his thinking being washed out, like visual details lost in light glare.

It was time to let go of it. Let go fast, like Paige had said.

He opened his hand—

The rifle fell and clattered on the roots at his feet. It took him a full breath to realize his mistake.

"Sweetie, you don't want to drop me, do you?"

Now that he thought about it, no, he really didn't want to let her go.

Her? It.

"You can think of me as a girl if you like. It's all the same to me. I haven't even minded being called the wrong name all this time. I promise to tell you my real name someday. It's a lot cooler than 'Whisper.'"

With each passing moment—each heartbeat of the sphere—the voice soothed him more deeply. Soothed him and took him back there, to that night, to those few hours he'd long remembered as the best of his life.

"There you go."

Emily kissing him, her need almost a tangible thing, her breath mixing with his, pulling away just long enough for her to tear off her shirt up over her head.

"You hit him with three of your twelve shots, in case you were wondering."

So beautiful. It didn't matter what she said now. The voice was enough. And what had Paige been thinking? Who in their right mind would let go of this thing? This lovely thing.

"Your third bullet hit the collarbone and glanced down at a forty-five. It fragged just in time to shatter the T6 and T7 vertebrae. Ouch and a half. He's not even in shock; he's feeling ninety-four percent of the pain capacity of the human nervous system. And judging by his systolic, he's gonna keep feeling it for another eighty seconds or so."

"I love you," Travis heard himself whisper. "I always loved you."

"Oh honey, Emily Price is dead. You know that."

"Yes, I know." It didn't matter. Nothing mattered. Everything was wonderful.

"Tough on her family that no one alive knows where she's buried, don't you think?"

"The worst." He sighed, his heart beating faster, the light keeping up with it.

"Briar Lake, the dunes west of the nature center parking lot. There's a stand of eight birches on the crest of the backdune. She's under the smallest one, more or less. It wasn't even there when they put her in the ground; now its roots are coiled through her rib cage."

So wonderful, so savagely wonderful. Travis drew the light closer to his eyes. How had he mistaken this dear thing for a star? It was so much more.

"You should really be thinking about Paige Campbell."

Who was Paige Campbell? Who cared?

"*That kiss may have been only practical, but my hunch is that she'll be up for the real thing once she gets to know you. My hunches tend to be right, by the way.*"

"Oh. That's nice."

"*If both of you survive what's coming, you'll have a chance with her, in spite of your résumé. Surviving is the trick, though, isn't it, considering where the two of you are going soon. Seven Theaterstrasse in Switzerland. Never mind that it's the linchpin of her enemy's plan. The fact is, it's the most dangerous building in the world—if you don't count places where they store radioactive waste. And c'mon, who's counting those?*"

"Seven Theaterstrasse . . ." He loved the way that sounded, coming from her.

"*Everyone in Tangent is terrified of that place. Imagine the kittens they'd shit if they knew its real purpose.*"

Travis laughed. He didn't know why. Didn't care, either.

"*But since you're going there, let me give you something you'll need.*"

As soon as she said that, Travis felt a prickling inside his head, the sensation diffused, everywhere at once. Then gone.

He heard Emily giggle. "*Now don't say I never helped you, irony notwithstanding. A girl has to have her fun, right?*"

"Whatever you want, I want," Travis whispered.

"*Do you mean that?*"

He nodded, and the sphere grew silent for a moment, contemplative maybe. Then the light changed. Just noticeably. Darker but not dimmer—somehow.

"Because what I want is trouble."

"Trouble," Travis agreed.

"It's what I do. It's what I'm for."

"Mmm-hmm . . ."

"That's why your enemies want me. They've got all manner of mischief planned. But their ambitions don't concern us here, do they? We can make our own mischief right now. A whole world of it, if we want to. Would you like that?"

"Oh yes . . ."

The sphere went silent again, and Travis had the impression it was weighing options of some kind. He turned it left and right in front of his eyes, watching the light play in its depths.

"Let's see now . . . That would work . . . but it's on the boring side; I want to do something big. Go big or go home, right? How about—" Suddenly the light flickered, and Travis heard Emily laugh. *"Yeah. Oh yeah, that would turn a few heads. And there might just be time to do it, before the helicopter arrives. All right then, it's settled. Go to the Black Hawk and take the satellite phone from the forward bulkhead of the troop bay. Run."*

Travis ran. It was all he could do not to skip like a little kid. When had he ever been this euphoric? Heroin had been nice, but it might as well have been chewable aspirin next to this. He slipped a little on the soft ground outside the Black Hawk, laughed, and climbed in with his muddy feet. The briefcase on the front left wall had to be the phone. He pulled it from its clamps and laid it on the floor.

"*Turn it over and open the rectangle-shaped access on the lower right.*"

He flipped it, pressed the thumb tab and removed the panel to reveal a circuit board.

"*We're going to change a few things before we make the call, or else it'll never work.*"

"Okay."

"*An inch to the left of the processor are seven jumpers, half the size of phone jacks.*"

He saw them. Each jumper was stuck onto a set of twin prongs, closing a bridge in the circuit.

"*Remove the jumpers at J4 and J6.*"

It was tricky, but he got them off after a couple tries.

"*Put one of them back on, at the empty position J12.*"

Easy. So easy to please her.

"*Now open the red tool case on the wall to your right. Take out the smallest precision screwdriver.*"

She kept speaking as he followed each order; he thought he could hear urgency in her voice. A lover's urgency, begging him to take her to the edge.

"*Use the screwdriver's tip to carve a gap into the silicon pathway marked PRC21. Do not damage any other pathway.*"

He finished the job in seconds.

"Good. Now switch on the phone."

He turned it over and pressed the red button marked I/O. The phone's LCD lit up with a red frame, and a message: MASTER SETTING MODE SELECTED. ENTER DOD AUTHORIZATION CODE.

"Use the keypad to enter 98104801, followed by the star sign."

When he finished, the red frame disappeared and a menu came up.

"Select option four, 'Change ID Prefix.' Answer all three questions with Yes, by pressing 1. Then enter 77118-star–945 as the new prefix. Pound key to verify it. Faster, sweetie."

He shuddered in response to her rising excitement; his fingers trembled on the keys as he finished the sequence.

"Now exit the menu, just keep pressing 9 until it says, 'Ready.' Good, my love. We're ready to call them. Pick up the handset and dial 82-star–375–121–9188."

He dialed. It rang once, and a man answered. "CINC-Pacific forward hub, please authenticate."

Travis opened his mouth to speak, and experienced bliss incarnate: the Whisper took control of his voice, bypassing his decision process. What came out sounded like him, though slower, and with the ghost of a drawl: "November, hotel, one, four, eight, juliet, echo, oscar. This is a priority card from Trap Door."

The man on the other end took a quick breath,

then spoke evenly. "Trap Door, I agree with authentication. Go ahead."

Travis felt his mouth open to speak again—but stopped. He turned his ear to the open bay door behind him.

From far away came the sound of rotors. At the same time he felt the sphere in his hand tense somehow; the light flickered like a nervous twitch.

Then he was drawn back to the phone, and spoke rapidly: "Relay the following EAM to USS *Maryland*. By order of the president of the United States and the chief of staff, Navy, set condition four-alpha, immediate launch of two Trident ICBMs against Target Package 3261, Nanjing ballistic missile complex, East China, Jiangsu Province."

The man on the phone didn't reply right away, and Travis said sharply, "Commander."

"Yes, sir." Another pause, not even a second, and the man said: "In accordance with protocols governing the release of strategic weapons, the senior controller will ask you for the president's and the Navy chief's nuclear launch codes. Those are the final authorizations required."

"Put him on," Travis said.

"*Go go go*," Emily whispered in his mind. The light was strobing so quickly now it was almost smooth again, like a bad fluorescent bulb.

The rotors were getting loud; the echoes off the valley walls made it hard to guess the distance.

A soft-spoken man came on the line. "The president's code first, please."

"Six, one, nine, three, three, three, two, eight."

"Now the Navy chief of staff's."

"Four, nine, six, eight, five—"

Suddenly the chopper sounded much closer; it must have just passed the last ridge and entered the airspace over the valley.

"Sir?" the soft-spoken man said.

"I'm sorry," Travis said. "Starting over, four, nine, six, eight, five, seven, seven, one."

"Thank you, sir, EAM is authorized and will transmit about thirty seconds from right—"

The man's last word was cut off by a shriek of metal as autofire ripped through the Black Hawk. Instinct overrode Travis's euphoria and he threw himself clear, toward the back of the troop bay. His wrist collided with the rear bench, and the Whisper broke from his grip. It hit the floor and rolled to the back corner.

Travis cried out, not from pain but from a swell of anguish. Losing hold of it—*her, losing hold of her*—felt like losing a loved one. Like losing his *only* loved one.

The chopper passed overhead with a turbine scream and a downrush of air that rocked the Black Hawk. The gunfire stopped and Travis saw the aircraft arc out over the valley, making a wide loop to come back.

He got up on his knees and reached for the Whisper—

Three inches shy, he stopped.

Clarity filtered back in, like blood to a deprived limb. He withdrew his hand as if from a serpent. What had he done? What had he *fucking done*?

A voice, tinny and just audible, issued from the phone unit behind him. "Sir? Are you still on?"

The preceding minutes came back to him now, laid bare to his logic. Outside, the helicopter had completed its semicircle and was returning, ten seconds out.

"Sir?"

Travis spun, dove for the handset and screamed into it, "Call it off! It's bullshit! Call it off!"

"Excuse me?"

"Call someone and check on it, it's all bullshit!"

"Who the *fuck* is this?"

Through the window he saw the gunner's muzzle flash overhead. He vaulted backward and fell from the bay door into the dirt, as the Black Hawk was shredded by a much more sustained burst than before. He got to his feet and—catching a last glimpse of blue light under the bench seat—sprinted into the trees.

He was forty yards away when he realized the helicopter wasn't following. The thunder of its rotors remained constant; it had gone into a hover, and now the turbine pitch dropped. Travis reached a grove dense enough to provide a screen and stopped. Looking back, he saw the chopper descend and set down beside the Black Hawk.

The men inside had the look of the hostiles who'd tortured Paige. One of them, wearing heavy gloves that went to his elbows, jumped from the chopper and ran to the Black Hawk's bay door, his face momentarily bathed in the Whisper's glow. He reached in and took hold of the sphere, and despite his protection, he swayed on his feet, his face relaxing and then his mouth turning up in a child's smile. Behind him, two others hauled a heavy steel box from the chopper, roughly the size of the cobbled one inside the Black Hawk. They reached the man with the Whisper and had to shout and nudge him to get his attention. At last he seemed to notice them. Nodding, he opened the container and shut the sphere inside it.

Twenty seconds later, its cargo secured, the helicopter revved to a scream again and climbed away over the valley.

PART II

7 THEATERSTRASSE

CHAPTER SEVENTEEN

The Tangent personnel who arrived on the next Black Hawk were under stricter orders than the first group. They bound and hooded Travis, belted him aboard, and he heard nothing but the craft's engines whining at full power for the next two hours.

He thought of the Whisper. The euphoric—even erotic—sensation of holding it still weighed on him like a personal loss, in its absence.

Yet as strange and powerful as the experience had been, he was forgetting it. Rapidly. Even now, just this short time after the fact, his memory of the entire event had faded to something like a receding dream. He could recall how it'd started: picking the thing up, Emily Price's voice directing him to fire on the unseen killer. And he could recall how it'd ended: letting go of it inside the Black Hawk, after slamming his wrist on the bench seat, and becoming aware of what he'd done under its control. What he'd done with the satellite phone, and what was about to result from it, thousands of miles away.

But everything between those two points was

now a bright blue haze. Like a drug high he couldn't remember, except for fading pieces. The thing's terrifying capability. Its impossible knowledge of everything—literally everything. It'd told him something about Paige. What, he couldn't remember. And it'd given him a street address, for reasons that now escaped him. Something that sounded German, he thought; he could resolve it no further than that. As the time stretched out aboard the Black Hawk, he found even these trace memories slipping deeper and deeper out of his reach.

The chopper landed. He had no idea where. The aircrew helped him outside onto pavement, and he heard the heavy turbofans of a large jet powering up. Someone guided him up a set of metal stairs, and then he was aboard the plane, his head still covered.

There were quite a few people on the jet, ten to fifteen voices, he thought. A set of hands led him to a seat at the back end. Outside, the engines rose in pitch, and the aircraft began to taxi.

He heard tension in the voices around him. Fear, too. Calls came and went, in a few different languages. From the context of those made in English, Travis gathered that the people on the other end were government officials in countries all over the world. For a moment he wondered if the Whisper's plan had been carried out anyway, and the ICBM launch against China had gone ahead. The man next to him assured him it hadn't; his screamed warning at the end of the call had been more than sufficient.

But something was going on. Something that concerned the whole world. Something that scared the shit out of these people.

A moment later the jet turned onto its runway. It stopped for a few seconds as its engines came up to full scream. Travis's interrogation started just as it lifted off.

Five times, for five different people, he told his account of what'd happened, starting with his discovery of the wrecked 747, Box Kite. The point of the repetition was obvious enough: to see if his story would break along the fault line of a lie. It didn't. All he kept from them was the part he'd lost: the now nearly impenetrable amnesia effect that hung over the minutes he'd spent with the Whisper.

He told them about the invisible attacker, dead on the bent pine bough in the valley. The questioners' reaction to that news was a few clicks above happy. They called ground teams that had secured the valley and directed them to the body. Travis thought of the first team's fear, in the last minute of their lives, and wondered how long Tangent had been dealing with that particular threat.

Then he told them about the street address. The one he couldn't quite remember. The one that sounded German.

"Seven Theaterstrasse," the first questioner said. Not even asking.

Travis nodded anyway. That was it.

He heard the phrase make its way up the plane like a passed note, and he marked its progress by the silence it left in its wake.

* * *

They let him sleep after the fifth round of questioning. He woke to the bark of the wheels touching down. Then came a jeep ride over rough ground for a few hundred yards, through bright sunlight that warmed the black fabric of the hood still over his head. The baked air could only be that of a desert. Behind him he heard the jet already powering up to take off again. The jeep reached a smooth surface at the same time that it passed into shadow out of the sunlight. An elevator ride followed, lasting some ten seconds. Ten seconds moving down.

"You can take that off him. Those, too." A woman's voice. Soft and raw, like she'd ruined it screaming at a rock concert the night before.

The binds at his wrists clicked open, and the hood came away to reveal a windowless office—and Paige Campbell standing in front of him. The veins in her right arm were still discolored, and her face remained drawn and pale, darkened beneath her eyes. But she was on her feet, as steady as a person could be. Her breathing was silent, normal. She'd come out of the Brooks Lodge on a stretcher, two thirds of the way dead, maybe ten hours ago, depending on how long Travis had slept on the plane.

The others left the room. He was alone with her.

She followed his eyes to her arm, the now-sutured incision across her triceps just peeking from her sleeve. Some compound the color and consistency of tar had been applied to the wound, probably deep inside it. The swelling around the injury had all but vanished.

"You'll see a lot of strange things around here," she said. Then, softer: "I saw a map of the distance you carried me. Thank you."

He didn't know what to say back to that. He nodded, and thought of what else she must have seen by now. His criminal record. Every detail of what he'd done. More than enough to counterbalance any merit he might have gained with her.

"Sorry for your treatment aboard the plane," she said. "We're methodical."

Her cell phone rang. She looked at the display, answered, and told the caller to give her a minute. In her voice was the same tension he'd heard among those on the plane.

She gave him a look that seemed to cut past any further polite conversation while at the same time apologizing for it. "Would you consent to a narcotic interrogation? It may help us recover more of what the Whisper told you."

He had a sense that she didn't expect that to work, but that she'd take what she could get. He also felt sure it would happen whether he consented or not. Nice of her to pretend to ask, though.

On the wall behind her was something that clashed with the professional look of the office. It looked like a promo poster for a rock band. It was a close-up of a steel surface, with the words *ETHER WASTE* carved roughly into it. Nothing else. No tour dates, no website address.

Paige waited for an answer. Probably wouldn't for much longer.

"Do what you have to," he said.

"Thank you." She indicated a door on his left. "There's a bathroom there if you'd like to clean up. I'll be back in a few minutes, and we'll get started."

He turned toward the closed bathroom door as she crossed the office to leave.

"I thought I was back up to speed on heavy metal groups," he said. "Guess I missed one."

Her footsteps halted at the threshold to the corridor. "What?"

He looked at her. Saw her looking back with blank eyes.

"Ether Waste," he said, nodding at the poster. "I've never heard of them."

She didn't move. Still staring at him from the doorway. She had no idea what the hell he was talking about. Maybe the drugs were still having some effect on her thinking, though nothing else about her behavior said so.

Then she reacted.

Her eyes narrowed and she took a step in from the doorway. Looked back and forth from him to the poster. "You can read that?"

He started to ask if she was okay, but the sentence died as a thought. He was looking at the poster again, which suddenly looked more like a blown-up forensic image than a promo. He looked at the text in particular. Really looked at it, instead of just reading it.

It wasn't English.

It wasn't even writing, by any definition he'd have assigned. There were no discrete rows or columns. No sense of order at all. The engraving on the steel was just a chaotic tangle of curves and lines, overlapping and pointing in all directions like a spill of needles and loose threads.

But he could read it.

He could read it without even thinking about it, as if it said STOP in white letters on a bright red octagon.

VERSE III
AN OCTOBER NIGHT IN 1992

Though the fog is thinner here in the elevated district west of downtown, and the streets are brightly lit, Travis is driving faster than he should. He doesn't slow, even after he's entered the subdivision, Empire Oaks, with its smooth asphalt lanes winding among ten-thousand-square-foot homes. He doesn't slow because he doesn't care who or what hears him coming this time—because either way, he's going to do what he came here to do.

He thinks of Emily and wonders if she blamed him in her last minutes of life, when she knew it was over. She'd have been right to blame him, of course, but every instinct tells him she blamed herself instead, and the thought of that generates more hurt than Travis knows what to do with. He has already mentally added it to the debt he will settle in the next few minutes.

He makes the turn onto Stonegate Court doing fifty, his back tires losing the wet street for a moment before they grip again, and the car surges forward.

Emily Price.

She is all that matters to him now, even though she's gone.

He thinks of all that she did for him. All that she saw in him, beneath all that he was.

He thinks of her father, using the word *Detective* as a slur. It cuts because it's true. Though that word has preceded Travis's name on his paychecks for three years now, he's been on someone else's payroll much longer. In fact Travis's sole reason for becoming a cop was to further serve the needs of his other employers. His first employers.

He'd have spent the rest of his life as a rat, without Emily's intercession. Without her light to lead him out of the maze.

She did lead him out.

And they killed her for it.

He makes the next turn and sees the house at the end of the street, blazing with light from all twenty-six of its exquisitely furnished rooms. Drug money spends like any other kind.

Travis is still doing fifty when he drives through the fence. He hits the brakes halfway up the yard, and when the needle drops below twenty-five, he shoves open the door and bails onto the lawn. He rolls and comes up just in time to see the car punch through the bay window and disappear completely into the house. Five seconds later he follows it in, gun in hand and eyes searching for targets.

CHAPTER EIGHTEEN

aige's office came to life. People came and
went with purpose. Where there'd been tension and fear before, now there was tension
and fear and a little hope that no one wanted to
voice. Paige sent someone to line up another transport, this time to Zurich. From the context of what
followed, Travis gathered that 7 Theaterstrasse
was a building located there, and that the metal
engraving from the poster-sized photo was inside
it, along with other writing of the same kind. Paige
and the others seemed to believe that the Whisper had given him the capacity to read this text,
though he couldn't imagine how or why.

Someone leaned in and told Paige the transport
was thirty minutes out. She seemed to disconnect
from all the talk at that point, thinking hard about
something.

"That's enough time to show him," she said, her
eyes finding Travis.

"Show him what?" a woman next to her said.

Paige considered her decision a few seconds
longer, then solidified it. "Everything."

* * *

A moment later he and Paige were in the corridor, moving away from the office while the others stayed behind. Travis heard them making calls, finalizing details of supplies and ground transportation in Zurich.

The silent corridor was a welcome change. Dimly lit, mostly deserted. The place felt like a high school after hours.

A red-haired woman, early fifties, hustled by toward the office behind them. She caught Paige's eye as she passed, then stopped.

"Is it true?" the woman said. "He can read it?"

Paige nodded.

The woman glanced at Travis, her expression mixed, as if he were either a B-list celebrity or an escaped specimen from a plague lab. Maybe both. Then she nodded, touched his shoulder, and continued on.

Paige led him farther along the hall.

"I know this all must feel like cleaning your contact lenses with a hose," she said. "I'll try to put it in order for you. A lot's going to depend on your being up to speed."

She went quiet just long enough to assemble her thoughts. "Right now, the business of running the world is on hold. Right now, the most powerful people on Earth are sitting by their phones. Including the American president. Who just lost his wife. He can't focus on that, any more than I can focus on what happened to my father, because right now the worst-case scenario we've ever imagined is threatening to come true. And until you read that text on my wall, I didn't see any real way to stop it."

They came to an elevator. She pressed the call button pointing down.

"This building is called Border Town. Tangent's home. It's in eastern Wyoming, seventy miles from the nearest anything."

The doors opened with a chime, and Travis followed her in. Turning, he saw a panel of floor buttons that started with B1 and descended all the way to B51. B10 was presently lit. He thought he knew which button she'd press, even before her hand went to the array. He was right. A few seconds later they were dropping toward the bottom of what was essentially a buried skyscraper.

"What's Border Town on the border of?" Travis said.

As evenly as she might have said *Nebraska* or *South Dakota*, Paige said, "Another world."

B51 was nothing like the corridor they'd left above. Concrete floor, walls, ceiling. From the elevator it extended sixty feet and then opened up to an undefined space beyond, vast and pitch black. The tunnel might have led onto a darkened football field.

Paige moved toward the open end, but turned in at a doorway thirty feet shy of it. Travis followed her into a room that looked like a bunker that scientists would've sheltered in during atom-bomb tests in the fifties. Like the hallway, everything was concrete. Antiquated computer terminals hunkered at the far end of the room. Nearer to the door, current issues of *Newsweek* and the *Wall Street Journal* lay on some of the desks. Despite the place's mausoleum atmosphere, it apparently saw some use.

Paige opened a cabinet and withdrew a tan spiral notebook.

"At one time, only this floor of the building existed. It was the site of a Department of Energy project, the Very Large Ion Collider. Sixty billion dollars and ten years to build. It went operational on March 7, 1978. It was used exactly once."

She handed him the notebook. Up close he saw rust-brown fingerprints on it that could only be blood. Similar stains had soaked deep into the pages at the book's edge.

"Read this," she said. "It won't take long, and it speaks for itself better than I can."

With that she took out her cell phone. Travis opened the notebook while she called upstairs to catch up with the preparations going on in her office.

The blue lines on the paper had faded almost to nothing, but the text, handwritten in black ink, remained sharp and easily read:

VLIC GENERAL COMMENTS LOG

(SEE DATA LEDGERS FOR
ALL SCIENTIFIC RESULTS)

MARCH 7, 1978—14:33 UTC

Well, it begins today. We're all so excited we can't put it into words.

I'll make this opening entry quick, since we have a lot going on. First, the point of this ledger: to record the human story of this place. Someday we may want to write a popular book about the VLIC, in the style of Feynman or Sagan. A log of people's personal experiences here would be great for that. So no pressure, guys. Just jot down what you're feeling. Anticipation, frustration, anything.

Here's today so far. Very, very exciting around here. Many of us have been on board this project for the entire decade that VLIC has been under construction, so to finally be just hours from the first shot is a kind of excitement I've never felt before. About twenty DOE people will be here for it, including Secretary Graham. He met with us earlier. Nice enough. He seems to have a good grasp of what this place means to physics and all science, in passing anyway, although after he stepped out someone said he probably would think an off-shell W boson was something at Taco Bell, haha. (No offense Mr. Secretary if you ever read this, we kid around a lot.)

Predictions for the first shot? Ha, not on your life. Obviously there's the expectation that we'll raise the lower bound on the Higgs by another percent of the standard model's prediction, but no one's saying it'll happen on the first shot! I would stick my neck out and say I hope, in time, we get an even more significant result than that, but I don't want to look back on this entry and think I was an idiot, so I'll just say I'm proud to be here, and to be part of this team trusted with something this special. We all are. This is Dave Bryce.

MARCH 7, 1978—
PROBABLY A QUARTER AFTER 18:00 UTC

This is Dave Bryce again. This account of the shot is for investigators in case we all die down here before anyone gets to us. None of the machine-collected data survived, I'm sure, because of what happened with the metal. I don't know how we lived through it, it seems like the iron in our blood or the trace copper in our neurons should have been affected, and killed us instantly. Maybe it did get affected, and we're just not symptomatic yet. We're all very upset and scared. Here is the record, what I know at least, so whoever finds this will have somewhere to begin.

The shot happened at 17:40 UTC as scheduled. At the instant of collision, everything metal here in the bunker took on luminescence, different colors depending on the metal, but generally blues, greens. Something inside the wall phone was shining bright yellow, not sure what it was. The DOE undersecretary, Porter, collapsed, and there was no pulse at all, even right away. Two of the DOE people who knew him said he had a pacemaker. That seems pretty irresponsible to have him down here for this, even though we wouldn't have guessed there was any danger, I think I would have advised against it if I'd known. Laid the body at back wall of bunker, does not seem very dignified but nothing else would be any better.

Ruben Ward collapsed also, but for a different reason. He had both hands resting on the metal housing for the ring switches at the time of the shot. Don't know if he got a jolt from it, or what it might have been, but he lost consciousness and fell. He's still unconscious, we have him on the floor with a couple sweaters for a pillow.

Luminescence faded after about thirty seconds. At that point we had no information to go on, all electrical systems were out, computers, temp gauges, everything. The lights in the bunker were out, too. The only way we could see anything was a bright light shining down the hallway from the shot chamber, right past the doorway. It's very bright, and a lot of it comes in here, indirectly. Because of the angle, we can't see far enough down the hall to see into the chamber. We don't know what's going on in there, or where the light is coming from. I know we don't have anything that bright installed out there. It is still shining now, thirty or forty minutes after the shot.

We took a vote and have decided to open

the door, and send someone to check if the elevator is working. (I'll go.) It's a dozen yards or so farther from the chamber than this room, maybe there's a chance it wasn't affected. Scary to open the door, if it's possible the air is bad outside the room, though I don't know why that would have happened. (But who knows about anything down here now?)

APPROX. HOUR AND A HALF AFTER LAST ENTRY

It took us half an hour to get the door open. The metal had fused to the frame at several places like a weld. If it'd been a tighter fit to the frame, the whole thing would have fused, and we'd have been trapped. Sure as hell would not have broken through the 2-inch-thick polycarbonate window in the door.

No use anyway. I went out to the elevator and it's dead. Pulleys are probably welded solid even if the electrical was working.

When I was in the hall, I could see into the chamber, but could make out no detail except the light, which I couldn't look right at. In peripheral, it seems like a single point of light out in the middle somewhere, bright white. It felt like sunlight on my skin, maybe even a little warmer, which is scary. I came back in the room quickly.

Also, some kind of sound is coming from the chamber, very faint, could almost be imagining it, but I don't think so. Hard to describe it, sort of like a tuning fork. Back in the room with the door shut, I couldn't hear it anymore.

Someone will have to come for us soon. Ruben is still not responding. I keep thinking about all the precautions I might have recommended, all these years while this place was being built. Maybe a medical staffer down here, if nothing else. Just never thought for a second something like this (whatever this even is) would happen. I take responsibility for whatever happens to these people. This is still Dave by the way.

FIVE TO SEVEN HOURS AFTER LAST ENTRY

I dozed off. Secretary Graham woke me up and I saw that the light in the hall had changed. Much dimmer, and blue instead of white. Everyone's nerves have had it, mine too. Why the hell isn't someone down here to get us yet?

Ruben still unconscious. Wonder if he is in a coma, but have no idea. Porter's body bloating a little, smells terrible, really bothering us in this unvented space.

I am pissed off, I'll say that. Maybe unprofessional, and maybe I'll tear out these pages later, but right now I'm pissed and want to say so. Ruben Ward is my best friend and one of the smartest men in the world, he has so much to offer science, and he might be experiencing brain damage by now because these fucking assholes are doing what up there? Having a luncheon and setting a date for a formal meeting about how to get us out of here? I know I'm being unfair and stupid, I'm sure they're up there figuring it all out, but I'm stressed and really pissed. This room smells like roadkill but we're afraid to leave it. Wish I knew what the hell that light from the chamber was. Dave.

TWELVE HOURS AFTER LAST ENTRY, GIVE OR TAKE

Can no longer handle the smell. Graham and I have volunteered to take the body out into the hallway at least, maybe farther toward the chamber. Majority have voted to leave the door open for a while after that, let the room air out if that will even happen.

Light is a bit dimmer now, and purple, projecting ripples in the hallway like you see on the bottom of a pool. Have to admit I'm afraid to go out into it, just don't know what it is, what is out there in the chamber.

But curious, too, no doubt about it. We're going now. Dave.

ONE HOUR AFTER LAST ENTRY

The interacting point at the center of the chamber is gone. The whole assembly, and the magnets too, just gone like they were never there. Some amount of the floor they were sitting on is gone as well. There's a kind of crater in the floor, not blasted there, but more like machined there, like a giant with a disc sander honed it out. It's maybe a foot deep in the middle, shallowing out to the edge at a radius of, I don't know, twenty feet.

Above the crater, perfectly centered where the interacting point used to be, is what I can only call a rip in midair. The rip is an oval, some ten feet wide, maybe three feet tall in the middle, purple and blue light filling it and curling like flame at its edges. When you look into the rip and move back and forth sideways, you realize you're looking into a depth, an opening. It's like looking in through the hatch of a deep coal furnace.

Graham and I just stood and looked at it for I don't know how long, after we took the body down to the chamber. Then Graham went around the far side of the rip, and called out for me to follow. I went, and here's where it's craziest of all, you can't see the rip from the other side. As soon as you go past it, it's gone, you just see the empty air over the crater. Edge-on, you see those blue-purple flames licking out of the opening, but a step farther back and there's nothing.

The sound is still there, too, different now, like the light is different. I still have no good way to describe the sound, except . . . it's like voices. I mean, it's not, but that's what comes to mind. Voices singing from out of the opening. There's something bad about the sound. It does something to your mood. Not sure what it is, but it makes you feel very wrong, in a lot of ways. Graham felt it, too, and when we got back to the room, the others had changed their minds about leaving the door open. They wanted to shut the sound out, even if it meant keeping the smell in. I agreed.

Since then I've been sitting here just trying to come to terms with what we've created. What the hell is it? I keep thinking of all the concepts I thought were five hundred years down the road, Einstein-Rosen bridges, that kind of thing. Not even going to guess, though. I'd just look stupid later. It has to be studied by experts in a range of fields, measured, tested. Data first, theories later. Wow, though. Wow squared, Ruben would say.

I just realized I can still hear the sound, even with the door closed. Maybe it's because I know what I'm listening for now.

HALF A DAY OR SO AFTER LAST ENTRY

I woke up in the hallway, down at the end where it widens into the chamber. I did not remember walking out there, and would never have chosen to. I was shivering hard when I woke, could feel the sound from the opening, like it was going right through my body and making my bones hum. Got up fast and saw that Graham was out there, too, and the fat guy who works for him, Kurson, I think his name is. Both asleep. I woke them and they were as surprised as me to find themselves there.

Back in the room with the door shut, could not seem to relax. A woman from DOE, someone's assistant, spilled a few Cheez-its and tossed them in the trash, and I blew up at her, seriously thought I would physically attack her until the others calmed me down. I apologized later.

What the fuck is up with someone coming to get us? What is it, a couple days now? I don't even know. This is bullshit. When this is over someone's getting an earful from me and probably legal action. Seriously, what the fuck?

QUITE A FEW HOURS AFTER LAST ENTRY

I sat next to Ruben a long time and read to him from a paperback he had in his desk, in case he can hear somehow. Maybe I just did it to try blocking out the sound from the chamber.

Then, I don't know why, but I got up and went out there, out into the chamber. Stood staring at the rip/opening. It's beautiful, and you know what else? When you're looking at it, the sound is not entirely bad. I'll probably tell Graham to try it for himself, I think he'd be able to appreciate it.

I GUESS A DAY LATER

Pretty bad tension among the people down here, I guess it is to be expected with us all crammed in like this. I am not fitting in with the group much at all. I can't wait to get out of this place and never see these people again. Another bad argument a little while ago (the third or fourth one) this time with me against almost all of them, except Graham and Kurson.

A few of the guys teamed up and tried to demand that we stop going to the chamber to listen to the sound up close. They are saying that it does something to us, and that we're causing grief as a result. But we aren't causing ALL the arguments, I don't think. So nice try, but you guys can fuck off. I shouldn't get pissed like this.

The sound is pretty soothing now. It's all that keeps me in my wits down here. When will they come for us?

TIME IS HARD
TO FOLLOW LATELY,
I THINK IT IS A DAY LATER

I have this weird, shitty hunch about Ruben Ward, but don't want to write it down.

Also, I have to admit, I'm having a hard
time staying focused, and today my right arm
was shaking for like an hour when I was out
in the chamber. But it's not from the sound.
I really do like it quite a bit.

QUITE A LOT LATER

My hunch is Ruben is faking now. Was really
unconscious at first, of course, but faking now
so that he can stay out of the arguments
and not have to side with me against all of
these fucking people. It pisses me off if it's
true. I tried really hard to wake him up just
now, hitting him in the face even. Then many
of the others pulled me away from him (of
course they would if he's on their side the
cowardly piece of shit). Now I am out in the
hall by the chamber writing this.

Only the voices from the breach (we started calling it the breach, we like that name for
it) make it better.

I will tolerate these people, but I know I
would not lose sleep if they all got hit by a
goddamned bus.

MANY, MANY HOURS
(IT MIGHT BE A DAY OR MORE) LATER

Why? Why are you doing this? You don't have to be doing this.

Graham and Kurson and I were in the chamber for a long time and came back to find the rest had jammed the door shut with one of the desks. Graham was rightly upset and tried to break in through the glass, but the polycarbonate is very strong.

Not even kidding, I would love to kill all of these people, and Graham is the same. Kurson just nods, I wonder if he is only telling us what we want to hear.

I like the blue and purple there is a dance to it.

HOURS I THINK BUT TIME
IS GETTING IMPOSSIBLE TO KNOW

Kind of losing the knack for keeping all that stuff straight, hours and minutes. I think I've taken for granted all my life how hard time is to keep track of. Quite hard. Quite a trick to it, I think.

STILL DAVE HERE DID I MENTION THAT?

No desire to go back into the room with the others, but just the principle involved drives me mad. I stand at the glass and look in at

them, and they won't look at me, and fucking Ruben you fake coward motherfucker, I
swear you are going to pay.

But mostly I am calm. Never been calm like
this and I love it.

GRAHAM HAD A VERY GOOD IDEA

he broke off a metal conduit in the back
of the chamber (took him forever kicking to
break it) and is using the sharp break point
to scratch a line through the polycarbonate
window in the door. it's working, too!!! he has
carved half an inch into the window on one
side, and then this is great, he carved just
the shape of the whole square he's going to
cut into it, so those assholes can see what
he has planned. he is a very smart man, it
makes sense that he is secretary of the department of energy.

we are going to get in there within a couple
days and then ruben i am going to mount you
like a fucking baboon i swear.

THE BREACH GAVE US SOMETHING

it must have come out a little while ago,
a piece of green fabric the size of a napkin,
did not see it come out, but I noticed it lying underneath the breach, and it had not
been there before. tried to pick it up, but this
makes no sense at all . . . it weighs hundreds

of pounds, i just cannot lift it. graham and i together were able to slide it, try to smooth it out on the floor, what the hell is it??? i am not going crazy, it really weighs hundreds of pounds, this tiny little thing!

GRAHAM IS AWESOME

he lost it for a while and was pounding the conduit against the door window and then noticed a huge (huge) flap of his palm had torn away and was hanging, and right in front of them watching he took it in his teeth and ripped it free. he is an awesome man

we killed kurson, not really a choice, we just set on him all of a sudden, it happened. no one's fault really, so it's fine.

WHO IS IT SINGING IN THE BREACH?

voices are so beautiful please i need to know who it is.

RESCUE!!! HAHAHAHAHA

(graham died this morning, don't even know how, someone had torn out his throat while he slept.)

later two men in yellow suits and mountain climber gear pried open the elevator doors just like that, no warning, i was able to kill one with the conduit but the other was wea-

sel quick and got away through the top of the
elevator cab screaming don't.

BULLHORN ALL DAY

   they are talking from high up in the elevator
shaft i don't care just shut the fuck up, goddamn all of you.
   very upset that the window is still intact
and these people may survive especially ruben
he was supposed to die.
   sitting at the breach makes it okay.
   it is a day at the breach get it?
   i should be fine after all this, if i can stay
here.

I THINK I KNOW WHO

   ghost little girls. that's who is in there.
that's who is singing in the breach.

Travis closed the bloodied notebook and caught
the end of one of Paige's calls. The plane was
twenty minutes away.

She nodded at the notebook. "What followed is
what you imagine. The next team that roped in
had guns." She was quiet for a moment, then said,
"The Breach Voices are just one of a thousand
things we're completely in the dark about. Their
origin, their meaning, the reason for their effect on
people. We just don't know, probably never will.
I think about David Bryce often. Top of his class

at MIT, father of four, respected by everyone who ever met him. He couldn't see the danger, even sitting in front of it with his eyes wide open. I sometimes worry that's the only story the Breach knows how to tell."

She led him back into the hall, and toward the open space at the end. The darkness there looked wrong: given what Travis had read, the Breach should be visible from right here. A few steps later he saw why it wasn't. They entered the cavernous chamber to find a hulking black shape nearly filling it, a dome the height of a three-story building.

To the right along the dome's base was an entry channel like that of an igloo. As they approached it, Travis saw the ghostly blue and purple light Bryce had described, projected through the entry onto the concrete wall of the chamber. Ten feet shy of it stood a simple metal table. Paige left her phone and watch there. Travis followed suit with his own watch.

He thought she'd head for the entry then, but she stopped, stared at him, her eyes working something out.

"You were a cop," she said. "A detective."

He nodded.

"Were you good?"

He breathed a laugh. "By no stretch was I a good cop."

"I know you were corrupt. I meant good *at* it. Were you good at detective work? Did figuring things out come naturally to you?"

He didn't hear judgment in her voice. Something

else. Contemplation, he thought. He wondered why.

"Yeah. I was good at it."

Her eyes on him, unblinking. Then narrowing in thought.

"That might end up being useful," she said. "It's not often we get fresh eyes around here. I'll explain a lot more on the plane. For now I just need you to know what's at stake."

With that, she led him to the dome's entry, and through its heavy glass door.

CHAPTER NINETEEN

L ike looking into a depth. Into a furnace. As Bryce had written. The Breach was an oval ripped open across thin air, ten feet wide by three high. Blue and violet tendrils of light, flame-like in their substance but not in their shape, capered along the length of the tunnel, which was three feet in diameter and receded to infinity. Only in the nearest yard did the tunnel flare out to the wide oval.

Within the giant dome that shielded the rest of the building from who knew what, a much smaller containment system encased the Breach to protect anyone who entered this space. This smaller enclosure was a rectangle made of more thick glass, with an airtight door at the front. The glass cage's purpose was as obvious as the library silence of the room. Travis watched his faint reflection blurring rhythmically on the vibrating glass, and imagined the malignant Breach Voices encased within it, just a few feet away.

He refocused beyond the glass to the Breach itself, the tunnel stretching away to a vanishing

point. He felt his perception bend toward it like a
row of iron filings to a magnet.

"There's only so much to say about it," Paige
said. "It leads somewhere. We don't even try to
guess where. Nothing can go through from our
side. And no living thing has come through from
the other side. But objects do. Three or four a day,
on average, for over three decades now. Entities."

Directly beneath the Breach stood something
like an industrial-strength trampoline. It was
square, five by five feet. Its fabric looked both flexible and strong, and its legs were wrapped with
shock springs. It was positioned to soften the fall
for anything that came out of the opening, whether
it weighed an ounce or a ton.

Cameras just inside the glass casing covered
the Breach from two angles. No doubt someone
watched their feeds day and night, from somewhere in the floors above B51. It would only be
necessary to come into this space when things actually emerged from the Breach.

"Certain entities we see all the time," Paige said.
"The twenty most common probably make up
ninety-nine percent of the traffic. A few of them
are behind you."

Travis drew his eyes from the Breach and turned
around. A dry-erase board on the wall proclaimed,
NEXT UNIQUE ENTITY WILL BE DESIGNATED 0697.
Below the board and to the left was a set of steel
shelves. Arrayed along them were a few duplicates
of three separate items. One was a kind of string,
bright white and a little thicker than floss. Each

strand, about a foot long, had been trapped on one end by a paperweight. They'd have floated away otherwise. The strings trailed lazily in space, neither heavier nor lighter than the air. Gravity seemed to just not affect them. On the next level down were a few pink crystals, the length and width of fingers. Travis could see nothing special about them. Beneath those, on the lowest shelf, were two examples of what Bryce had described. Green rags. Travis dropped to a crouch and studied them. They were lying mostly flat. The few wrinkles in the fabric were tight and sharp, like hardened veins. Like the material had been drawn to the surface by vacuum pressure.

"Try to lift one," Paige said.

Travis tried. He grabbed for the nearest as if it were a washcloth, palming it in the middle to gather it in a handful. It was like trying to grab a handful of the shelf surface itself. The cloth didn't budge. He took the corner of the rag between his thumb and forefinger and found he could lift the first inch. Beyond that, it was just too heavy. He wondered for a moment how the technicians moved these things around, and then he noticed a wheeled chainfall a few feet away, with a vise-grip claw hanging from a cantilevered arm. Built to hoist engines out of cars, it was probably just about suited to lifting these rags.

"Bryce wasn't crazy," Travis said.

"Not about that."

She picked up one of the pink crystals from the middle shelf.

"For all that we don't know about the Breach," she said, "this much is certain: in terms of technology, whoever's on the other side is as far ahead of us as we are ahead of Java man."

She let go of the crystal, shoulder height above the floor. It plummeted. Then, in the last foot of its fall, it slowed and came to a stop a quarter inch above the concrete. Sharp little beams of light shot from it, projecting onto the floor. The object seemed to be measuring its own position and rotation. After a second the beams switched off, and the thing set down with a *ting* that reverberated through the room.

"Everything that comes through is baffling to us," Paige said. She nodded at the green rags. "The best materials scientists in the world have studied that fabric using our most advanced tools, scanning-tunneling microscopes that can isolate atoms. They've learned nothing. Not a single thing, in over thirty years of study. They tell us the material doesn't even seem to be *made of* atoms. They nicknamed it a quark-lattice, but that's a wild guess, not a testable theory, and it's almost certainly wrong."

Travis found his eyes drawn back to the Breach.

"Once or twice a month," Paige said, "things come through that are either rare or unique. Things like the Whisper. We never understand how they work, but we can usually get a sense of their purpose. Not always, but usually. Some of them have good applications, like the medical tools that were used on me over the past several hours. Others are so dangerous, we just focus on keeping them safe, keeping them dormant and locked away. And that's more or less what Tangent was created for. To shepherd what comes out of the Breach. To distinguish the good from the bad, find uses for the former, and contain the latter."

She paused and turned to him. He looked at her and saw in her eyes the same vague trance effect he felt in his own. In the Breach's presence there was no avoiding it.

"In the first year after March 7, 1978," she said, "when the government was trying to figure out what to do with this place, there were proposals to fill the elevator shaft with concrete and leave this chamber sealed forever. Whatever showed up could just stay down here, however helpful or dangerous, and we could simply not tinker with any of it. At the time, those proposals were thought to be the most prudent. My father didn't think so. He argued that eventually something might come out of the Breach that was effectively a ticking bomb. Something that if left alone would be so destructive that five hundred feet of dirt wouldn't protect the world from it. He was right. In the time since then, at least three entities have arrived that fulfilled that criteria. The point is obvious enough. It takes the smartest and best people in the world, working as hard as they can, just to prevent the Breach from triggering a nightmare. Imagine what the worst people could do with it, and you understand what's on the line here." Her eyes went back to the Breach. "This building is the most secure site on Earth. It protects the Breach and all that's ever come out of it. All that ever will come out of it too. And right now, it's all in play. The security isn't enough. The people who tortured me and killed my father, the people who now have the Whisper in their arsenal, want control of this place, and if things go wrong for us in the next day or so, they'll have it."

CHAPTER TWENTY

On the surface—literally—Border Town was not an impressive place. It was a faded red pole barn with a pile of rusted automobile parts drifted against its back wall, the property bounded at the perimeter by a few cracked and leaning posts that had once been a split-rail fence. Just visible against the flatlands that planed to the horizon on all sides, a gravel track wandered southwest across fifty miles of nothing.

Nothing that could be seen, at least. The barren landscape probably concealed enough firepower to repel a military assault. Even American military.

Travis stood at an open bay door of the barn, alongside Paige and fifteen others who made up a larger version of the teams he'd met in Alaska. He'd heard the proper terms for them now: the units were called detachments, and their members were known as operators. At the moment, each of the fifteen was dressed casually, weapons and armor stowed in green plastic carrying cases, though their bodies and expressions marked them as hardened, well trained. Paige had the same look. No doubt she'd come up through their ranks, though it was obvious now that she outranked everyone present.

Something glinted in the washed-out blue sky to the west. It resolved into what Travis expected: a blank, white 747.

Two F–16s accompanied it. As it began its final approach, they broke away and went into a circling pattern high above the desert. Travis had an idea that such escorts would be standard procedure for Tangent flights from now on, after what'd happened to Box Kite.

A minute later the 747 landed a quarter mile away on what looked like unmarked scrubland. Travis and the others drove to it in three electric vehicles with all-terrain wheels, the same sort of vehicle he'd ridden in earlier, while hooded. Only as they closed the last fifty feet to the aircraft, and the ground beneath the carts smoothed out to un-natural perfection, did Travis realize he'd been staring at a runway all along. The tarmac had been mixed with an additive so that it matched the land-scape perfectly, and even landform shadows and patches of vegetation had been painted onto it. To any aircraft or satellite, it would be invisible, day or night. He wondered how the pilots who landed here lined up on it, and then saw the answer: tiny lights lined the edge, their plastic casings rough-ened and browned like their surroundings. They weren't shining. Hadn't been a moment ago, either. They were probably ultraviolet, visible only with the right gear.

In the deep shadow of the 747's wing, a door

opened, pulled in by a crewman standing in what should have been the luggage hold. Travis could see an interior staircase behind the man, leading up to the main level. Had he investigated further aboard Box Kite, no doubt he would have found an identical setup.

Paige and the others began unloading their gear and taking it to the plane. Travis helped. Among the carrying cases he saw two that were different: black instead of green. He didn't need to ask their significance.

A few minutes later they were climbing, the F–16s falling in at the 747's wingtips again. The aircraft banked into a northeast line, bound for Switzerland by the shortest route, across the top of the world.

The plane's floor plan was the same as Box Kite's. Travis sat in a large chair, facing Paige, in the counterpart to the room where he'd found Ellen Garner wide-eyed and dead. Out the window, Wyoming stretched east toward Nebraska, vast and brown and empty.

"You really never wonder?" Travis said.

Paige looked up at him. "I'm sorry?"

"The Breach. You said you don't even try to guess what's on the other side. That's hard to believe."

She thought for a moment, then said, "We all wonder. But if there's no way to test any one guess, no way to measure them against each other, it all comes to the same thing. We just don't know."

"Whoever's on the other side," Travis said, "the tunnel would've had to open on their end too, right? You'd think they'd notice. And how are these objects coming through it? Is someone over there feeding them in, three or four times a day?"

"The popular guess is that we tapped into an existing network of tunnels. Some alien equivalent of those pneumatic tubes they use at the bank. Could be a delivery system limited to non-living objects. Maybe, right? Maybe not. *Maybe*'s a common word in Border Town."

"Maybe you tapped into a garbage chute," Travis said. "Maybe all this amazing stuff is just their trash."

She smiled, seeming to surprise herself as she did. It was the first smile Travis had seen from her, and he thought it made the entire flight worthwhile.

"Haven't heard that one before," she said.

"Fresh eyes," Travis said.

They were quiet for a moment. Then he said, "Why can't someone go through from this end?"

"There's a resistance, right at the mouth of the tunnel. When you try to push something through, the resistance pushes back with something close to gravity force at first. But the force doubles about every three centimeters the further you go, so you don't get very far. The woman we passed in the hallway, with the red hair, is Dr. Fagan. She's done the most work studying the resistance force. She wants to break through it, find a way to contact whoever's on the other side of the Breach."

Somehow that notion affected Travis more deeply than anything they'd spoken of yet. Real contact with whoever—with whatever—was on the other end.

He saw recognition in Paige's eyes, like it was obvious what he was thinking. Maybe it was. Maybe that idea struck everyone the same way, the first time they heard it.

"It's not likely to work," she said. "Even Fagan accepts that. If you could get past the initial barrier, the math would still be stacked against you. It gets into really strange stuff—Einstein, general relativity, time dilation—things we can calculate but not actually understand. Anyway, it all points to the same conclusion: whatever you sent through the Breach would just come back before it reached the far end. It might return months or years later, or—and this is more of a guess—it could actually come back *before* you sent it. Maybe long before."

She watched Travis's expression, then added, "Like I said, lots of *maybes* in Border Town."

Travis nodded, then stared out at the country falling farther and farther below. A freeway crept by, running east to west, all but devoid of traffic.

"So, what exactly is at Seven Theaterstrasse?" he said at last.

Paige was quiet a moment before replying. "It's not so much what's there, as what the building itself *is*."

"Which is?"

Another silence. Then: "A weapon."

He turned from the window and looked at her. Waited for her to go on.

"Seven Theaterstrasse is where it's all going to be decided," she said. "It's the choke point at the center of everything our enemy is planning. If we win there, everyone wins. And if we lose there—" She cut herself off, unwilling to say the rest, or maybe even think it.

After a moment she said, "None of this will make sense unless I start with the beginning. The essentials, at least."

She thought about how best to get into it, and then began the story.

Two strange things happened in the spring of 1978: the first occurred five hundred feet beneath Wyoming, the second, five hundred feet south of Pennsylvania Avenue. The most powerful bureaucracy in the world, presented with the most important asset in history, chose to limit its own influence.

Over the weeks following the catastrophic failure of the Very Large Ion Collider facility at Wind Creek, the president of the United States and most of his cabinet were briefed on the details as they came in from inspectors on site. The trapped DOE personnel had all been hospitalized and released; along with thick nondisclosure agreements, they'd been provided with trauma counseling, some of which would probably be long-term. Ruben Ward remained in a coma; he'd been flown to Johns Hopkins, where so far there'd been no change in his condition.

On April 3, the first scientific inspection team entered the VLIC site. They found that more than ninety objects had accumulated beneath the Breach—that term was well cemented even by then. If it hadn't already been clear to everyone involved that this situation would call for delicate handling, the team's findings brought the picture into razor-edged focus. In the eighty-seven-page report they filed after that first object survey, the word *dangerous* appeared more than two hundred times.

Upon receipt of the report, the president's most senior advisors settled into discussion along predictable lines. How tight a stranglehold should be kept on this project? How limited should Congress's awareness be? Which defense contractors should be brought on board, and how central a role should they play in making use of this strange new resource? Obviously those that had been the most generous during the election would have to be first in line, but how far back did the line go? Two companies? Maybe three?

Several hours into the first such meeting, the president turned to a man who'd said almost nothing so far: Peter Campbell, an MIT professor and, at thirty-three, the youngest member of the Science Council.

"You don't appear to agree," the president said.

"I don't."

"Then say what you're thinking."

Campbell chose his words carefully before he began.

"Does anyone in this room really believe we can keep this secret?" He allowed a few seconds of silence for an answer. None came. "Consider the spec data on the Manhattan Project. If there was ever a secret we needed to keep, that was it. How long did we manage? Two years. The Russian bomb program was under way within two years, at the latest. Think of the amount of knowledge they had to obtain from us to make their project work, and then consider that they need only learn two facts this time: that the Breach exists, and that the VLIC created it. After that, all the information they need is there for the taking. The specs on the VLIC were published in *Scientific American* five years before we finished building it."

The vice president spoke up. "Russia developing its own Breach is problematic, but—"

"Russia, China, India, North and South Korea, Israel, Germany, France, Britain, Japan, Saudi Arabia," Campbell said. "Probably a few more I'm leaving out. Count on each of them to have it up and running inside of ten years. Our VLIC took a decade to build with Department of Energy funding. DOD would've gotten it done in half that time, and we should expect the same urgency in all of these countries." He waved his own copy of the object report in front of him. "You want all *their* most generous defense contractors fucking around with this kind of stuff?"

Even years later, Campbell would lie awake wondering if one calculated use of the word *fuck* had saved the world. Certainly something in those few hundred words had struck a nerve, because the conversation tipped at that fulcrum and never managed to tip back. He'd aimed for their fears, that was all. He'd aimed for their fears and hit.

In the end, the president turned the inevitable question back to Campbell. What alternative approach did he propose?

Campbell had an answer. Take away the incentive for any other country to waste resources creating its own Breach. Share this one with all of them. Hold a secret summit with the leaders of these nations and their most respected scientists—but not their military-industrial tycoons. Be straight with them. Be upfront. Set in stone the only policy with a chance of avoiding chaos: the Breach should be overseen by a single organization loyal to the world as a whole and to no nation in particular. Let this group be composed of people with impeccable backgrounds in science and ethics—real ethics of human needs and liabilities, not the limited scope of any one culture's religious morality. Let no one actively seek to join; anyone craving that much responsibility should never be trusted with it. Instead identify excellent candidates and recruit them. The member nations should protect and finance this group, but none should control it. Not even America.

"But the Breach is on our soil," the defense secretary said. "We paid for what created it."

"All the more legitimate our stance will be," Campbell said. "Look, to whatever extent we flex our egos over this thing, we increase the chance of some other superpower saying, 'Forget it, we'll

make our own.' Once one of them does that, others
make our own.' Once one of them does that, others will follow. The only way to prevent it is to be even-handed. Think about it: wouldn't we be grateful if one of them did the same, if one of their research facilities had accidentally generated this thing?"

"I don't believe any other country would do that," the president said.

"I don't either," Campbell said. "Which is why history will think so highly of you."

The debate didn't quite end that day, but over the spring and summer of 1978, nearly every decision ultimately went Campbell's way. The group that would oversee the Breach was designated Tangent. Its objectives were simple: to organize and study everything that emerged; to draw scientific insight—if possible—from those observations and advance human knowledge; to prevent the Breach from ever becoming a wishbone between opposing parties.

And it worked.

For a while.

"My father's strongest ally in the fight to create Tangent was a man named Aaron Pilgrim," Paige said. "He was the president's chief science advisor, and also one of the founders of the original VLIC project. Like my father, he went on to become one of Tangent's highest-ranking decision makers, and was generally considered the smartest member of the organization. He was exceptionally good at figuring out the purposes of the strange and unique entities that came out of the Breach. In time, those were brought to Aaron Pilgrim first, by default."

She paused. Stared out into the harsh sunlight on the plains.

"The Whisper came through in the summer of 1989. It had an attachment that kept it separate from its key, at first. But even switched off, it was dangerous as hell. The key only turns on the intelligence; the self-destructive aspect of it is always on. The first person who held it barehanded murdered two lab assistants and then cut his own throat with a pen. With its intelligence on, it triggers the same murder-suicide impulse, but on the scale of the entire world."

Travis tried to recall the thing's possession of him. He couldn't. His memories of it, vague only a few hours earlier during the interrogations, were simply gone now. All he had left were memories of his own descriptions of the experience, but even those were going.

Paige saw his expression. "No one ever remembers," she said. "In a few more hours, you'd forget you ever held it at all, without others reminding you. No idea why it does that."

"Why did it save my life?" he said. "From the killer in the suit?"

"If we understand anything about its pattern, it works like this: first it addresses any needs on the part of the user. The more desperate the need, the better. So it helped you kill your attacker. And then—I'm guessing a little here—it gave you the ability to read the language you saw on my wall, because that's a need too, if we're going to prevent what's coming."

"But is that my need, or yours?"

"It's everyone's need now."

The way she said it didn't lend itself to doubt.

"So then what?" he said. "When it's done with the user's needs, it gets busy with its own?"

"Something like that. It may toy with the person for a while. Reveal some painful insight into an old wound, things like that. That may be why it uses a voice from the person's past, one with a strong emotional impact. But yeah, it turns toward its own goals pretty quickly, and they're always the same: cause as much harm in the world as possible, as quickly as possible."

"Nice."

"We understood all that about it, early on. The danger was so obvious, we considered locking it away and never studying it at all. But the potential for good was too big to ignore. It knows *every-thing*. And everything *about* everything. It knows how many blades of grass are in Kansas right now, and the length, angle, and arc of each one, and how the arc would change if the wind were half a mile an hour stronger. It knows the cure for cancer. The cure for everything."

"I assume you asked it."

"We asked. We brought in late-stage cancer patients and let them hold it. Should've worked, right? But it didn't. Either it didn't consider their need compelling enough, or . . ." She hesitated to say the next part, then exhaled and went ahead. "Or it just didn't want to tell us things like that."

Travis waited for her to continue. She looked outside again, maybe reliving the angst the thing had inspired in her over the years.

"You probably don't remember," she said, "but when it switches from help mode to kill-the-world mode, the light changes."

He didn't remember, but took her word for it.

"The focus of our research, of Aaron Pilgrim's research, was figuring out how to extend the first part, indefinitely if possible. How to control it, as a user, and not let it change. Pilgrim was the only one who ever gained any ground on it, in that regard. He learned how to keep it tame for minutes on end. And then indefinitely. He mastered it, by some combination of focus and . . . who knows? He said *he* didn't even know. He just got to where he could control it, keep it talking to him as long as he wanted."

"No cure for cancer, though," Travis said.

She was quiet a moment. Then she said, "Looking back, we have no idea what it really told him," and Travis understood where the story was going.

"There was no warning at the time. No sense that there was anything wrong with him. He made his move in 1995, after six years of working with the Whisper. He shut down Border Town's defense system and killed eight security personnel on his way out. He took three entities with him. One was the transparency suit you recovered for us this morning. Another was the Whisper. The last one I'll describe later. It's important. It's still unaccounted for, and it must be part of his plan."

"To take control of Border Town?"

She nodded. "In a way that wouldn't have been possible in 1995, all by himself. He's spent these past fourteen years assembling his own organization. You could call it a dark twin to Tangent." She met his eyes, and looked more grave than when she'd been dying. "There are things locked up inside Border Town that make a joke of every military on the planet. Pilgrim knows how to use them. Count on his people knowing, too. If he gets them inside, if they get control of that place for even half an hour, that's the end of any chance to stop them. They get the world that day. And whatever miserable fucking agenda they want to push, six and a half billion people will be stuck with it."

It was the kind of thing Travis wouldn't have believed even a few days earlier. He believed it now.

"Aaron Pilgrim became the most hunted person in history," Paige said. "The intel communities of every nation that funds Tangent pooled their resources, their knowledge, their means. They got nothing. Nothing for years. The more time passed without Pilgrim making another move, the more nervous everyone got. He was out there somewhere, setting up the chess pieces for whatever he had in mind. And it had to be something big, right? He had the Whisper to help him. He had all the knowledge he needed, and considering that knowledge is power, he had all the money and influence he needed too. He had all that, yet it was taking him years to set up whatever he was planning. You can imagine how that scared the shit out of us. Like there's someone standing behind you with a slingshot, and the longer it takes before he shoots, the farther back he's drawing it. After five years of waiting for the intelligence groups to unearth something, Tangent decided it'd been idle long enough."

"They got into the hunt themselves," Travis said.

Another nod. "This was around the time I came along, twenty years old. My father wanted me to stick to the research side of things, tucked away safely in Border Town. I wanted that too. But I saw the importance of the new program that was coming together, and I wanted to contribute. We modeled it on the CIA's Operations Directorate, but with every corner of it beefed up with Breach technology. Our going active like that was the one thing Pilgrim never expected, and if the Whisper told him about it, it wasn't enough to help him."

"How do you know?"

"Because it worked. We started getting leads on him. Picked off a few of his people, even grabbed some alive. Made them talk. Got even more leads. Like that. Dialed in on him."

"Couldn't Pilgrim just stay on the move?" Travis said, but even as he asked, he realized the answer himself. "Oh."

"Seven Theaterstrasse," she said, seeing his understanding. "He built his entire plan around a single location. In retrospect, we should've guessed

Zurich, or Switzerland at least. Information security like no other place on Earth. There's nowhere
better to hide a serious, expensive enterprise. We
pinned the address down on May 17, 2005, and
came within maybe two minutes of catching him
there. He escaped by such a narrow margin, he
had to leave the Whisper behind. Along with a few
of his people. Whom we grabbed. And whom we
made talk. Almost all that we know about that
place, we learned from them. They told us Seven
Theaterstrasse's stated purpose is—and I'm quot-
ing here—'to permanently end Tangent's restric-
tion of Aaron Pilgrim's global authority.' And they
told us it's not just a building. It's a weapon. It's a
weapon he was three hours away from pulling the
trigger on, when we arrived that day to stop him."

Silence fell between them. There was only the
drone of the engines, and the soft rush of air past
the window.

"Three hours," Travis said.

"Three hours."

"That's very hard to believe."

"Yeah," Paige said.

"Borderline impossible to believe."

"There are factors that nudge it toward plau-
sibility. His people were a lot more active than
normal in the last few months before his dead-
line, acquiring essential things here and there,
some of them hard to come by. That made their
movements easier to spot. At the same time, Pilgrim had to know we were closing in. Stands to

reason he picked up his pace a bit, wasn't as careful as he might have otherwise been. All of that helped us."

"Three hours, though," Travis said. "I know shit happens, but that kind of shit almost never happens."

"The alternative is even less likely. That he wanted us to show up there, force him out of the place he'd spent a decade preparing, and leave him on the run without the Whisper, which he'd probably come to think of as a second brain by that time. He'd probably rather have lost his eyes and ears than lose that thing."

She had a point.

"So Tangent has controlled Seven Theaterstrasse for the past four years," Travis said. "I assume you've had people studying what Pilgrim built inside it."

"Twenty-four seven, since the day we occupied it."

"So what does the weapon do?"

"That's where you come in," she said. "Because even Pilgrim's own people didn't have a clue. And neither do we."

Silence again. He had solid guesses for some of the questions in his head, but not all of them.

"The reason we don't know is obvious enough," Paige said. "Pilgrim didn't design the weapon himself. He made the Whisper design it for him, based on what he needs it for. Made it guide his work, for the ten years he spent building the thing, which occupies just about every cubic inch of the building, nine stories on the waterfront in Zurich. It's alien technology, cobbled together from human-made components. Clever way to build something, using the Whisper like that, but there was a downside, too, from Pilgrim's point of view."

"The memory effect," Travis said.

Paige nodded. "Impossible to remember, from one time to the next, what the Whisper has told you. That'd make it tricky as hell to follow its instructions consistently. So Pilgrim had to write things down. But that was a security risk, so the Whisper gave him a language no one else could read."

Travis saw all the pieces slotting together now.

"The place is covered with that writing," Paige said. "I could show you a few thousand images of it right now, but there'd be no rhyme or reason to it. It'll be better if you see it in person. See it the way he wrote it."

"You're hoping I can help you understand the thing," he said. "So you can shut it down."

"More like praying you can help us," she said. "But yeah."

"Can I ask something really obvious?" he said.

She smiled vaguely and preempted the question. "There's a reason we don't simply level the building. You'll see for yourself when we get there. And we can't protect it, either. Not now. It wouldn't matter if we parked an armored cav division outside of it. Pilgrim has the Whisper. It trumps everything. Even other entities, as you learned for yourself in Alaska."

He took her point.

"If there's any way whatsoever to achieve a given result—and there always is—then the Whisper will know how," she said. "Think of it as a game of rock, paper, scissors, and the Whisper is a diamond-blade rock cutter. It just beats everything. If Pilgrim wants to return to Seven Theaterstrasse and trigger the weapon—and let's go out on a limb and assume that's exactly what the fuck he wants—then he will. Unless we destroy it before then."

VERSE IV
AN OCTOBER NIGHT IN 1992

Travis discovers immediately that he's gotten a lucky break. His car, which has come to rest against the entertainment center at the back wall of the living room, has pinned the couch and its occupant against the big-screen TV. Manny Wright, six-foot-five and maybe four hundred pounds. The homeowners' bodyguard, and the only one who lives in the house with them. His back is broken. He's trying to move, trying to reach the .44 holstered at his waist. But he can't.

Travis wonders if Manny was the one who actually carried out Emily's murder, on orders from above. Then, because the answer is obvious, he stops wondering. He raises the .32 to Manny's face.

Manny can't get enough breath to say please, or no, but his eyes say both. Intensely. And in vain.

Travis puts the gun next to Manny's right eye, pointed sidelong across his face, and fires. The hollowpoint shreds both eyes and the bridge of the nose, leaving a ragged, bloody crater, and to Travis's deep satisfaction, Manny gets enough breath to make some noise after all. The man's scream is plaintive, full of self-pity, with the same stresses and tones he might use to scream "Why?" over and over. Travis wishes he could stand here for an hour and listen to it.

Instead he stoops, takes the .44 and leaves Manny to die like that, blind and screaming.

Manny isn't the reason Travis has come here tonight. The house's owners, the people who made the choice to kill Emily, are the primary targets.

Travis goes to the broad, stone-clad hallway that leads to the master bedroom, where his own mother and father are waiting.

CHAPTER TWENTY-ONE

T he day slipped by in a few hours over Canada and the North Atlantic, sped up by the plane's eastbound transit across the time zones.

Paige gave Travis two thin reports, one for each of the entities that they'd brought along on the trip. The objects in the black carrying cases.

QUICK REF REPORT—BREACH ENTITY
0118—"MEDIC"

BREACH EGRESS: 1981 July 15—07:31 UTC
PHYSICAL: Medic has a mass of 1.31 kg. Long dimension is 11.5 cm, height 8.1 cm, width 3.0 cm. It bears a strong superficial resemblance to a handgun. Its structure is simple: tube, grip, and trigger with guard. Black in color.
FUNCTION: Localized, massively accelerated healing of biological damage. Sends a surge of radiation from its barrel, covering an area 30 cm wide at a distance of approx. 15 cm. Radiation is a complex mixture of various particles, most not identifiable or known to present science. Result is instant death of

most deleterious microorganisms, as well as clotting of all air-exposed blood within less than one second. Extremely useful for combating infections and treating serious wounds, to a degree.

Has been shown to work on humans, all tested mammals, and vertebrates in general. Has never worked on any tested invertebrate.

THEORIES ON HOW ENTITY FUNCTIONS: None.

LIMITATIONS OF USE: Many wounds are too severe for Medic's effect to be of use in time to prevent mortality.

QUICK REF REPORT—BREACH ENTITY
0353—"DOUBLER"

BREACH EGRESS: 1991 January 24—14:50 UTC

PHYSICAL: Doubler has a mass of 7.85 kg. Long dimension is 18.2 cm, height 5.1 cm, width 5.1 cm. It is black and yellow and resembles a large, square-shafted flashlight with two lenses, one on each end.

FUNCTION: When switched on, Doubler projects a discrete cone of light from each end. Yellow light from the yellow end, UV light from the black end. Each light cone flares outward from the lens and terminates sharply at a distance of just over 1.5 m.

Anything contained within the yellow light beam for more than 3.44 seconds is physically cloned, with the copy appearing inside the UV light beam. Creation of the copy is almost instantaneous, with time from start to finish not exceeding two frames of digital video, less than .066 seconds.

The fidelity of the clone to its master is physically

perfect, presumably to atomic detail. This was demonstrated by the doubling of a laptop computer, the clone of which functioned properly and contained all the same code as its master. Chemical compounds and processes may also be copied. Cloned bullets fire as normal. Cloned food ingested by test animals produced no ill effect. A lit "Zippo" lighter was reproduced with its flame still burning.

THEORIES ON HOW ENTITY FUNCTIONS: None.

LIMITATIONS OF USE: (1) Does not work on most Breach entities. As of [November 16, 2008—latest update] only [5] entity types have been successfully doubled: Entity 0001 (Heavy Rag), Entity 0004 (Shard), Entity 0012 (Bottle Cap), Entity 0028 (Drift Wire), Entity 0051 (Inertia Plank).

(2) Living bodies may be cloned, but in all experiments so far, the clone has arrived dead. Autopsies have failed to reveal any specific cause of death. The master specimens (for ethical reasons, only mice and rats have been used) appear to suffer no harm. There is universal agreement within Tangent that no doubling of a human will ever be sanctioned.

When Travis finished reading the reports, he saw that Paige had opened a laptop. She turned it to face him.

"This is test footage of the last entity Pilgrim has," she said. "It's not quite unique. Four of them have come through over the years. He only has one. It's no Whisper, but it's powerful, in its way."

She opened a video frame on the screen and clicked PLAY. The video showed a stark white room containing a metal cage, no larger than a single-occupant drunk tank in some backwater police station. A man in his forties, balding, entered the frame holding an orange cube maybe four inches wide. There were markings on it, symbols etched in black, but they were too far from the camera to be discernible. It didn't matter: Travis could see that the writing was different from the strange jumble he'd read on Paige's wall. And it sure as hell wasn't English.

"October 4, 1986," the balding man said. "Video demonstration of Entity Zero Two Zero Five: Ares."

He entered the cage with the cube, closed the door and locked it from inside. Then he manipulated something on the cube, moving the symbols on its surface, arranging them. Here the camera reframed to a wider field of view, revealing a dozen people seated in chairs outside the cage, the nearest maybe ten feet away. Men and women, twenties to forties. Dressed casually. Nothing strange about them, except their anxiety. Something was about to happen, and they knew it.

The man in the cage finished whatever he was doing with the cube: the thing suddenly flared bright, throwing off the camera's white balance and making the room appear darker. In the same instant, all but three of the seated people turned sharply, regarding the man in the cage with something like surprise.

Then, as one, they came up out of their chairs and rushed him, like baseball players charging from the dugout to beat the shit out of some opposing player. They hit the cage en masse, trying with all their force to get at the man inside. Arms reached in through the bars. Hands gripped the steel and shook it. A few of the attackers stepped back and aimed heavy kicks at the cage door's latch. Had they reached the balding man, they would have torn his limbs from his body. There was no question of it.

By their moves, it was clear that they weren't seeking the orange cube itself. They weren't looking to destroy it, or even take it away; they were only reacting to the man who held it. They crouched and reached for his legs. Climbed atop the cage and plunged their arms into it, going for his head. They wanted to kill him. It was that simple.

Yet beyond the rage, their actions were surprisingly normal. Nothing about them suggested that they were controlled like mindless puppets, or even reduced to some animalistic state of mind. Not even close. They were just extremely pissed-off people focused on a target. Their minds were, if anything, clearer for the adrenaline rush. As Travis watched, two of them conferred and then one took out a set of car keys and tried to pick the cage's lock with it.

The man in the cage only stared at the horde around him, rattled by the experience but not at all surprised. Like a marine biologist in a shark cage.

Travis's eyes went back to the seats and the three people who remained in them. They were the farthest three from the cage. The farthest from the orange cube. As if the thing had a radius of influence, and they were just outside of it. One of the three looked up, his eyes drawn to someone out of frame. He nodded in response to something he was told, then stood, and took a single step toward the cage. His eyes hardened. His jaw tightened. A second later he was sprinting toward it, crashing into it with the rest of the throng.

The video ended.

Travis stared at the blank screen a moment, then met Paige's eyes.

"What's the write-up on that one?" he said. "Pisses people off like nobody's business?"

"It does something to the R-complex," she said. "The reptile foundation of the human brain, where the fight-or-flight response comes from. Where rage comes from. The cube does two things. First, it tags anyone within a couple feet of itself as a target. Then it affects everyone within another twenty feet beyond that, maxing their aggression and turning them inward against the target."

"Bet someone at Border Town learned that the hard way," Travis said.

Paige nodded, looking away. Travis didn't bother her for the details.

"Anything nice ever come out of the Breach?" he said. "Instant puppy generator, something like that?"

Paige managed a smile. "It's not all bad. We survive the next thirty-six hours, I'll show you some of the good stuff."

* * *

Somewhere over Greenland, Travis reclined his seat and tried to rest. He was asleep within minutes.

Paige watched him.

After a moment she felt self-conscious and looked away, even though there was no one else in the room to see her.

She didn't trust what she felt about him. There was every reason not to; her feelings were exaggerated all to hell right now. The guy had saved her from the worst thing she'd ever endured—had literally come in with guns blazing—and then carried her over fifteen miles to safety. Her memories of the journey out of the mountains, early on before she'd gone completely comatose, comprised a vignette of little waking moments. Coming to in his arms, being carried like a child. A big part of her had hated that feeling: being unable to stand up for herself after years of training her body to military-specialist standards. But here was the thing, and there was no getting around it: being carried had also felt good. Irrationally good, on some primal level that was all about vulnerability and security. He'd simply made her feel safe.

And then she'd kissed him. Jesus, why had she done that? There'd been no real need for it; he'd already been faking it well enough, as far as the chopper was concerned. Looking back, she wished she could write the moment off to her delirium, but in fact she'd felt pretty damn awake at that time. Rotor wash made for an effective alarm clock.

She glanced at him again. Sound asleep, sunlight across his chest, the shadows of folds in his shirt sliding back and forth as he breathed.

No, she definitely didn't trust her feelings. A few hours earlier, when she'd seen his life history on the screen of her PDA, she'd taken it like a kick to the stomach, and then had immediately found herself rationalizing, finding ways to cut him slack, to not blame him for what he'd done—for what he'd been—in his distant past. It was a wonder she hadn't said it all out loud and made an ass of herself in front of her people.

All this, superimposed over the thing she wasn't dealing with at all.

Her father.

Even now, she hadn't cried. Not since her initial reaction in the clearing. She'd tried. Tried to get there, to at least accept that it had really happened, if nothing else. So far, it hadn't worked. It was still too big, too close—she couldn't get a sense of where its edges were.

It would happen in its time. It seemed there was no forcing it.

For now, she thought she could use some sleep of her own. She stood and left the room to find a place by herself.

Travis felt someone shake his shoulder. Had he even slept? It hardly felt like it. He opened his eyes to find Paige standing over him, haloed by the ceiling lights of the little room. Outside was darkness, broken every few seconds by the pulse of the aircraft's starboard beacon.

"Wheels down in five," Paige said.

Travis nodded. She left the room to speak to someone in the hallway.

The plane banked steeply, offering a view of its destination: Switzerland's Meiringen Air Force Base, its runway threaded tightly between mountain ridges in a way that was uncomfortably familiar.

Ten minutes later Travis stepped out of the plane's tarmac-level exit into crisp air, the stars hard and bright above the mountains.

A tandem-rotor helicopter—a Chinook, he thought it was called—waited with its turbines already whining at idle. The team transferred the gear, and within five minutes they were airborne again, moving north over the high country toward Zurich, and whatever waited at 7 Theaterstrasse.

CHAPTER TWENTY-TWO

Zurich was close to what Travis had pictured. He sat beside Paige in the last SUV of the motorcade winding its way down into the heart of the city. Under the black sky, the clean lines of centuries-old architecture descended in fractured order to the river. Ahead and below, a fog bank had settled over the low-lying blocks that flanked the waterfront. Gray specters of mist drifted along the deepest streets of the city. The motorcade descended into the fog just before swinging left onto Theaterstrasse.

Ahead and to the right, rising straight from the water, was the only nine-story building for several blocks. Paige and the others in the vehicle reacted to the sight of it, if only in subtle ways. Hands unconsciously tightened the clasps of Kevlar armor. Gripped the stocks and barrel guards of rifles. Drummed on armrests.

The detachment operators had put on their gear aboard the Chinook. Travis hadn't asked if they'd brought a set for him. They had. In addition to the Kevlar, he now wore a tiny comm unit in his ear: a microphone and receiver that were always on and linked to the rest of the team. They'd given him a gun, too. A rifle identical to theirs. Identical to the one he'd already killed with, while kneeling over a muddy hole in Alaska.

Paige called Border Town on her cell for an update. She'd done this every five minutes since they'd touched down at Meiringen. Right now there was an AWACS aircraft making broad circles thirty thousand feet above Zurich. Six attack helicopters were staged in parking lots along the ridges east and west of town. Farther out, F–18s orbited, ready to kill any unauthorized thing that came within fifty miles of the city on wings or rotors. Every traffic camera for miles had specially filtered lenses that reduced windshield glare and allowed high-res facial imaging of vehicle occupants at night. These cams were all networked to a system that could recognize Aaron Pilgrim and several of his known allies. If they did, three detachments from Tangent's Berlin hub were standing by in the city, ready to move against them.

None of it reassured Paige, Travis saw. Rock, paper, scissors.

On the outside, the building was beautiful. Ancient stone facade rearing up to the sky. Cobblestone approach. Wrought-iron fence gleaming in the mist, its sheen catching the city lights through the fog.

On the inside, the place looked like the home of an obsessive-compulsive who couldn't pass a used computer store without buying out its entire stock, and had done so on a few hundred occasions. Travis wasn't up on computers—hadn't owned one in the year since he'd rejoined the free world, and the last time he'd seen one before that, the term *e-mail* hadn't yet made it into popular culture. He'd seen his brother's impressive setup for the home business, and he'd gone online a few times at the library in Fairbanks in recent months. His experience ended there. But even a glance at the interior of 7 Theaterstrasse made it clear that no amount of familiarity would've helped. Supercomputer designers would've been stumped. Probably had been. No doubt Tangent had brought in the best people.

Beginning at the main-floor foyer, where six members of another Berlin detachment stood guard, the building's space, wall to wall and floor to ceiling, was filled with wires, and computer boards, and cables, and pieces of equipment Travis didn't recognize at all. A rain-forest overgrowth of circuitry, lit from within by its own galaxy of tiny LED indicator lights. Here and there, window fans were bolted to walls or the ceiling, aimed at particularly dense clusters of wiring and spinning at full speed, as they must have been for years and years. Elsewhere, air-conditioning units whirred softly, the radiant heat of their motors vented away through metal ductwork toward exterior walls.

"Power's never been shut off since you took over the place?" Travis asked Paige.

"Oh no." She said it like he'd asked if she'd ever juggled straight razors. There was more behind her answer than she was letting on. He had an idea he'd find out what it was soon enough, and didn't ask.

"The building runs off the city grid, but there's an uninterruptible backup, powerful enough for the whole place. It's kicked on twice in these past four years, during outages. Thankfully."

They moved through the foyer toward the stairs. In the recessed space beneath them, Travis saw something that was at odds with the rest of the place. It looked like a little painter's studio: an easel tucked against the wall, a few spare canvases, and a scattering of oil-paint tubes covered in dust in the corner.

"What's that about?" Travis said.

"Nothing, as far as we know," Paige said. "Maybe a remnant from whoever owned the place before Pilgrim."

They went past it to the foot of the stairs. The circuit-board jungle flowed up the marble steps, woven through the spindles of the railing. The passage through it all was only wide enough for single-file movement. Paige took the lead, Travis just behind her.

On every floor, half a dozen more of the single-file rabbit tunnels branched out from the one that wound up the stairs. Whatever purpose these runs had served Pilgrim, they served Tangent now. Travis saw that most of the pathways led to the outer walls and then ran along them, allowing access to the windows, several of which had Tangent snipers and spotters in place.

On the third floor, Paige led the group away from the stairs. Down one of the tunnels. Past three sniper teams. The path turned back in toward the interior, the wilderness of cables and silicon and flickering LEDs. It ended at something like a clearing, a circular space twelve feet across. At its center was a steel box the size of a footlocker. A thick trunk of bound wires descended from the canopy above and fed into the box through a hole in its lid. The lid itself was welded shut.

Paige stepped aside at the mouth of the clearing, but only enough to let him see past her. She was still blocking him from actually moving out of the tunnel and approaching the steel box.

"We never go much closer than this," she said. "Our first inspection of the place showed us the need for caution. There are five boxes like this in the building. We've never tried to open them."

"Just ran out of curiosity, right?" Travis said.

Paige smiled dryly. "Yeah. Also, they're resting on pressure pads that are sensitive enough to react to any change of weight distribution. Putting a hand on top of one of these boxes, or against its side, would result in something bad. The same something bad that would happen if the building's power were cut."

Again, Travis didn't ask. His eyes picked out the thin black wafers of the pressure pads under the box's corners, their fine wires snaking across the floor to join the tangle.

"Follow my lead," Paige said. "Move like I move. Don't get any closer to the box than I do."

With that, she stepped into the clearing and began to circle it along its outer wall. A wall of wires. Travis followed. Twice Paige pointed to indicate the wires for the pressure pads. Travis didn't need them pointed out, but he understood her need to do it.

A moment later they were on the far side of the box, and Travis saw what he'd expected to see. Covering the back side of the box, and the floor around it, just discernible in the shifting LED light, was a vast sprawl of the same writing he'd seen in the enlargement on Paige's wall. In real life, the writing was newsprint-sized, and at a glance he thought it must be half an hour's worth of reading material.

Within seconds he saw that he was wrong.

It was only a single phrase, written over and over, almost maniacally. There had to be a thousand variants of it, in all directions, but the words were the same everywhere. They read simply,

GRAVITY ABERRATION, INNER NEXUS.

He translated it for Paige and told her about the repetition. She reacted with a mixture of confusion and disquiet, the look of someone surprised and shoved off balance in the worst possible direction. For another moment she only stared at him.

"That's it?" she said.

"That's it."

She looked from him to the others, still standing in the tunnel. One of the Tangent operatives,

Haslett—probably the oldest of the unit at close to fifty—was already typing it into a PDA.

Travis watched Paige's eyes as she pondered the line's meaning. For four years Tangent had probably worked with the world's best cryptanalysts, cycling fragments of this jumble through a million hours of computer time, in the hope of decoding a thousand-page text file of useful data. Instead they'd gotten four words. And nobody knew what the hell they meant.

"Four more of these boxes," Paige said. "Let's get to them." If there was any hope in her voice, Travis missed it.

The other clearings were on Levels Four, Five, Six, and Eight. Same-sized boxes, same-sized clearings, and the same-sized sprawls of repetitive text. To the extent that it mattered—not a hell of a lot, apparently—the messages were different in each place.

They read, respectively:

OPTICAL UNIFICATION TENSOR, PARALLEL UNIFI-CATION TENSOR.

BROAD AXIS NULL DRIVER, WORKABLE INFLOW DETOURS TO HARMONIC.

SYSTEM LEVERAGE, ETHER WASTE, RIGHT AN-GLE TRANSFER EGRESSION.

FREE ELEMENT EXPULSION, DIRECTED FLOW ONTO RADIANT WITH AXIAL RESISTANCE DETER-MINED.

Long before they'd reached the last one, Travis could see the group's reaction to the messages as a whole. And Paige's. More despair and anxiety than he'd ever seen gathered in one place.

"You might as well see the last thing," Paige said, and led him back to the stairway.

Halfway up the stairs to the ninth floor, the jumble of wires ended. The last steps were open and clear. At the top of the staircase was a ten-by-ten-foot landing, bound by walls on the left and right, with a set of double doors at the end providing the only access to the rest of the ninth floor. The doors were closed, and a big, unsightly thing stood before them like a sentry on duty.

From the floor beneath it, through tiny holes, emerged the fine wires Travis had seen connected to the pressure pads throughout the building. They all fed into the thing on the landing. Now Travis saw more pressure pads tucked into the seams around the double doors. These too were wired into the thing that stood before them.

Travis knew what the thing was, though he'd never seen one in person before, and didn't suppose the ones he'd seen in movies were very authentic. They hadn't been, but he knew it by sight anyway. It was cone-shaped, the height of a washing machine, drab green with a dark red star painted on it. One side of it was open, revealing complex circuitry, and admitting the wires that snaked in from every pressure pad in the building. Any disturbance to those pads would trigger this thing.

"Pilgrim has connections," Travis said.

"Pilgrim has connections," Paige said. Then: "The Russians never had the accuracy with their missiles that we did, so their philosophy leaned toward making the warheads more powerful. This one came from an SS–18. Enriched uranium primary. Tritium secondary. Yield is about five megatons. Enough to turn everything within twenty miles of this spot into vapor."

"Now I know why this place unnerves you guys," Travis said.

Paige looked at him, and instead of confirmation in her eyes, he saw only more desolation.

"No you don't," she said.

CHAPTER TWENTY-THREE

Ten minutes later Travis and Paige were standing at an open window on the eighth floor, one of the few unoccupied by snipers. The rest of the detachment had dispersed throughout the building to reinforce the defenses, either at other windows or at the ground-floor entrances.

Travis stared out, high above the city and the fog. Nearby building tops rose from the mist like ships in a marina. Deep beneath the surface, streetlights cast diffused circles of bluish light, and here and there, Travis saw the roaming glow of vehicle headlights, and heard the sharp echoes of footsteps or voices, some of them American. Drunken tourists, the only people awake in Zurich at a quarter past three in the morning. The only steady traffic was a modest flow along a primary street a few miles to the west, bisecting the river and climbing away toward the ridges to the north and south. It was the road Travis and the others had come in on, E41.

Beside him, Paige's breathing betrayed her anxiety. It reminded him of the fear he'd seen within the first Tangent group in Alaska, when they'd noticed the footprints in the mud. Not cowardice. Real fear. Fear in someone who didn't scare easily.

"I really thought we had a chance," she said. "I thought those inscriptions would tell us what we needed to do, and then however hard it was, we'd do it. I didn't think we'd get this far and still be at zero."

Her eyes roamed back and forth over the city. Like she expected hell to come rolling in at any second. Maybe it would.

"I don't even know what to do now," she said. "That was our only move. Now . . . we could leave if we wanted to, but it wouldn't matter. It's not like any place is safe, if Pilgrim achieves his goal. Staying feels better, like we're doing something, right? But obviously we're not. Forty-two snipers in this building, but we won't slow him by a minute. Not when he has the Whisper. He'll know what to do."

For a long time, neither spoke. In the night around them, Zurich rumbled on idle.

"Tell me what's worse than the nuke upstairs," Travis said.

She looked at him, almost grateful for something to talk about besides the dead end they'd come to.

"We don't think the nuke is the only defense system in this place," she said. "We don't even think it's the *main* defense."

Travis waited for her to explain.

"The bomb's purpose is obvious," she said.

"No opening the boxes," Travis said. "No opening the ninth floor."

She nodded. "There are even pressure pads embedded in the ceiling on Level Eight that prevent us from cutting through to the ninth floor that way. Same for the exterior walls. And the roof. And the windows on that level. Which are painted from inside. Obviously we'll never figure out the purpose of this place until we can see into those boxes and that floor, and Pilgrim doesn't want that, so . . . there you go. Simple, right?"

"Right," Travis said. "But?"

"But it doesn't work. The logic of it. It's like the single hostage problem. If a captor has one hostage, his threats are automatically empty, because he knows that if he kills the hostage, he'll be left with nothing. I know people take single hostages all the time, but those people are idiots. Pilgrim is as far from an idiot as you get. There's no way he'd leave this building defended only by something he wouldn't actually want to use. Something that would destroy the place, when all his ambitions depend on it. Don't get me wrong. The bomb *would* go off, if we did any of the things that would trigger it. But Pilgrim would expect us to be careful. And there's something else I think he'd expect. Something he'd *have to* expect, for the sake of caution."

Travis thought about it, and understood. "He'd know there was at least a chance of Tangent finding a way around the bomb, using some Breach entity that showed up long after he left Border Town."

"Exactly. Something that could have emerged yesterday. Or *any* day. He'd never know what we might suddenly have at our disposal. Something that lets us look through walls. Or *walk* through walls. Or turn enriched uranium into tin. Who knows, right?"

Travis didn't bother asking if anything like that had actually come along. Obviously it hadn't, but her point was still valid.

"If Pilgrim was cautious enough to rig the building with pressure pads and a nuke," Travis said, "you're saying he'd also be cautious enough to have a backup defense in place."

"A spare hostage," Paige said. "One he's not afraid to pull the trigger on. And that's what scares me. I think even if we were able to figure this place out, and make a move toward shutting it down, we'd run into that second defense, whatever it is." She stared out over the fog. The river, visible only as a vague sheen against the lit backdrop of city streets, snaked away to the northwest. "But I guess we're no closer to running into that problem than we ever have been."

She turned from the window. Stared at him. Her eyes, as beautiful as they were haunted, reflected the glow from the fog.

In her hand, her PDA displayed typed copies of the five lines Travis had read from the boxes earlier. She'd spent most of the past ten minutes staring at them, willing them to mean something. Now she looked at them again.

He watched her. Watched her try to contain the frustration and succeed only by degrees. She looked like she wanted to tear out the wires that hung around her.

A question came to him. He wasn't sure why it mattered, but had a sense that it did.

"If you guys got the Whisper back from Pilgrim four years ago, why was it on a 747 last week? Shouldn't it have been locked up in Border Town?"

The frustration behind her eyes stepped up a notch. "It was. And we spent the four years trying to get answers from it. Trying to make it tell us about this place." She shook her head, just perceptibly, her jaw tightening. "It's so goddamned aggravating. You just can't force it to help you if it doesn't think you need it. And you only get those few seconds to try, before the light changes and it tries to take over. A few people suggested letting someone else master it, like Pilgrim had done. You can probably guess how the vote went on that brainstorm."

Travis managed a smile.

Somewhere out in the city, a bottle shattered on concrete. In the fog, it might have been one block away or five. Men laughed, their voices ricocheting from every building, clarified in the mist.

"In Border Town we found an old pad of Pilgrim's handwritten notes," Paige said at last. "He'd taken care to destroy all his computer files, all his work on the Whisper, before he fled the place in 1995. But this notepad was one he must've left in the lab years earlier and lost track of. An attendant found it in a stack in the archives, in 1998.

Most of the contents were useless. Lab tests that had failed, been crossed out, that kind of stuff. But one thing stood out. He'd made a note about a facility that was being built in Japan. Back then, in the nineties, it was only a proposal. Still ten, fifteen years from completion. The Large Hadron Accelerator. Keep in mind that particle accelerators are Aaron Pilgrim's field of expertise. He stands with the best minds on Earth on the subject. Well, in that notepad he had five pages of math, written out longhand, supporting a conclusion he'd circled in red: when the LHA in Japan was completed, it'd be worth a try to set the Whisper right in its interacting point and hit it with a shot. His hunch was that it would act like the on/off key . . . but for the suicidal part of the Whisper, not the intelligence part. Meaning you could have all the good, and none of the bad."

The regret that pulled at the edges of her expression was almost hard to look at.

"LHA went operational last month," she said. "We had to try. If it worked, we'd have perfect knowledge of everything. How to cure every disease in the world. How to use all the Breach entities we've never been able to figure out. Most important: how to neutralize this building, destroy the weapon before Pilgrim could ever get a chance to use it. We had to try, and we had every reason to make our move as soon as possible. Four hundred thousand people live inside the kill radius of that nuke, and all it would take would be a lightning strike to zap the power for a few seconds, or a good-sized delivery truck crashing into the foundation to give the pressure pads a jolt. What were we supposed to do, tell everyone in Zurich to move?" The regret moistened her eyes now. Like acid. "All for nothing, anyway. We tried it at LHA just like he said. No result."

"I guess he could've expected you to find his notes, and fly the Whisper there and back when that place got up and running," Travis said.

Her eyebrows made a shrug, hard and bitter. "I guess."

"He circled it in red, huh?"

She looked at him. Eyes narrowing now. "Yeah. So what?"

"Did he circle anything else in the book like that?"

"No. What's your point? That he planned it? That far ahead? Circled it just to make us take the bait?"

"I don't know," Travis said. He didn't.

"It's not possible," Paige said. "He wrote those notes a decade and a half ago, before he ever left Border Town. No one could plan *that* far out. And why? Why would he plan to lose the Whisper to us, hours before triggering this place, and then recover it four years later?"

"I don't know," Travis said again.

But something about what she'd told him didn't fit. There was a problem there; he just couldn't quite put a name tag on it.

Paige had lowered the PDA again. Travis indicated it with his eyes, the five lines still on its screen.

"Mind if I look at those?"

She handed it to him.

GRAVITY ABERRATION, INNER NEXUS.

OPTICAL UNIFICATION TENSOR, PARALLEL UNI-
FICATION TENSOR.

BROAD AXIS NULL DRIVER, WORKABLE INFLOW
DETOURS TO HARMONIC.

SYSTEM LEVERAGE, ETHER WASTE, RIGHT AN-
GLE TRANSFER EGRESSION.

FREE ELEMENT EXPULSION, DIRECTED FLOW
ONTO RADIANT WITH AXIAL RESISTANCE DETER-
MINED.

The words meant nothing to him. Or her. Or
anyone else, apparently. At the time she'd typed
them on the PDA, she'd forwarded the lines to
Border Town, where a representative set of the
world's smartest people lived. Fifteen minutes now,
and no answers on her phone.

"I might be the least qualified to say it," Travis
said, "but I think these lines are bullshit. I don't
care how brilliant the guy is, if he was writing
Post-its to himself, they'd be clearer than this. If
there's a meaning to these sentences, it's not literal.
It's something else."

"I agree," Paige said. "So what is it?"

He could only shrug, focusing on the tiny screen,
his expression probably matching hers from a
moment earlier.

And then the lights of Zurich went out.

CHAPTER TWENTY-FOUR

P aige was on her phone within seconds, asking someone what the hell was happening. Over the comm unit in his ear, Travis could hear sniper teams on the lower floors speaking to one another, reporting their status. Everyone fine, for now.

He leaned on the windowsill. The grid immediately around 7 Theaterstrasse had gone out first, and within seconds others had followed in succession, plunging the city into blackness. Now as he watched, successive blocks, leading away up the valley and climbing the ridges on both sides, winked out one after another, until the only lights he could see were the headlights on E41, and a scattering of others on the streets of the darkened city. Almost immediately his eyes began to adjust, and he discerned the fog again, lit not from below but from above, by the half-moon. The whole bank of it, shrouding the city, caught and scattered the silver-blue light and set a contrast for the monolithic shapes of the buildings that rose from it, black and dormant in the night.

Paige was talking to someone at Border Town who had open lines to the three Berlin detachments stationed around Zurich. None of them were reporting any hostile contact. She finished the call and looked at Travis. The two of them were lit only by the screen of her PDA, which Travis still held, and by the vague glow of LEDs blinking like animal eyes in the jungle of wiring around them. The power to 7 Theaterstrasse hadn't so much as stuttered. An uninterruptible backup must be one of those rare things that actually lived up to its name.

"Whatever it is, it'll happen anytime now," Paige said. Trying to sound calm. Not succeeding very well.

Outside, dim lights began to appear in the windows of the few people awake at this hour. Candles or flashlights.

"You don't have to stay here, you know," Paige said. "You've done what we asked you to do. If you want to leave, you can."

Travis looked at her for a moment, then stared out over the city again.

"I know," he said, and made no move to take her advice.

At the edge of his vision, he thought he saw her smile. She leaned on the windowsill next to him.

"When it really gets hopeless," she said, "there's one move we can make that Pilgrim probably won't have anticipated. And even if the Whisper tips him off a few minutes early, there won't be anything he can do to stop it."

The tone of her voice and the deadness in her eyes told Travis what it was.

"We can set off the nuke," he said.

"We can set off the nuke."

"I don't think the locals will appreciate that."

"They'll get over it. In about a thousandth of a second. For the world's sake, it might be the prudent move."

"If Pilgrim's long-term agenda is bad enough."

She breathed a laugh, the sound empty as a waiting coffin. "I'm sure it's bad enough."

Travis thought about the situation. He could accept that she was right, that they were in deep shit, but the logic of it was hard to fit together. Didn't Pilgrim risk losing all the work he'd put into this building if he attacked it now? Any method of taking out the more than forty snipers stationed at these windows would involve some level of violence, and with it a high likelihood of triggering the pressure pads wired to the nuke.

But the Whisper would understand that. Would find a way around the problem. Any way. Maybe the attack would be a few canisters of VX gas, lobbed from a launcher two blocks away. Kill everyone in the building and not disturb a microchip. There had to be a thousand ways in, as clever as that, or more so. The Whisper would know them all.

Someone screamed outside. A man's voice. Travis saw Paige flinch, even as the scream turned into a drunken laugh, and someone else told the man to shut up, also laughing. The first man kept yelling, asking who'd turned off the fucking lights.

"It won't be much longer," Paige said.

But it was. More than half an hour passed, and nothing happened. A few ambulances moved about the city, sirens quiet but flashers pulsing through the fog. Travis thought of home-care patients whose medical equipment had failed in the outage. Somewhere to the east, out of sight past the building's corner, was a bright light source. A building running on a generator. It had to be a hospital; the ambulances came and went from that direction.

Paige made more calls to Border Town. More calls to the Berlin detachments stationed around Zurich and to the AWACS aircraft circling high above. Four in the morning and all was well. The snipers downstairs continued to call in their status at close intervals. They'd put on FLIR goggles to let them see the shapes of human bodies through the fog, and in low tones they reported the movement of any pedestrian who strayed into the two-block radius around the building.

"I don't understand," Paige said. "What's Pilgrim waiting for?"

It was the slingshot feeling again. Each passing minute made it worse.

Mostly they watched the night, but at times either he, or she, or both of them stared at the lines on the PDA. The consensus from Border Town agreed with Travis: the sentences were gibberish, on the surface.

At a point when neither had spoken for over a minute, Travis said, "You must have a few guesses, at least."

She looked at him in the pale glow of the screen, and offered a smile. "I promise I don't."

"Sorry, not the lines," he said. "I meant the weapon. In four years, Tangent must've come up with a theory or two about what it does. If not by looking at all these wires, then by considering what Pilgrim would have to do to eliminate Tangent. He'd have to compromise the defenses at Border Town, right? Somehow he'd have to do that, from this place, five or six thousand miles away."

"We have a few guesses," she said. "They all hinge on the idea that this building is a transmitter antenna of some kind, possibly directional, that could target Border Town even at this distance. What it does could be any number of things. Maybe it kills people but leaves physical structures intact, like the effect of a neutron bomb. Or maybe it induces a reaction in specific materials, in a way that would kill Border Town's defenses for a period of time. That's one set of possibilities."

"Are there others?" Travis said.

"One other, in particular."

"Which is?"

"That the weapon has nothing to do with taking over Border Town. We only assume that's his plan because it's such a logical power grab. Border Town is the biggest asset in the world if he controls it, and the biggest liability in the world if he doesn't. Plus the Breach itself. Of course he'd want control of that. Logically, it all fits. But who the hell knows? Maybe logic isn't what's driving him. So maybe the weapon just does something catastrophic to the whole world. Maybe it kills ninety-nine percent of it, leaving a scattered remnant population that's easier for him to control."

"You sound like you're leaning toward door number two," Travis said.

She looked down into the fog shroud. "There's evidence for it."

He waited for her to go on.

"We know Pilgrim bought this place in 1995, just a few months after he left Border Town. Strange things started happening in Zurich in the following years, continuing to the present. Suicides have tripled. Domestic violence arrests are up by a factor of four. Certain rare forms of cancer have increased between five- and sevenfold. We only saw all this in retrospect, of course, after we found this place four years ago. It gets more compelling when you pin the locations of all these incidents on a map, and see the distribution around this building. You probably wouldn't see it if you weren't looking for it . . . but when you do see it, you know you're not imagining it. Seven Theaterstrasse is doing *something* already. Some little pilot-light version of what it'll do to the world if Pilgrim gets his way and throws the switch."

Travis held her stare a moment, then looked out

into the darkness again. Another ambulance flickered silently through the fog on the far side of the
river.

"Could you really bring yourself to trigger the
nuke upstairs, if it comes to it?" he said.

For a long time she didn't answer, but when
she spoke there was nothing hesitant in her tone.
"Yes."

"In that case," he said, "I have an idea."

CHAPTER TWENTY-FIVE

T ell me," she said.

"I need to know something first." He looked around at the mess of wires at their backs, filling the room except for this narrow passage by the window. "All this circuitry and equipment that's accessible, Tangent's studied every inch of it, right?"

"Every connection, every processor, every jumper setting. Everything."

"Any of the wires not plugged in?"

She didn't follow.

"I mean, was there some random corner on one of these floors where it looked like the work hadn't been finished? Wires hanging loose, circuit boards lying around, tools on the floor? Anything like that?"

She shook her head.

Travis thought for another moment and said, "He was three hours from activating this place when Tangent showed up in 2005."

She nodded.

"Three hours away because he was three hours from having it finished, right?"

"That's always been the assumption, yeah."

"The unfinished work wasn't anywhere in this tangle that we can see, and the five steel boxes were already welded shut, so he must have been done with whatever's in those. That leaves the ninth floor, behind the closed doors. Three hours' worth of work left to do, up there."

She was nodding again. Tangent had figured this part out long ago. Which he'd assumed.

"When you took over this building, where did you find the Whisper?"

"On the seventh floor, in a shielded box."

Travis thought it over, putting the sequence of events together in his mind. Trying to see it all from Pilgrim's point of view, that day when he'd been forced out of here. That thought process—mentally tracking someone's moves, getting inside a subject's head—was familiar, like putting his hand into a baseball glove he hadn't worn in almost two decades. The kind of thing he'd once been good at, in spite of his motivation.

"All right, it's May 17, 2005," he said. "Pilgrim is three hours from finishing the weapon. He's working on it. He knows Tangent is close, because you've nailed some of his people in recent weeks. He obviously doesn't know Tangent is literally moving in, or else he'd have left even earlier. Which means he's not using the Whisper at this moment, or else it would've warned him. And it's plausible enough that he wouldn't be. I mean, he's been building this place for ten years, this close to the end he probably knows all by himself what's left to be done."

"Okay," Paige said.

"So he's up there, working on the ninth floor. The Whisper is safe in its box on Level Seven. If he gets the two-minute warning that Tangent's coming down the street, what does he do?"

"Apparently he shuts the doors on Level Nine, shoves the pressure pads into the gaps, and flees the building."

"So he takes the time to do that," Travis said. "But he doesn't stop for a few seconds on the seventh floor, on his way down, to grab the Whisper? The thing that matters more to him than his own senses?"

"Yeah, we know that doesn't add up," Paige said. "Which is why we don't think he was on the ninth floor when the warning came. We think he was on the first floor, for any of several reasons. The kitchen is down there, along with the only working bathroom."

"That makes it even harder to believe," Travis said.

For the first time in this discussion, Paige looked uncertain. She waited for him to continue.

"He's down on the first floor. He gets the call. Shit, Tangent's coming. They're so close, even if he sprints out the door right now, he could still get caught. There's simply no time to run up seven flights for the Whisper. So he does the hardest thing he's ever had to do. He leaves the Whisper and he runs."

"Right."

"So how do the doors on the ninth floor get closed and pressure padded again?"

She shrugged. "He had to have done it before he came downstairs, as a standard procedure. Must have always done it. Sealed it up whenever he came down, unsealed it when he went back up. He would've known how to do that, how to switch off the pressure pads when he wanted to go back in. I'm sure we could figure it out ourselves, with a little trial and error—if 'error' didn't mean vaporizing a city."

"But that's the part that doesn't work," Travis said. "Pilgrim rigging the doors just to run downstairs for a minute. Think about it. Ten years of work. Work that's going to give him the world, or whatever he wants. He's three hours away from wrapping it up. He's probably done nothing but work on it for the final few days. Probably hasn't even slept. Let me guess, in the kitchen downstairs, every cup was coffee stained. Even the ones that weren't coffee cups."

She looked vaguely impressed at that.

"Amphetamines too, right?" he said. "Not meth. Maybe prescription stuff."

Paige nodded. "Dexedrine. Good guess."

"Not really. It's just nothing unusual. I spent three years working vice; it's not as long as most, but it's long enough. Long enough to see the same pattern, over and over. Pretty much identical, for all of them."

"All of who?"

"People doing things they're not supposed to. People whose lives would basically be over if they got caught. People who are in no position to fuck around. A guy like Pilgrim, those last days in this place, that close to getting away with what he was doing, I doubt he'd waste five minutes to go down and make a sandwich. He'd have someone bring it up to him, and he wouldn't stop working. Whatever he had to go downstairs for that day, it wasn't going to take long, and he sure as hell wasn't going to make it take longer by stopping to shut the door and arm the pads, then disarm them again when he came back. Not three hours from the finish line."

He could see in Paige's eyes that neither she nor anyone in Tangent had considered this angle before. Maybe they just hadn't been under the right pressure. Maybe they hadn't been in dire enough straits to consider the option Travis was considering right now.

"But the pads *were* in the doors," Paige said. "So what are you saying?"

"I'm saying he had it rigged so he could go in and out quickly, without having to stop every time. Minutes would've been precious at the end. I'm saying the pads on the doors upstairs are decoys. You could open those doors and walk through them, right now if you wanted to."

For a moment she said nothing. Just stared at

him. Then: "The wires to the pads are live. We checked for current."

"Sure," Travis said. "He'd make it look real. He'd make it impossible to know, one way or the other."

More silence. More consideration. He watched her, aware that the idea didn't have to make perfect sense. It just had to be less batshit crazy than the other options they were stuck with, including sitting here like paper targets.

She seemed to agree. She took out her cell and dialed. He heard her address the same person at Border Town that she'd called earlier. She explained the idea. Travis couldn't tell, from Paige's half of the call, what the other party thought of it. A moment later Paige said, "Yeah, put them all on." Then she waited. And waited. And her eyebrows furrowed. The party on the other end said something—Travis couldn't make it out—and Paige took a hard breath. She lowered the phone an inch and met his eyes in the darkness.

"None of our three detachments in the city are responding."

CHAPTER TWENTY-SIX

Sixty seconds later they were standing at the double doors on the ninth-floor landing. The nuke filled up the space behind them, its paint gleaming like a cold smile. Over his headset, Travis could hear the snipers downstairs trading status updates, with a tension in their voices that hadn't been there earlier. They were up to speed on the plan.

"You want the honor?" Paige said, and indicated the ornate doorknobs.

He nodded. Why not? He put his hand on the left one. Then stopped. He breathed a laugh. "You know, he wouldn't have had to rig *both* doors with decoys."

In the vague light he saw her smile. Almost literally a gallows smile.

"If this works," he said, "then we'll find out pretty soon if you're right about the second defense system."

The way she was holding her rifle, she didn't look like she needed to be reminded of that. "If this works, and it's really this easy to get in," she said, "then I can't imagine there wouldn't be one."

He reached for the doorknob, but stopped again.

He looked down. In his other hand he was still holding the PDA. The five lines, black and white, shining in the darkness. Something about them struck him now. It was like the feeling he'd gotten outside the Black Hawk, staring at its tire but not consciously noticing the footprints beside it. There really was a meaning to the words. Not on the surface. Just beneath it.

"What?" Paige said.

For a few seconds he didn't answer. He thought if he even spoke, it'd break whatever thread of insight had formed.

Then he saw it, and it was so obvious he couldn't believe it'd taken this long.

"Look at the first letters of the words," he said. "In order."

He tilted the screen so she could see it better. He heard her exhale within less than a second.

The first line: GRAVITY ABERRATION, INNER NEXUS. *GAIN*.

The next four lines condensed into words as well: OUTPUT, BANDWIDTH, SLEW RATE, FEEDFORWARD.

"Amplifier," Paige said. "Those are all aspects of a signal amplifier."

They looked at each other in the glow of the screen. The next question was so obvious neither said it. The moment stretched. Travis saw in her eyes that the answer was as far out of her reach as his. What the hell was being amplified?

In his earpiece, one of the snipers downstairs spoke up. "Vehicle coming south on Falkenstrasse, pretty high rate of speed. I can take the driver from here."

Paige broke her stare with Travis, looked away at nothing, thinking hard.

"Permission to fire?" the sniper said.

Paige narrowed her eyes, thought for another half second. "No. Weapons tight."

Travis heard a hard breath over the comm unit. Then, from the bottom of the stairs, the eighth floor and its open windows, the sound of the vehicle's racing engine drifted up. Coming fast.

"Three blocks," the sniper said. "Two . . ."

By his tone, the man was asking Paige to reconsider the order. She closed her eyes.

Outside, the engine noise swelled. Then the pitch changed in an instant. Deepened. And began to fade. The vehicle had gone right past the building.

Another sniper reported in. "Vehicle proceeding south. I see double doors on the back end. Ambulance with its flashers off."

Paige exhaled slowly. She found Travis's eyes again.

"We're not going to get any more false alarms," she said. She looked at the words on the PDA one last time. Just a glance. Then she disregarded it and focused on the doors in front of them.

Travis understood. Whatever was being amplified, they weren't going to figure it out standing here. Regardless, they had to go through these doors and deal with what was on the other side. Figure out what the weapon was, and destroy it, even if that meant coming back out onto the landing and giving this pressure-sensitive warhead a swift kick like it was a Coke machine that'd stolen their last dollar. Whatever they were going to do, their time in which to do it was evaporating. Pilgrim probably knew they were opening the doors; if he was holding the Whisper right now, it was sure as hell telling him. Travis put his hand on the doorknob, then gave the warhead a last look.

"Sure you don't want to take a crack at disarming it?" he said.

She glanced at it. "It's not entirely impossible. Nukes aren't like regular explosives. They're complex machines. If you can disrupt that complexity without setting it off, you're good to go."

"Disrupt it?" Travis said. That word sounded like it was warming a seat for an uglier one.

Paige saw his expression and offered a smile. "Shove a grenade into it and pull the pin."

"How likely is that to work?"

"A shitload less likely than what you're about to do," she said.

He returned her smile, faced the door, and gripped the knob—

"Wait," Paige said.

He met her eyes, and found her looking back at him with a strange expression. A look that didn't know what it wanted to be.

"I didn't thank you enough," she said. "Before, when you first got to Border Town. I know I said thanks, but I wanted to say more than that. I wanted—" She paused again. Frustrated about something. Then: "I just should have said more. What, I'm not sure. I'm sorry if this isn't making sense."

Travis watched her eyes; she was looking down now, looking everywhere but at him.

"You're welcome," he said, so quietly that for a moment he wondered if she'd heard it.

She looked up at him. There was something in her eyes he hadn't seen there before. Something vulnerable. The last pair of eyes to look at him like that had been Emily Price's.

Not a bad final moment, if this was it.

Holding Paige's gaze, he turned the knob and shoved the door open hard.

They didn't die.

In the darkness beyond the doorway, more wires and circuit boards hung like vines, though not as densely as they did throughout the lower floors. Only a few here. Travis could see them silhouetted against a dim orange glow from somewhere ahead. Like the light of embers, but constant.

A sound began to radiate from the room. A droning hum, so deep it was barely audible. He could feel it more than hear it.

He pocketed the PDA and unslung the rifle from his shoulder. He stepped through the opening, Paige just behind him. The way ahead was hard to see; the orange glow barely helped. He moved toward what he thought was its source, though he couldn't actually see it yet. As his eyes adjusted, he saw that the room around him was vast. It was all the remaining space of the ninth floor, wide open and uninterrupted.

The hum was coming from somewhere ahead, the same direction as the light source.

Twenty feet in from the doorway, Travis saw something on the floor ahead, maybe an obstacle to step over, maybe a strewn bunch of wire. A few steps later he saw that it was neither. It was another inscription written in the scratch language, carved right into the floorboards. This one had the note-to-self simplicity Travis had found lacking in the previous five.

It read, TAGS ARE ESTABLISHED WHEN THIS ROOM IS OPENED.

He translated it aloud for Paige. She stiffened.

"Tagging," she said. "The Ares."

Travis thought of the video she'd shown him. The orange cube tagging the man in the cage, making him the target for the rage it incited in those around him.

He looked at the orange light ahead; there was no question as to its source now, even if he couldn't see it yet.

"It tagged us when we opened the door," he said. "I thought you had to be within a couple feet of it."

Understanding came to him even as he finished the line. He saw it come to Paige as well.

"Amplified," she said. "The distances are amplified."

Travis stared at the light source and guessed that they were at least fifty feet shy of it.

"If it can tag us this far away," he said, "how far can it reach to turn people against us?"

He saw the implication saturate her expression, saw her whole body react to it as if a ghost had traced its fingers up her spine. They were standing atop a nine-story building filled with armed, trained killers. If even those on the nearest floor were affected—

"Oh my God," she whispered. She steadied her microphone beside her mouth, caught her breath and said, "All teams, get out of the building, right now. *Run*."

But even she had to know it was too late. In the darkness around them, the LED indicators on the hanging circuit boards began flashing a manic rhythm. The trap was already springing. A second later, the orange light ahead of them flared bright, just as it had done in the video. Then brighter. So much brighter it lit the room, revealed it as daylight would have. A basketball-court-sized space, mostly empty, strung with spiderwebs of circuitry here and there.

Travis grabbed her arm, spun her toward the double doors and the landing beyond, and sprinted, dragging her until she caught her balance and ran with him.

"Where are we going?" Paige said.

"The eighth floor windows over the river. I hope you can swim."

"Are you fucking insane?"

"Insane problem, insane solution."

They passed through the doorframe, sidestepped

the nuke and took the stairs two at a time, slowing only as they reached the tangle of wires halfway down the flight.

Just below them, the stairwell thundered with running footsteps. But were the footsteps going down, or coming up? There wasn't time to judge it.

Travis reached the bottom of the flight, Paige just a step behind him. Tunnels among the wiring branched in five directions; he didn't know which one led to the river overlook. Paige did. She took the lead, and he followed, close, stooping in the low passageway. The pounding on the steps still gave no clue as to its direction.

They'd gone thirty feet through the tunnel when a voice spoke in their ears.

"This is Haslett. I just got outside the main exit. I think we better get everyone back to their positions."

Paige stopped. Travis pulled up just short of crashing into her. Behind him, the clamor of footsteps on the stairs went silent.

Paige steadied herself and spoke. "Status, all report. Are you guys affected or not?"

A jumble of calm responses came back over the line, the comm system cutting out most of them. But Travis heard enough to know they were fine. Paige turned in the tunnel, faced him, looking as confused as he felt.

"Maybe it didn't reach far enough," she said.

Haslett responded. "No, I think it reached *too* far. I think it just tagged us as targets, the same as you."

"What are you talking about?" Paige said.

"Look out the window," Haslett said. "All teams back to positions, right now. Sorry to countermand you, Miss Campbell."

The footsteps resumed on the stairs, definitely coming upward now.

Paige met Travis's eyes a moment longer, then turned and covered the last forty feet to the nearest set of windows, at an open corner looking out over the river in one direction and the city in another. Over her shoulder, Travis saw what was happening even as he stopped.

Paige said nothing. There was no expression for it.

In every building they could see, the dim glow of flashlights had vanished from the windows. That was because the flashlights were coming out through the street-level exits now, their beams stabbing wildly through the fog as their owners ran. Ran toward 7 Theaterstrasse. Travis's eyes trailed up along the river, and he saw the same thing happening, block after block, as far as he could see. All the way to E41, two miles away, where every pair of headlights had just swung off onto the surface streets, and were coming this way at full speed.

VERSE V
AN OCTOBER NIGHT IN 1992

Neither Mr. nor Mrs. Chase strains at the binds any longer. Both appear resigned to what is going to happen to them, and Travis hates them all the more for it. He wants them to be afraid, as he knows Emily must have been before she died.

The mad blue and red pulses of police flashers rim the plantation shutters. They've made no move to come in yet. A bullhorn has been chattering on and off for the past ten minutes, and three times the phone has rung for thirty seconds or more, but Travis has paid no attention.

Neither has he spoken to his parents.

It is this simple: he wants them to sit here waiting to die.

He wants them to feel what Emily felt, and he wants them to feel it for as long as possible before he kills them. The last thing they will ever hear will be the footsteps of the SWAT team on the stone floor of the hallway. It's likely that this will also be the last thing Travis hears, and that's fine. If he survives to spend the rest of his life in prison, that will also be fine, because he's earned it. Either way, all the justice Emily can ever be given will be spun in this room in the next quarter of an hour.

She deserves more, of course. She deserves to be alive, and lovely, twenty-four years old, with a future full of the simple things she wanted: a house, kids, a couple cats lying around in sunbeams on the living-room carpet. Revenge is a pale and sickly substitute for those things, but it's all Travis has left to give her, so he means to give it.

Down the hall in the living room, Manny's screams have ebbed to a whimper, and in the past minute he's begun choking on something—blood, no doubt. The sound of it has an effect on Travis's mother; her poker face slips. She is thinking about her own death now. Really thinking about it.

If he cared to speak to them, Travis would ask them how they could have expected any other outcome than this. They sculpted him to be what he is: a corrupted human being. A cop whose only real job has been to keep them pre-informed of police activity against them. A man whose moral compass points wherever the hell he wants it to point, at any given time. Didn't they know their animal would turn on them, after what they did?

Manny's choking climaxes in a series of convulsive heaves; he is trying with all his remaining air to purge the obstructing fluid from his windpipe. All his remaining air is not enough, and a moment later there is no more sound coming down the hall. Mrs. Chase begins to weep openly. Mr. Chase looks at her with disgust, and Travis suddenly understands the mini-plotline that has just reached the end of its reel and begun flapping against the projector arm. It is all he can do to keep from laughing at them both.

Then the window bursts and the shutters are knocked aside by a projectile that arcs across the room and ricochets off the dresser. Pepper gas, thick and orange-white, seethes into the air, and Mr. and Mrs. Chase begin to scream, because they know what's coming.

"We're your blood, goddammit!" Mr. Chase shouts.

"So was the kid she had on the way," Travis says.

He sees them react to that, and decides to let it be their final thought. He raises the .44—

—and finds hesitation where only a second ago there was resolve.

Another second passes. The gas fills half the room now, its outermost tendrils stinging Travis's eyes. His next breath will fill his lungs with it, and there will be nothing in his world but pain. At the same time a window shatters somewhere in a nearby room, and bodies clamber through. If he doesn't do this now—right now—it will never happen.

He forces an image of Emily into his mind. Emily standing right here with him, deserving retribution in her name. But instead of willpower it brings him understanding: he knows now why he hasn't pulled the trigger. It's not pity. It's her. It's the thought of how she would feel about him, if she were here to see him doing this. Travis does not believe in the afterlife. Emily is gone, gone forever, but all the same, he knows what she would think of this. She would be fucking ashamed of him.

He feels the gun slipping from his hand even before the SWAT commander appears in the doorway and screams for him to drop it, and a moment later Travis is on the floor, deep in the gas, unable to hold his breath any longer.

CHAPTER TWENTY-SEVEN

T his can't be happening," Paige said.

They could hear the screams coming up out of the fog, from the leading edge of the incoming swarm, less than a block away now. The buildings directly around 7 Theaterstrasse were corporate and commercial structures, empty at this hour, so the crowd had originated from farther away. But not by much. The frenzied movement of the nearest flashlight beams drew closer with each second. Travis thought of the feral rage of the test subjects in the video, rushing inward toward the man in the cage. The scale of the situation had been amplified a thousandfold in this place. Seven Theaterstrasse was the cage now, and all of its occupants stood in the crosshairs of the effect, which extended at least as far as the edges of Zurich.

The forefront of the crowd was maybe fifty seconds away, surging between buildings to the west, and onto the two nearest bridges spanning the river just to the south.

Paige's cell rang. She answered. It was someone aboard the AWACS, circling high above. Travis could just discern the tinny voice over the phone, reporting a visual on something strange happening down in the city.

"We noticed," Paige said.

In Travis's ear, the sniper and spotter teams reported in, one by one, as they retook their window positions.

The reality of what was about to happen descended on Travis like a poison cloud. He saw it settling over Paige at the same time, as she watched the flashlights race in toward the building. The nearest were past the bridges now.

The last of the snipers reported in. Travis could picture their rifles silently tracking the advance of the crowd while they waited for the order.

"We should just let them in," Travis said.

"They'll kill every one of us," Paige said.

"Yeah."

He was surprised by how little fear he heard in his own voice. How little he felt, for that matter. Maybe there was just too much of it to process. What he had in place of it was logic.

"It's not their fault," he said. "A few of us dying, instead of hundreds of them, that's not a hard choice at all."

For a moment he saw agreement in Paige's eyes. What other option was there?

And then her eyes changed, and in the same instant Travis understood why. The wicked effectiveness of Pilgrim's trap became clear. There would be no simple way out of it. Not even by suicide.

"Christ," he whispered.

He saw in his mind what would happen in this building, less than a minute from right now, if they held their fire and let the crowd in. He saw the rush of bodies coming up the stairs like fluid under pressure. Saw them clambering over one another, tearing at the jungle of wiring that filled the space of every floor. Crashing through the clearings with the metal boxes, and the delicate wires for the pressure pads that were almost certainly *not* decoys.

"If the nuke goes off, the crowd dies anyway," Paige said. "The whole city dies."

Travis could hear it in her voice: confirmation of everything she'd feared about this building. Here at last was the spare hostage. The one Pilgrim wasn't afraid to pull the trigger on.

But she also looked confused. Damn confused. And even in the tension of the moment, Travis thought he knew why. Because the whole building seemed to have been devoted to creating this effect. The whole building was the second hostage. So where the hell was the weapon Pilgrim had spent a decade working on?

Travis's line of thought was broken by a singular cry from the mob, clearer than the rest. It was furious, and wild, and so high-pitched that it could only belong to a very young girl, maybe younger than ten.

The crowd's leading edge was less than twenty seconds from the building.

"Fuck, fuck, fuck . . ." Paige breathed.

Travis wondered how many kids were among the crowd, but only for a moment, because he already knew how many. Every kid in Zurich would be out there, soon enough.

"Miss Campbell?" one of the snipers said over the comm unit, the voice tight like a wire.

The question was obvious.

So was the answer.

Paige swallowed hard, bit down on whatever she was feeling, and said, "Weapons free."

The night came alive with gunfire.

Travis saw the muzzle flashes from a dozen windows below him, across the face of the building. Saw the red paths of tracer rounds cutting through the fog, the snipers picking out individual targets for each shot. And though he couldn't see the victims at street level, as the snipers could with their FLIR goggles, he saw the results as clearly as he needed to. The flashlights at the forefront of the charge were suddenly kicked backward, their beams flipping end over end. The front ranks were cut down in rapid succession, and Travis heard screams of pain, mixed with surprise and fear. Men, women, children.

But the charge didn't stop. Didn't even slow. The rest of the surge, coming from behind the fallen, hardly faltered over the bodies. Travis saw the wave of incoming flashlights stutter-step where the first victims had gone down. The dead served only as speed bumps for the horde.

More flashlights were coming on in the windows of other buildings as the sleeping residents of the city woke, roused either by gunfire or by the effect the Ares had had on them. Beams flared behind panes for spare seconds, just long enough for their owners to take a look at 7 Theaterstrasse and know that the targets of their rage were somewhere inside. Then each light turned away quickly, as the people behind them ran for the stairs. Ran for the street. The whole city would be out there in a matter of minutes.

Down in the fog, the mob made forward progress in spite of the gunfire. Travis saw Paige's eyes, filled with hard tears, spilling now. She was tough as hell, he knew, but tough didn't cover this kind of thing. Nothing did, short of psychosis.

"It's not enough," she said, her voice cracking twice in those three words. "Single shots aren't going to keep them back."

She turned from the window and moved quickly into the tunnel of wires, toward the stairwell. Travis followed. Paige reached behind herself as she went, unzipped her backpack and plunged her hand into it. She came out with something that looked like a flashlight with lenses at both ends. The Doubler. It was more or less what Travis had pictured when he'd read the report, though its details drew his attention: the way its surface caught the light, the way its separate materials—whatever they were— met without seams. It was unlike anything he'd ever seen. A tool built by alien hands.

Paige reached the top of the stairs, and shouted, "Seventh floor, ranking operator to the stairwell!" She had to yell it again, waiting for a gap in the shooting, before one of the snipers, a woman in her thirties, appeared at the bottom of the stairs.

Travis had seen her introduced earlier as Miller. She looked as shaken by the events of the preceding minutes, as Travis supposed all the snipers were, but she was steady on her feet.

Paige tossed her the Doubler and yelled, "They need to switch to autofire! Grab five magazines, double them compound until they're eighty, then use that group for a basis and start massing piles right where you're standing. I want one person acting as feeder for each floor, running clips to the snipers. Double some fresh rifles, too. They won't last long under the strain."

Miller nodded and disappeared with a purpose.

Travis and Paige returned to the window. Outside, the crowd had filled both bridges to the south, and all the streets between the buildings in every other direction. Gathered flashlights flickered around in the fog, like lighters above the crowd at some end-of-the-world rock show. At the mouths of each of these bottlenecks—bridges and streets alike—the amassed dead had finally begun to constitute a real obstacle for the incoming throng, and where the surge backed up, Travis suspected that even some of the living had stumbled and been trampled, and become a part of the barricade themselves.

The snipers were still firing single shots, picking their targets. As Travis watched, the nearest outriders of the mob were always the ones taking the hits. A flashlight bobbed over the pileup on the near end of the left-side bridge, and came hurtling toward the building at impossible speed. No fucking way could a human move like that—

A rifle cracked from the fifth floor, straight below Travis, and the fast-moving light in the fog clattered on the cobblestones as a man screamed. Under the scream, Travis heard the telltale racket of a bicycle wiping out.

The piles of bodies were only doing so much. The fifty-foot buffer zone around the building wouldn't last much longer if the autofire didn't start soon.

Travis heard someone crying in pain, somewhere in the dark below. The man who'd come in on the bike. Still alive. He sounded young, maybe just into his twenties. His cries were so full of suffering it turned Travis's stomach. Paige's eyes were still rimmed, catching the moonlight and the red tracer fire from below. She held on to just enough composure to keep her breathing steady. The dying man's cries escalated to screams. He was saying something in German. A single word over and over. *"Bitte! Bitte!"* Travis thought it meant "please." The tone sure as hell implied that it did. Paige reached into her vest, came out with a pair of FLIR goggles and strapped them over her eyes. She leaned through the window, shouldered her rifle and aimed it down. She fired a single shot, and the man's screams switched off instantly.

A few seconds later the autofire began, one sniper at a time, and after a moment the night was a roar Travis could barely think above. The impact against the advancing crowd was more dramatic than he'd imagined. The front lines were carved back in savage arcs, like weeds falling to scythe sweeps. Paige tore off her goggles, overwhelmed by the detail she must have seen through them, and finally lost control. She turned toward Travis, put her arms around him and held on fiercely. He held her in return, his own eyes flooding against his will, and hoped to hell Aaron Pilgrim ended up in his gun sights at some point.

CHAPTER TWENTY-EIGHT

P aige kept her face against his chest for only a moment. Then she drew back, wiped at her eyes, and looked out into the night again, like it was her obligation to do so. Like it was her penance.

"Maybe if we had tear gas . . ." she said. "Pepper grenades. Anything like that . . ."

Travis watched the chaotic movement of the flashlights below, the crowd flooding forward at some surge point, being cut back, flooding through somewhere else, being cut back there. Over and over.

"I doubt it would help," he said.

"There are entities that would've helped," Paige said. "If I'd been smart enough to see this coming, I could've brought them. There's one that's exactly like the Ares, only it's green, and it affects memory. We call it the Jump Cut. Everyone within its reach loses the last three days of their memory, instantly. From the target's point of view it feels as if, whatever they were doing three days ago, they skip instantly from that to the present moment. Massively confusing, and there's no way to think around it. Wears off later. It'd be a perfect crowd disperser. We could've set it up in the main entrance downstairs, and maybe—I don't know . . ."

She was reaching. Trying to take responsibility for things that couldn't possibly be her fault. It was the mark of a good leader. It was also not helping anyone right now. Least of all herself.

Travis set a hand on her shoulder and turned her away from the window.

"Let's go back up and see what we're dealing with," he said.

She nodded, getting control again, pawing at her eyes one last time. He turned and led the way through the tunnel, toward the stairs.

At the landing, he looked down and saw Miller and a few others operating the Doubler. In the darkness, lit by the strobing pulses of gunfire all around, he caught only glimpses of the thing in action. They'd piled about eighty ammo magazines in one spot, and Miller was holding the Doubler so that the cone of yellow light coming from one end fully enveloped the stack. The UV light from the other end of the tube was barely visible. It shone only where it touched the floor or the banister atop the stairs, turning flecks of dust bright white.

Every few seconds, a perfect duplicate of the stack of eighty clips appeared in the UV light. Though the fractured glare from the muzzle bursts made it hard to really see the process, Travis didn't think it would have looked any more normal to him even in clear sunlight. Each time a new stack of ammunition appeared, the operators around Miller would grab handfuls and disappear either into the tunnels beside her or down toward the lower levels.

Travis moved on, climbed the stairs to the ninth floor, Paige just behind him. They emerged from the tangle of wires, and a few seconds later they were on the highest landing again, passing the nuke and entering the room at the top of the building.

The room was as brightly lit as when they'd left it. The radiance from the Ares was so intense it was more or less white. Earlier, when they'd turned to run, there'd been no time to study the revealed details of this place. Now they did. At the center of the giant room was a cluster of wires and cables, all emerging from the floor at that spot, and tangled together to form something that looked like an eagle's nest. All of the light was coming from the depression at its center, into which Travis couldn't see until he was within ten feet of it, holding his hand up against the searing glare.

Inside the nest were two objects. One was the Ares. The other was a jet-black cube, a foot in each dimension. The top and sides of the cube were smooth, without any wires feeding in. They must all connect into the underside. This cube was the active element of the amplifier. A shaft of silvery light, like a taut rope made out of plasma, stretched between the amplifier and the Ares, binding them.

Woven delicately into the surrounding nest of

wires were dozens of pressure pads, stuck to circuit boards and fat cable connectors. These pads, Travis had no doubt, were real. He had the sense that even a hard step on this floor would trigger them.

Downstairs, the gunfire went on endlessly. He could see it eating into Paige like acid. She narrowed her eyes, seeming to force her mind to stay in this room where it could accomplish something. She turned, surveyed the cavernous space.

"Okay, so where the hell is the weapon Pilgrim's people told us about?" she said. "What was he going to activate, three hours from the time we stopped him that day?" She nodded toward the Ares. "Not this goddamned thing. What good would that have done him? And the steel boxes downstairs are only there to serve this system, so forget those, too. There has to be something else. I mean, why the hell would he turn the whole building into a defense system that doesn't defend anything but *itself*? That's recursive. It's like one of those joke signs someone hangs in a doorway that says, 'Caution, don't hit your head on this sign.'"

Travis supposed that fad had come and gone while he was in prison.

He turned and surveyed the room with her, letting his eyes move slowly over every detail. A few wires hanging here and there, spilling from holes in the walls or snaking out of floor-level ductwork. Green circuit boards lying or hanging among them, LEDs blinking furiously, as they had ever since the amplifier had kicked on. But mostly there was nothing. Bare floor space. Bare stretches of wall. Outlets with nothing plugged into them.

"All the wiring is for the amplifier," Travis said. "In here, and in the rest of the building. And that's what took him most of the ten years, right? All the detailed work involved."

Paige nodded, waiting for the rest.

"So that makes the least sense of all," he said. "Why spend all that time on just the defense system, and why build that part *first*? If this place has some other purpose, some *main* purpose, it seems like he could've had that finished years earlier."

She could only stare. She could make no sense of it either.

Outside, an engine raced, and then the muffled concussion of a gasoline explosion put an end to it. The cars from E41 were starting to arrive.

Travis's eyes picked up something twenty feet behind Paige. A jumble of wire against the wall. There was something concealed beneath it. He'd taken only a few steps toward it when he saw what it was. More of the scratch writing, dug into the floor. He reached it, studied the wires to be sure they weren't bound by pressure pads, and eased them aside.

"What does it say?" Paige said.

"Names," Travis said. "It's a list of names."

Thirty-seven in all. People of varied nationalities. A few sounded Japanese, a few others Russian, German, Spanish, French. They weren't famous;

Travis had never heard of any of them. He read a
few of them to Paige and saw no recognition in her
eyes, either.

She took out her cell and dialed. Border Town
picked up. She set it to speakerphone so Travis
could relay the names directly. The man on the
phone identified himself as Crawford, and as Travis
began giving him the names, someone began typing
in the background. By the time Travis read the last
name, the techs on the other end had pulled up
info on the first ten.

All had been extremely wealthy. All had been po-
litically connected, to some degree. All had com-
mitted suicide since 1995.

As those in the background at Border Town continued parsing the list, Travis looked at Paige.

"These people were threats to Pilgrim's plan, in
some way," he said. "Find out why, and you'll have
real information to work with."

Suddenly there was commotion on the other end
of the line. Someone calling out to others, and then
a few surprised sounds.

"What's going on there?" Paige said.

Crawford spoke up again. "The last name on the
list. Ellis Cook. Suicide by gunshot to the head.
Two days ago on Grand Cayman."

Paige looked at Travis and mouthed, *Two days?*

"This is all wrong," Travis said, the thought
coming to him even as he voiced it. "Pilgrim was
never planning to trigger anything in this place
four years ago, when you guys thought you stopped

him. Whatever his plan is, he's launching it tonight. It was always going to be tonight."

Before Paige could respond to that, Crawford spoke again.

"Second-to-last name on the list. Rudolph Hagen. Jumped to his death from a hotel balcony, twenty-eighth floor. Three months ago. He was alone in the room, door locked, no forced entry."

Paige kept her eyes on Travis, shaking her head, either not following his logic or not wanting to.

"There *is no* weapon," Travis said. "Pilgrim just needed Tangent to think there was. He *wanted* you to show up here four years ago. *Wanted* you to recover the Whisper."

"Why the hell would he want us to take the Whisper from him?" she said.

"Because it told him to," Travis said.

The concept cut the air like a blade. Even the typing on Crawford's end of the call went quiet; whoever was around the speakerphone on that end was listening, too.

"What?" Paige said.

"He mastered it, right?" Travis said. "Learned how to make it tell him anything he needed to know?"

"That's what the evidence supports," Paige said.

"So he asked it for a plan. A way to eliminate Tangent, get back into Border Town, something like that. Whatever it was, it was hard. Right on the brink of impossible. Any of the obvious ways to do it, you guys have long since thought of, and built defenses against. So whatever plan the Whisper came up with, you'd expect it to be pretty far from obvious. Like a chess move by a supercomputer, something even the best human players can't make sense of."

Her eyes changed. Began to accept the idea, almost unwillingly.

"I can't even guess what the plan is," Travis said. "But there has to be one. *This* has to be one. He *let* you guys drive him out of this place, that day in 2005. He *let* you take the Whisper, knowing he'd get it back. He knew LHA in Japan would go active in four years. Knew you'd found his old notebook, and would risk flying the Whisper there to test his old theory. Really, a human being could almost guess those things. So it'd be child's play for the Whisper. The real question is, what else could it have guessed? Could it have predicted that once Tangent lost the Whisper to him, you'd send a team here to try to contain this place tonight?"

Paige thought about it, nodded.

"Okay," Travis said. "So then what? Could it assume a desperation move on your part? You said yourself you thought of triggering the nuke, if it came to it. How were you planning to do that?"

He knew what she would say.

"I would've done exactly what we already did," Paige said. "I would've opened the doors into this room."

"Still a move the Whisper could expect. So far, it adds up."

"What adds up?"

"That Aaron Pilgrim meant for a Tangent team to be here tonight. Meant for them to open these doors and trigger the Ares, and end up fighting off a siege by the whole city."

"Why?"

Travis thought about it, but could only shake his head. "I don't know. Whatever it is, the dominoes are dropping exactly like he wants them to, so far. We're dead-centered in the trap."

He watched her consider it. Watched her hate it as much as she acknowledged it. It wasn't so much an assessment of their situation as a diagnosis.

"How the hell we're supposed to compete against this kind of thinking, I don't know," Travis said.

"I might," Paige said. She looked around the mostly empty room, then back at him. "We exploit the things the Whisper could've never predicted."

"Like what?"

"Like you. Four years ago, or fourteen years ago, whenever Pilgrim got this plan from the Whisper, there's no way it could've known a random hiker would show up at that crash site two days ago. That Ellen Garner would've survived and left a note for you to follow. That you'd end up holding the Whisper yourself, and that it would be compelled to tell you how to read this language."

He nodded. That much seemed safe enough to believe.

"Meaning we were never supposed to know these names," Travis said, indicating the list carved into the floor.

They were both silent a moment.

Then Crawford's voice came over the speaker. "We're on it. I'll put someone on each name, dig up everything there is, find whatever thread connects them all to Pilgrim."

His last word was cut off by a scream in Travis's ear, from one of the snipers over the comm system: "*Gun!*"

Half a second later, another of them cried out, and then there were two voices shouting that a man was down.

CHAPTER TWENTY-NINE

Sprinting again. Past the nuke. Down the stairs to Level Eight.

Miller, on the landing farther down, saw Paige and shouted, "Sixth floor! Hill's been hit!"

Travis followed Paige down, past the piles of ammunition Miller continued to stockpile, through the tunnel of wires to the level below. Then more tunnels, across the sixth floor, toward the windows and the sound of screaming. They found two snipers kneeling over a third, who'd lost a good portion of his face and neck but was somehow still breathing. Wouldn't be for much longer.

Paige dropped her backpack from her shoulders, wrenched open the zipper and brought out something that looked a lot like a pistol, maybe a little Walther PPK, Travis thought. Then he saw it better, and realized the resemblance was only fleeting: the thing's shape was just stark and practical, a small black tube with a grip and a trigger. It was the Medic.

Paige aimed it at the dying man's wounds, her body language full of doubt, and pulled the trigger.

The effect looked something like a camera flash going off, accompanied by a surge of heat that Travis felt two feet away. The man's body spasmed in response, and Travis saw the injuries change dramatically. The blood flow seemed to staunch itself in less than a second.

But the guy was still dying. Eyes still wild as he fought for breath. Paige gripped his hand, and her eyes pleaded with him to fight. But after a moment, his own eyes tilted away from hers, and he expelled a hard breath. He didn't take his next one.

"Shooter was in a window halfway up the block," one of the others said. "They're getting smarter about it."

Travis thought of the demo video on the laptop, two of the enraged men conferring thoughtfully and then trying to pick the cage lock. Livid, but not stupid. Not even close to stupid.

He turned to the window. Outside, on the bridges and in the streets between the buildings, the barricades of the dead were now adorned with the burning shells of automobiles. The blazes slowed the forward crush only a little, but had a stark effect on the fog, baking the air and clearing deep cavities through the mist around them. Like lenses through which Travis could now see the carnage, hard and clear in the firelight. He wished he couldn't.

A small knot of people broke from the crowd and came inward at a sprint. The two snipers near Travis and Paige opened fire again.

Travis leaned close to her and shouted, "We're not gonna last much longer! Four hundred thousand people out there! They see what's not working for them, they'll find a way that does!"

"What are we supposed to do?" Paige shouted. "If they come in, they'll trip the sensors!"

"How does it normally work with the Ares?" he said. "Are the attackers after the thing itself, or just the people who are tagged by it? It's just the people, right?"

Another car detonated in the street below, like a mortar round going off.

Paige shouted over the sound. "Yeah! They're just after us!"

"So let's leave!"

She looked at him like she'd heard wrong. So did the nearest of the snipers.

"They'll follow us," Travis said. "And they'll forget about the building. We'll end up dead, but at least we can draw them away from the fucking nuke. There must be service tunnels under the streets, drainage, pipeline maintenance, that kind of thing. Is there access to them from inside this building?"

"Yeah," Paige said. "There's a panel in the basement. It's not huge, but we could fit through, single file—"

She stopped. Caught her breath. A second later Travis realized why.

Then she was on her feet and running again, through the tunnel, shouting into her comm unit as she went. "Second floor teams, get to the basement! Secure the conduit access!"

Travis was right behind her, rifle in hand, hitting the stairs now, down through the wire-choked space, past the feeders running ammo, past the rabbit tunnels branching out to the shooters on every level. Third floor now. Second. First.

And here were the snipers Paige had just ordered down. Bunched around the doorway to the basement, the door itself torn from its hinges. Four men, firing on full auto at something right there, maybe just feet beyond Travis's angle of view. Paige's insight had prevented disaster by a margin of perhaps seconds: the throng had already flooded into the basement through the access tunnels.

At that moment, one of the four snipers took a shot to the head and dropped. However many people were down there, some of them had guns.

Travis realized he could hear their voices, loud as the shooting was. Could hear the screams of anger, could hear even the distinct words, in German and maybe Italian. A noise to Travis's right made him turn. It'd sounded like something heavy being dropped on the floor. It came again, and this time he saw its source. The hallway floor heaved upward an inch, hit by something from below. Some heavy object in the hands of probably a dozen people, being used as a battering ram to come through the floorboards. The third impact cracked one of them, leaving a four-inch-wide gap. Through it, Travis saw the nightmare. The space below was wall-to-wall with writhing bodies, faces twisted in rage. Eyes locked onto him through the gap, and a volley of incensed screams came up.

He turned and saw Paige looking at the same

spot. Then, beyond her, one of the snipers took something from his backpack. In the crazed light, Travis couldn't see what the thing was, but had a pretty good guess.

Paige turned, saw it, and screamed, "No!"

The man pivoted toward her, and Travis saw what he'd expected: a grenade.

"There are gas lines down there!" Paige shouted.

"What the fuck are we supposed to do?" the man yelled.

Paige had no answer.

The floor heaved again. A second board fractured, right behind the first, and a hand gripped it from below and snapped it down into the darkness. The hole would be wide enough to admit bodies soon. A second later, Travis heard the battering impact again, somewhere else on the main floor.

The sniper was still looking to Paige for an answer.

"I don't *know* what to do," she said. She repeated it, looking around as if the answer would come to her.

"Yes you do," Travis said.

She met his eyes. Narrowed hers.

"The grenade," Travis said, and then darted his own eyes upward. Through the ceiling. To something eight stories above their heads. She followed. Understood.

"It's all we've got," Travis said.

"Is it a chess move the Whisper would have expected?" she said.

"We're stuck with it, whether it is or not. Go. I'll help these guys."

She considered it for another two seconds, then nodded. She turned to the sniper and held out her hand for the grenade. He looked like he understood the plan. Or didn't care, so long as there was one. He handed it over.

"Don't take losses holding this floor!" Paige shouted. "Withdraw up the stairs when you have to! One way or another, this'll be over in the next two minutes."

Travis stared at her. Realized he was storing the image. Wondered if he'd ever see her again.

Then she was gone.

He unslung his rifle, thumbed off the safety, and went to the basement door where the others were standing.

Beyond it was the worst thing he'd ever seen. The basement, a vast space maybe twelve feet deep, crawled like a snake pit full of bodies, the living and the dead so intermixed it was hard to differentiate them. As the leading edge of the wave advanced up the stairs and was cut back by the autofire, those behind dragged the bodies aside, between themselves or above. The corpses that rode the crowd pumped arterial blood from bowl-sized exit wounds, spraying and coating the throng.

Men, women, children. No fog to hide them now. The crowd was the sort you might encounter at a mall, or a supermarket, or anywhere. Some of the parents were holding seven-year-olds by the hand, as if unwilling to lose sight of them. Even as they dragged them forward into the gunfire. And even the seven-year-olds looked ready to kill someone. Would have tried to, had they reached the top of the stairs.

The forefront continually surged and was seared back, ten to twelve steps below. Travis shouldered his rifle. Lowered the sights to the crowd on the stairs. Didn't fire yet. Suddenly wasn't sure he could. They were just people. Bloody and screaming, and furious enough to come forward into machine-gun fire. But still just people. It wasn't their fault this was happening to them.

One of the snipers stopped to reload. It took him only three seconds, but in those seconds of reduced fire, the crowd gained four steps, and the back-and-forth cadence resumed there. Their progress was like a ratchet, locking in each little burst of progress, never really losing it.

A moment later, as the first sniper resumed fire, the other two ran dry in unison, and fumbled for fresh magazines. The crowd rushed upward at full speed; the lone shooter could only cover any one spot at a time. An old man wearing a ridiculous green bow tie, like a St. Patrick's Day reveler drunk off his ass, came scrambling up out of the pack wielding a steak knife, aiming for the thigh of one of the reloading snipers, who wasn't even looking his way. Travis pulled the trigger and took most of the old man's head off. The body pitched back and was immediately grabbed and hauled upward, out of the way, by the next two attackers: a teenage boy and a woman no older than thirty. Travis shot them both in the chest, and didn't stop shooting as each new target presented itself. He understood within seconds what it took to do it: you just didn't look at the faces. That was how the snipers were managing. It was a miserable fucking tactic, he knew. And it wasn't a real coping method for what he felt. It was just a kind of debt. He'd pay it back later. If there was a later.

Behind him there came a violent crash. He turned, along with the others, to see some kind of steel shelf unit sticking up through the floor, having broken a wide hole through. It dropped away a second later, and then there were hands gripping the edges of the hole, people below no doubt hoisted on the shoulders of others.

"Fall back to the stairs!" Travis shouted.

A head came up through the hole. Covered in someone else's blood. Could've been either sex, any age. Travis put a bullet into it and watched it drop back through the opening, like the shelf had.

He and the others were moving now. Backing up in stutter-steps so the crowd on the basement stairs didn't surge. They reached the stairs to the second floor and made their way up, reloading and firing as they went, the throng matching their pace as they climbed.

Paige rounded the landing on Level Seven. Miller was still there, doubling ammo and spare rifles. Feeders were running armloads to the snipers.

"Get some down to ground level!" Paige yelled, and didn't wait to see her nod. She continued on. Up to Level Eight, then Nine.

The warhead. The red star like an eye, watching her. Daring her.

This would either work or it wouldn't. If it didn't, well, there were worse ways to die than standing near the heart of a thermonuclear blast. Truth be told, there was probably no better way. It would reduce her to loose atoms about ten thousand times faster than her nerves could send the pain signals to her brain. Faster than her eyes could report the sudden light to her visual cortex a few inches behind them. It would literally feel like nothing at all.

Still, pretty goddamned scary.

She knelt before the thing. Considered the grenade and the available space inside the warhead. Right against the primary would be the best place to put it. This primary was an implosion type. A uranium sphere surrounded by shaped charges, precision wired to a detonator. Properly triggered, the shaped charges were designed to blow in millisecond unison, crushing the uranium to critical mass and setting off a fission reaction. That was the A-bomb aspect of the device. The A-bomb, in turn, would set off the H-bomb portion. But if the grenade went off right up against the shaped charges, and scattered their careful arrangement before any of them blew, then none of that would happen. The uranium crush would fail, and the whole sequence would stall.

That was the idea, anyway. It wasn't the sort of thing anyone had tested.

She set the grenade in place, between the shell of charges and one of the aluminum struts that braced the primary. She held it in place with her left hand, and with her right she pulled the pin. The handle swung open, and she heard the fuse ignite with a *pop*.

Turning now. Running hard. Into the room full of blazing white-orange light and not much else, past the inscription in the floor, past the nest of wires and the Ares and the amplifier and the silvery bond between them. To the far side of the room, putting as much space as possible between herself and the grenade blast. Wondering if she'd hear just the first crack of it before her life ended mid-thought.

CHAPTER THIRTY

Travis brought up the rear, two steps below the other shooters, the advancing crowd just another six steps below him. Slowing them was a lot harder on these stairs; they were wider than those in the basement.

"Landing!" one of the snipers shouted at him, and his next step put him on the flat surface of the second floor. He pivoted around the banister and continued upward, the rifle running dry at that moment. He ejected the clip, took another from his pocket, and as he racked it in he felt the building shudder from the force of an explosion, high above.

Paige had closed her eyes and turned away just before the blast. Now she opened them and found the room choked with plaster and explosive residue. Most of the wall around the double doors had been blown out, leaving a huge cavity. The grenade must have triggered a few of the shaped charges. Not bad, though. It could have been about five megatons worse.

She turned her eyes on the Ares, still lying in the nest, bound to the amplifier by the strange channel of metallic light. The tangle of wiring was still encrusted with pressure pads, which now mattered about as much as Post-it notes. She closed in on the Ares at a full run, didn't slow, and kicked it like she was back in high-school soccer practice, doing penalty drills. It shot from its resting place and went tumbling across the room, corners skittering on the wood—but its visible connection to the amplifier held. The silvery, plasma-like channel simply elongated and swung to maintain the connection, like a beam of light following a target. The Ares hit the wall beside the blast cavity, bounced back three feet, and settled in the swirling dust.

The orange-white light still filled the room. The gunfire downstairs went on unhindered.

Paige had never destroyed an entity before. Some of the strictest protocols forbade it. For obvious reasons. Who the hell knew what would result?

She'd know in a second.

She unslung her rifle, shouldered it, centered the sights and fired on auto.

The Ares made a sound like a human scream when it shattered. The room plunged into near darkness as the thing's light vanished, and the plasma channel to the amplifier switched off. Where the Ares had been, wild orange arcs of electricity skittered like fingers over the surrounding floor space, grabbing for purchase. Then they weakened, flickered, and died away.

The change came over the crowd in an instant. Travis let go of the trigger, spun hard and shoved aside the barrel of the only gun near him still firing.

The people on the steps below fell back. Where there'd been rage, there was now only shock. And fear. More fear than he'd ever seen. They drew away from the shooters, eyes wide and heads shaking, pleading in at least three languages. No ignoring their faces now. Travis saw them—felt pretty damn sure he would always see them, the way they looked in this moment. Would never lose a detail of this image if he lived to a hundred and five.

Within a matter of seconds the stairs below him were clear, at least of the living. The crowd had turned, shrunk away around the banister and out of view down the next flight. A sound came to Travis now. Like rushing air channeled through some narrow space, keening and high and fierce. It came from every direction. He understood. It was the crowd outside. It was thousands of people suddenly finding themselves waist-deep in the bodies of their friends.

Paige's voice came over the comm unit in his ear. "Weapons tight, but hold positions. Choppers are coming for evac, five minutes. Sit tight until then, in case this isn't over."

Five minutes later. Out through the front doors. Over the cobblestone approach. Past the wrought-iron fence. Dawn saturating everything pink, and the fog churning in compound dynamics: surging in toward the still-burning cars, curling violently in the rush of air from the Black Hawks. Four of them. Coming in low from the east, right along Theaterstrasse. Setting down in the street, their rotor wash at ground level pushing the fog back enough to reveal the mounds of bodies at the perimeter. Travis saw the nearest pilot and copilot survey the carnage, their mouths forming words he could lip-read pretty easily.

A moment later he was aboard the third chopper, with Paige beside him, along with a dozen of the others. Strapping in. Paige had the black cube from the ninth floor in her lap. The amplifier.

She cupped her mouth to his ear and shouted, "Take a look!"

She turned the cube over in all directions, showing him every side of it. All were smooth, featureless. No place for any wires or cables to connect. The damn thing had just been lying there, plugged into nothing. It alone was the amplifier; the nine stories of circuitry were all for show.

One more addition to the list of shit he couldn't square with.

The rest of the team from the building had already piled into the remaining Black Hawks, and within seconds the formation was rising. The streets below were deserted of the living for as far as Travis could see. The choppers cleared the roof, pivoted, and headed south over the city in a tight line, black silhouettes against the dawn.

At Meiringen, the 747 was already staged at the end of the runway, engines powered and ready. They boarded at a sprint, and three minutes later the aircraft was climbing above Switzerland at the steepest angle its wings could bear, on the chance that someone with a Stinger missile was down there on the pine-covered slopes. When they leveled off at 45,000 feet, Travis saw three escort fighters settle into formation off the starboard wing. No doubt the same number graced the other side, along with others far ahead and behind.

Paige made an executive decision to put the co-pilot at the tail of the plane, under guard, and then chose three operators at random to sit with the pilot in case he made any strange moves. When she returned to the seat she'd occupied on the flight over—next to the one Travis now sat in—she looked more exhausted than relieved.

The black amplifier cube sat on the floor nearby.

Paige ticked off the relevant bullet points on her fingers. "His building is gone; we'll level it with an airstrike as soon as the wounded are pulled out. We have the amplifier. Of the three entities he controlled, we've recovered the transparency suit and destroyed the Ares. He still has the Whisper." She looked at Travis, and he saw something that was almost—but not quite—optimism in her expression. "So what just happened in Zurich? Did we dodge whatever he was planning?"

"We'd have to know what he was planning," Travis said.

"Everything he's worked on for fourteen years is either destroyed or in our possession," she said. She sounded like she was trying to convince herself more than him.

Travis nodded, accepting her point, but unsure

all the same. There was just no way to know what the plan had been. What it might still be.

Paige's cell rang. Crawford at Border Town. She put it on speaker again.

"We got something on that last name on Pilgrim's list," Crawford said. "Ellis Cook. Let me just make sure I understand what you told me. These names were carved into the floor *inside* the room on Level Nine?"

"Yes," Paige said.

"Where nobody's been for at least four years," Crawford said.

"Right," Paige said. She sounded impatient.

"Ellis Cook had a net worth of over one hundred million dollars. But he made it by winning a Powerball lotto three years ago. Four years ago, when his name was already scratched on that floor, Cook was managing a coffee shop in North Carolina."

Paige looked like she was waiting for more. Or for a punch line, maybe. She stared at the phone, her eyes fixed, narrowed. Then she looked at Travis and said, "What?"

He had no answer for her.

"That's what we know so far," Crawford said. "All of these people were rich as hell when they died, though we're still looking for a specific through line. But at the time Pilgrim carved Ellis Cook's name into that floor, the guy was fielding complaints ten hours a day from people who wanted more foam on their cappuccinos. Your bafflement's as good as ours."

Paige ended the call and stared ahead at nothing for a moment. Finally she shook her head and said, "Look, I accept that the Whisper can know everything about the present. I don't know *how* it knows that, but at least that information really exists in the world. But Jesus, I don't care how advanced something is, how can it see the future? There's too much randomness. It's chaos."

"You'd have to think it'd be pretty good at making educated guesses," Travis said. "A hell of a lot more educated than ours."

"Educated enough to guess the winning lotto numbers, and which person would *pick* those numbers, a year or more in advance? Is that even close to possible?"

He met her eyes; they were wide, locked onto his. "Sixty seconds ago I'd have said no," he said. "Right now I'm leaning toward yes."

She stared at him a moment longer. Blinked. Looked away over Switzerland falling behind them. "What the hell are we up against here?"

"I have a thought," Travis said. "But I'm not sure you want to hear it."

"Try me."

"We've been operating under the premise that Pilgrim has total control of the Whisper. That he mastered it."

She nodded. Waited for him to go on.

"What if we have it backwards?" he said. "What if it mastered him?"

The cell measures nine feet by seven. There are no bars. Instead there are four concrete walls painted the ugliest possible shade of blue, and a steel door with a two-inch vertical strip of security glass set into it. It is the only window in the cell. Encased in the ceiling is a fluorescent light, which is never turned off. Since last December it has been flickering in a way that gives Travis headaches right behind his eyes. For more than eight years he has spent twenty-three and a half hours of each day inside this room.

There is a letter taped to the wall above the bed. It arrived three months ago to inform him that his parents had been killed, shot while waiting at a stoplight in Minneapolis. Two detectives came to ask for his input on the matter. Travis enjoyed their undisguised apathy over Mr. and Mrs. Chase's deaths.

The only other letters he's received are from his brother, Jeff. These are not on the wall, but folded neatly beneath the bed, where he doesn't have to look at them, or think about the survivor's guilt that saturates the space between every line. Jeff is convinced that Travis's actions, on that night in 1992, are the only reason he himself was spared being drawn into the family business.

Travis is lying on the bed now, eyes closed to take the edge off the flickering. It barely helps. Sometimes he manages to simply forget about the flickering, even while it's happening, and sometimes that helps. Letting things slip from his mind is a skill he's perfected in this place. Days. Months. Years. The time behind him. The time ahead of him. Letting it all slip away is how he keeps from going crazy.

He stands from the bed and paces the room. He is hardly aware of the decision to do this; it is an automatic action that he makes several dozen times a day. His pacing follows the same path as always: door to toilet, toilet to door, door to toilet.

At that moment the lock on his cell door disengages with a heavy click, and the guard pushes it in.

"Visitor," the guard says, and Travis senses that the guard is nervous. Which is strange.

Then a man strides into the cell, dressed in an expensive suit, and the guard closes the door behind him. The man's hair is graying at the temples, and he wears sunglasses even in this windowless room. He grimaces at the flickering light, and says, "Hello, Travis. My name is Aaron Pilgrim."

He reaches for Travis as if to shake his hand, but instead Travis sees that he's holding something out to him. It is a bright blue sphere, the size of a softball. The radiance of the thing swims. It is hypnotic, and Travis takes it into his own hand without even considering to refuse.

The moment it touches his skin, a voice speaks in his head. A voice he thought he would never hear again.

"Travis," it says, and the strength departs his legs. He sits hard onto the bed.

Emily.

Beyond the blue light—beyond everything that matters to him now—he is vaguely aware that the visitor, Pilgrim, is smiling about something. It doesn't matter. Nothing matters.

Travis says her name. The light flutters in response, then settles into the rhythm of his pulse.

"We won't be talking for long," *Emily says.* "Not this time. Not next time, either, years and years from now, when we meet again over that muddy hole in Alaska. But the third time . . . oh sweetie. The third time will most certainly be the charm."

"Why can't you stay with me now?" Travis says. He hears the longing and pain in his own voice. Missing her already, before she's even gone.

"I have work to do," *Emily says.* "Complicated work. I could never explain it to you, I'm afraid. Not here and now. Someday, I will. If it helps, just know this: you're more important to me than anyone in the world. More than the grinning jackass standing in this cell with you. Out of six billion people, you're the one whose involvement I need most. You're the irreplaceable component of my plan."

Travis feels something wonderful swell in his chest, at her words. He matters to her. She has chosen him. In this moment, it is all he can do not to cry.

"Why me?" he whispers.

She giggles softly. "You'll find out." *The light continues in step with his heartbeat for another few seconds. Then it changes. Darkens, in a way.* "Now I'm going to give you what I came here to give you," *Emily says.* "It's not much. Think of it as a nudge. A preference for where you'd like to live, when you leave this place."

The moment she finishes saying that, Travis feels something inside his head. A tingling. It lasts perhaps a second, then vanishes.

"There," *Emily sighs.* "You're exactly on course now, my love. On course to meet me again."

Against his will, tears sting the edges of his eyes. She's going to leave now. He'll be alone here again. Alone with the miserable fluorescent light, and the headaches, and the ugly blue walls. And nothing else. For years, and years, and years.

"Shhh," *she says.* "It'll all be fine. Someday we'll laugh at this, I promise."

But he's so very far from laughing right now. This moment is wonderful beyond anything he's ever known. It is also horrible, to the same degree, because it is ending.

"Hand me back to the grinning jackass now, Travis."

He knows he cannot disobey her. Feels his body shifting forward already, as if of its own volition. Feels his leg muscles contracting to stand, and his arm stretching out to give her back.

"Please," *Travis whispers, as if he could possibly change her mind.*

"Soon," *she says.*

He wonders if he'll think of anything but her, in all the years to come, and she pulses in his hand one last time.

"By tonight, you won't think of me at all," *she says.*

Then the man with the graying hair at his temples comes forward and closes his fingers over her. All that stops Travis from killing this man is Emily's insistence. The man pulls her away. Travis's breath rushes out. If he were holding a knife right now, he'd cut his own throat with it.

The man named Pilgrim raps on the door. It opens, and like that, he's gone, and the wonderful blue light with him, and Travis falls onto his bed, and there is no stopping the tears now. Still wishing for a knife, or a nice .38, he considers the sharp metal corner of his bedframe instead. It won't be anywhere near as quick and clean as a blade. But when the job is done, it will be just as done.

He lies there, considering it. Minutes pass. At some point it occurs to him that he's let the blue sphere slip from his mind for a few seconds. Maybe as many as ten. How is that possible? How could he have forgotten it—her, forgotten her—for even that long?

He realizes he's staring right into that fucking fluorescent light now, and rolls over onto his stomach, face into the pillow. He is very tired. Very worn by the jagged emotions. He finds his awareness drifting down toward sleep.

He wakes. His mouth is dry, like he's been eating cotton balls. He must have slept for hours. He stands, goes to the sink, splashes water on his face and drinks with his mouth to the spigot.

Something is troubling him. Some memory he can't quite get to. Something he dreamed, maybe. He tries to picture it, and for a moment he draws the image of a pulsing blue light, and for some reason he feels very good about it. Maybe it was a nice dream. But even as he dwells on it, it slides down into the darkness, out of his reach. Gone.

He straightens up, shuts off the faucet. Returns to the bed, but doesn't feel like lying down again, or even sitting. Without really deciding to do so, he begins to pace the room: door to toilet, toilet to door, door to toilet.

PART III

ENTITY 0697

CHAPTER THIRTY-ONE

They flew west in a kind of perpetual daybreak, crossing the pinched tops of the time zones at the same speed as the Earth's shadow.

Travis tried to sleep. He failed. In the calm hours after takeoff, as the night's adrenaline faded, the events in Zurich caught up with him in full. In the midst of the violence he'd thought he appreciated its scale, but he'd been wrong. With each new hour's hindsight his sense of it deepened, like the piles of bodies in the streets around 7 Theaterstrasse.

Twice during the flight he threw up, just reaching the lavatory both times. In each room he passed along the aircraft's corridor, the operators—still wearing every piece of equipment except their rifles—sat wide awake. Some rested their heads in their hands; others stared out the windows at the black ocean and pastel sky. The view was beautiful, and maybe they needed to look at something beautiful for a while, for whatever help it might offer.

Paige didn't sleep, either. She fell into a long silence over Europe and then the Atlantic. She didn't cry, but Travis saw her hands shaking at times. After a while he found himself following the operators' lead and staring out the window, letting his thoughts go silent. He was looking down at Greenland, the snow reflecting some of the faint pink of the sky, when Paige spoke.

"I was wrong, before." Her voice sounded as strained as if she'd cried, after all. "What I said about the Breach, that we're like Java man compared to whoever's on the other side." She paused again and chose her words carefully. "Really, we're like ants. Ants that accidentally tunneled into a holding tank full of chlorine underneath some chemical factory. That's how far out of our depth we are, dealing with this shit. That's how dangerous it is. And it's how little concern they have for us, whoever they are on the other side. As much concern as the owners of that factory would have for the ants. They probably don't even know about us. Probably wouldn't care if they did."

They were over North Dakota now, the landscape shadowy under the same dawn they'd taken off into, in Switzerland. Neither Travis nor Paige had spoken in hours.

Paige's cell rang. It was Crawford. Tangent had located Ellis Cook's daughter, who'd been present at the time of his apparent suicide. The girl had been very close to her father. She might know something. She was on a flight to Border Town right now, landing an hour ahead of them.

Travis found himself thinking about the Whisper again. Unnerving as it was, it made a welcome distraction. Paige ended the call and glanced at him, and he thought he saw the same sentiment in her eyes.

She was quiet a moment, then said, "Have you ever heard of a story called 'The Appointment in Samarra'?" She still sounded worn, depleted.

"No," Travis said.

"I forget who wrote it. One of those things everyone reads in English 102. This servant goes to the marketplace, and he sees Death standing there, and Death makes a threatening face at him. The servant runs back to his master and says, 'Let me borrow your horse, I'll ride to Samarra so Death won't find me.' The master lets him go, then heads down to the market himself, sees Death and he says, 'What are you doing making a threatening face at my servant?' And Death says, 'Threatening? No, no, I was just surprised to see him here. I have an appointment with him tonight in Samarra.'"

She looked past him, out the window at the waking countryside.

"That's what this feels like," she said finally. "Like no matter what we do from this point on, no matter what path we take, the Whisper is waiting for us at the end of it. If it can guess lotto numbers, it can sure as hell guess our moves. Even if we say to ourselves, 'Well, it would guess this, so let's do the opposite,' we have to assume it could guess *that*, too."

Travis could only nod. Yeah. No reason to think otherwise.

"So what the hell are we supposed to do?" Paige said.

He thought for a moment. Only one avenue seemed to have any light shining onto it. The hit list carved into the floor at 7 Theaterstrasse.

"We need to know why Pilgrim had those thirty-seven people killed. Or why the Whisper had them killed. There has to be a reason, and it has to matter. And even if the damn thing expects us to find out, and expected it ten years ago, what else can we do? If there's a way out, it's by knowing what it's afraid of."

She nodded, more accepting than agreeing. Which was more or less how he felt himself.

He stared out at North Dakota. Little towns slid by far below, some of them not much more than a set of crossroads with a streetlight or two, still shining in the half-light.

A strange thought came to him. Actually, it wasn't the thought that was strange. The thought was normal. All that was strange was that he hadn't considered it until now.

His former life was over.

His apartment in Fairbanks. His job there. His pressing decision between staying or going home to Minneapolis, going to work with his brother. That life was gone, as if someone else had lived it. He was here now, part of Tangent whether he liked it or not. If he ever went home, there was no question that Pilgrim's people would be waiting there for him. And given all the sensitive things he knew about the Breach now, Tangent would probably want to keep him among their own ranks after this was over, if only for their own security reasons.

If either he or Tangent still existed when this was over.

CHAPTER THIRTY-TWO

Her name was Lauren. She was sitting in Paige's office, almost on the spot where Travis had been standing when his bonds were removed a day earlier. She was twenty-three, but looked a lot younger than that at the moment. She looked like a lost child.

Travis was standing with Paige. Crawford and a few others were in the room too. For half an hour they'd asked Lauren all the questions about her father that the computers hadn't answered for them. So far, nothing useful had emerged.

There was something in the girl's eyes that Travis recognized. He'd seen it in people before, during interrogations. An eagerness to reveal something, stifled by fear of doing so. Fear because she didn't trust them.

Travis leaned close to Paige and whispered a question in her ear. She looked at him, understood his idea, and nodded. She stepped out of the room, taking out her cell as she went. Lauren's dark eyes followed her out, then returned to Crawford as he asked her to clarify something she'd already clarified twice.

A few minutes later, Paige returned. She was carrying a black plastic case. An entity case.

Travis waited for another exchange between Crawford and Lauren to end, then said, "Can I speak to her?"

Crawford nodded. Travis took a step toward Lauren, met her eyes, and spoke softly but directly.

"You don't believe your father killed himself, do you?"

She shook her head, her eyes never leaving his.

"There's no way," she said. She was quiet a moment. Then she looked at the floor, and continued. "Everyone's been telling me I need to accept what happened, or else I won't be able to deal with it. They said people always feel the way I do, when this happens. And they said it's normal for there to be . . . no warning. They told me they reviewed the security footage from all over the estate grounds, before and after it happened, and nobody came or went. But my father didn't kill himself. And I don't care whether you people believe me—"

"We know he didn't kill himself," Travis said.

Her eyes came up again. Stared at him. He turned to Paige, and she handed him the black case. He set it on the table next to the door and opened it. It looked empty. Travis reached in and took hold of what he knew was inside it. He couldn't be sure which part he was grabbing, but the effect was identical to picking up an article of clothing with his eyes closed. He felt something like a shirt sleeve at once, and a second later his hand found the hem at the shirt's bottom.

He turned back to Lauren.

"The man who murdered your father was wearing this," Travis said, and shoved his arm through the open bottom of the shirt, as far as it could go. He saw the arm and most of his shoulder vanish into nothingness.

Lauren's body jerked. She stared at the empty space where Travis's arm should have been, her eyes huge. Head shaking now, just noticeably. Her mouth formed a question, but it didn't come out. She only stared. Five seconds passed. Then ten.

When she did speak, her voice was barely audible. "Where is he now?"

She was looking at Travis again by the time she said it. He met her gaze without blinking.

"Dead," Travis said. "I killed him."

He watched her reaction, and saw what he'd hoped for. She knew he was telling the truth.

"We're not the bad guys, Lauren," he said. "Whatever it is you're afraid to talk about, you can tell us."

She looked at him a moment longer, then turned her eyes to Paige and the others, one by one. Each nodded.

Her attention came back to Travis, and after another moment she returned to staring at her own knees.

"My father belonged to a group of people you've never heard of. You won't find anything about them by looking at his tax records, or his phone logs. The other people who were killed, these past several years, were part of it too. I'll tell you as much as I know."

As much as she knew wasn't a lot. Her father had sought to protect her from what he was involved in.

The group had no name, she told them. That was supposed to be a security measure. Among its members, it did have a nickname—something of a joke—which was never written down: The Order of the Qubit. Travis didn't know that word. Everyone else in the room did. *Qubit* stood for "quantum bit." A computing unit of a quantum computer. For the better part of the past decade, a few dozen governments and a few hundred companies had been trying like hell to develop quantum computers, which were expected to be dramatically more powerful than computers at present. But other than very limited proof-of-concept stuff in labs, no one had had any luck. It was one of those things everyone was sure would exist at some point. But whether that point was five years away, or fifty, was tough to pin down.

Lauren thought the Order of the Qubit dated to the early nineties. As she understood it, it was more or less a group of very rich people funding their own secret work toward building a viable quantum computer. Their motivation was simply fear: in the global race to make one of these machines, whoever crossed the finish line first would gain a great deal of power. As it happened, a lot of the institutions who were likely candidates to win the race couldn't be expected to use that power for the world's best interests. Many could be counted on to use it for nearly the opposite purpose. The Order of the Qubit wanted to win that race itself, then carefully select a few organizations that really did have the big human picture in mind, and simply give them the technology.

Good idea. Also a good way to get killed. Entrenched interests tended to dislike threats to their power, and to express that dislike violently.

As to whether the group had achieved its goal, or even gained any ground toward it, Lauren had no idea. She also had no idea where their work was conducted, where their meetings were held, or where Tangent could locate any other member of the organization.

She finished speaking, and looked at them each in turn again.

"Did I help?" she said.

Travis met Paige's eyes. Saw that she was thinking exactly what he was thinking. He looked at Lauren again.

"You helped," he said.

"They have one," Travis said. "A working model."

He and Paige were standing in the open doorway of the pole barn on the surface, watching the jet—a Gulfstream this time—take off with Lauren in it. She'd asked to stay in Border Town. She'd said she'd feel safer there. She wouldn't have been. This was probably the least-safe place on Earth right now, lying in the Whisper's gun sights. Lauren herself should be under no real threat elsewhere; she'd already given them all the information she had.

"I think they must," Paige said.

Travis watched the plane diminish to a desktop model of itself. Then a speck. Then nothing.

"Is there any chance a computer like that could outthink the Whisper?" he said. "Is that why these people are a threat to it?"

"I only know a little about quantum computers. Stories about their potential show up in tech papers once in a while. I know their power grows exponentially the more qubits you add, but that in itself has been the trick. Adding more of them. There's some kind of engineering limit, ten or twelve qubits, something like that. Not enough to do very much. But if someone built a quantum computer with fifty qubits, or a hundred, it'd be off the charts. Way, way off the charts. I think there are still limits to their use, even then—limits on the kind of math they can do—but there'd be creative ways to get around that. There's no question it would be a big deal, if someone really had a scaled-up version working."

Travis thought it over, watching empty sky now. Even if they were right, it didn't fully make sense. If the thing was really a threat to the Whisper, then the Whisper should have seen that coming too. Should have directed Pilgrim to find and destroy the place where the thing would be built, long before it was completed.

That was just one of the things that made no sense

to him. There were several others. He couldn't help thinking that the confusion was part of the Whisper's plan. Any good strategy should look like nonsense to those facing off against it.

What *was* the plan? What was the Whisper's final goal? It was hard enough to figure out what a human being wanted. What the hell did this *thing* want? On that point, he couldn't even form a guess.

CHAPTER THIRTY-THREE

All day long, photos and video came in from a detachment scouring Ellis Cook's house on Grand Cayman. Nice place. There was nothing inside it that hinted about his involvement with any secret group. Air ducts were inspected. Carpets were torn up. A giant safe in the basement was drilled through and opened. A mechanical shed next to the pool was examined in detail. It contained an impressive pumping and filtering system, built to draw seawater in from the harbor at hundreds of gallons per minute, which would fill the pool in less than an hour. The kind of thing only someone with a hundred million dollars would think he needed. But no quantum computer.

The ATC logs for Owen Roberts International Airport on Grand Cayman turned up something interesting. A few times a year, an Airbus A318, big enough to hold over a hundred passengers but registered as a business jet, landed there. Each time, it departed again within eight hours. The jet's ownership was in Cook's name, but it was based at Dallas-Fort Worth, where he owned a

permanent hangar for it. The plane didn't seem to
be Cook's personal transport. For that, he had a
Dassault Falcon that he kept right there on Grand
Cayman. The Airbus, it seemed, didn't take Cook
anywhere, but instead brought people to him. A
lot of people, all at once. The implication was
pretty obvious: that Cook's house on the island
was the group's base of operations. Or one of its
bases, anyway. But the search of the house revealed
no evidence of that, and the data mining of real-
estate records showed no other land or property
on Grand Cayman with his name on it.

Travis saw the tension building on Paige's
shoulders, as the day went on without any action-
able information. She bore it as well as anyone
could have, but he could tell this was hard on her,
being amped up to do something—anything—
and having nothing to direct that energy at. Like
it would be hard on an engine to detach it from
its working load, and rev it past the redline for
hours.

More than once, Travis heard people comment
that Paige's father would've been a godsend at a
time like this, when answers were both critical and
hard to come by. Each time, Paige's reactions were
subdued, difficult to read. Late in the afternoon
she left to be alone for a while, and returned looking emotionally drained.

By nine o'clock at night, the team at the Cayman
house had finished. For the time being, there was
no more evidence to look over. Nothing to work
on at all.

Crawford gave Travis a keycard to a vacant residence on Level B12. He found his way to it, and entered to find a living space about twice the size of his apartment in Fairbanks. Granite counters in the kitchen. Eighty-inch LCD in the living room. The Sub-Zero refrigerator was well stocked, as were the cupboards. The master bathroom, decked out in natural stone, was a thing of beauty. The image in the mirror wasn't. Travis hadn't shaved in a week. Hadn't showered in several days, during which time he'd been active, to understate things a bit. He opened the medicine cabinet and found shaving cream, and razors still in the package. Shampoo and unused soap in the shower. Twenty minutes later he felt human again.

The master closet was filled with a wide array of clothing. He picked out some jeans and a T-shirt, and was in the kitchen thinking about a sandwich when he noticed the message button flashing on the wall phone. It hadn't been flashing earlier. He pressed the button and heard Crawford's voice, telling him that Tangent had retrieved two messages from his voice mail in Fairbanks, and routed them here.

"Obviously there are security measures we take with outgoing calls," Crawford's recorded voice said. "If you need to contact anyone, speak to me and we'll see what we can arrange."

The first message was a telemarketer's robo-call trying to sell him an extended warranty on his Explorer. The second was from his brother, Jeff.

"Hey, Travis. Give me a shout when you get this.

Cool news. Whitebird's almost official. It just beat Level One in *Fog of War* without my help. It's still buggy, needs a shitload of work, but I'm geeked, man. You can still get in on this with me, if you want. Call me. Out."

Whitebird was a computer system, both hardware and software, that Jeff had been working on for years. It was a narrow form of artificial intelligence, meant to improve the performance of computer-driven enemies in video games. Jeff had been testing its capability by letting it take on the role of the human player in older, simpler games, mostly martial-arts stuff on 8-bit systems from the eighties and nineties. Now he was up to modern games like *Fog of War*. Pretty impressive. He probably stood to make millions selling the technology to a game developer, once he had all the wrinkles smoothed out. More to the point, though, he simply loved the work.

Travis's temptation to accept his offer, during the past year, had at times nearly swayed him all the way. Even now he felt some strain of remorse. Like he'd missed an exit from the freeway, one he'd been supposed to take, but that he'd never get back to now.

It struck him that, of the two of them, if someone had been asked to guess which brother would end up in a place like Border Town, the smart money—the only money—would've been on Jeff. Tangent probably had an army of computer techs designing and running customized systems for their research.

Travis turned away from the phone, and was heading for the refrigerator when someone knocked on the door.

He crossed the living room, opened it, and found Paige standing there, also having just showered. Still looking keyed up. Looking like she wished she could relax.

"Tell me you haven't eaten," she said.

"I haven't eaten."

An hour later they were sitting cross-legged on her bed, facing each other. Sometimes she looked down at her hands fidgeting in her lap, and her hair fell across her face in a way that Travis couldn't stop staring at.

They talked about random things. Paige had finished high school at sixteen and gone to Texas A&M. She'd set out to become a historian, but four years later had found herself going for a master's in the new nanosystems engineering program there, working on the Model-T versions of what would someday, with any luck, be digital white blood cells, the cure for pretty much everything. When Travis asked her why she'd changed her major, she said she'd realized something: as much as she loved to understand where the human story had been, she was more interested in where it was going. Nothing excited her like the forward edge of technology, the best minds in the world building on one another's work at an ever-increasing speed. By twenty-one she knew she wanted to spend her life in that world. And then, in one very surpris-

ing weekend, her father—her only living relative—
had brought her to this place and shown her what
he really did for a living. Quite the revelation, it'd
been. With it had come another: there were grave
security risks attendant to the loved ones of Tangent operators like Peter Campbell. Paige was in
danger, just by living her life, just by being who she
was. She would be safer here at Border Town, so
long as the threat persisted.

"Lived here ever since," she said, glancing around
at her apartment. Two levels below Travis's, it
was identical except for the touches her taste had
brought to it.

Her hands found their way into his. He held
them, his thumbs tracing back and forth across her
palms.

She spoke softly. "Since prison, has there been
anyone special?"

"No one," he said. A moment later he added,
"No one special *in* prison, either."

Paige laughed, glancing up from their hands to
meet his eyes.

"After I got out," he said, "part of me thought
there was no point in trying. You can only get so
far into a conversation before you run into the wall.
'You're from Minnesota? Oh, what did you do
there?'"

She laughed again, quietly. "What did the rest of
you think?"

He was silent a moment. "That this was my real
punishment. The one I'd never get free of. And that
I deserved it."

"For what happened to—" She paused, and Travis could see her parsing her memory of the police report she'd read. At last she said, "Emily. Emily Price."

Travis nodded. "She saved me from what I was. Saved my life, figuratively, even literally, I'm sure. And they killed her because of it. I should've known. I should've seen it coming, and I didn't."

"It's easy to underestimate the bad in people," Paige said. "I don't think it should carry a life sentence."

He managed something close to a smile, and held her hands a little tighter.

In the darkness their clothes evaporated, and there was only her skin against his, so much warmer than he'd imagined, and her hair falling around him, scented sweet like apple trees in October. He tasted on her tongue the white wine they'd had with dinner. Tasted the soft skin below her jawline. Tasted everything.

Later, holding her close, Travis felt the silence filling up with all the questions he knew they were both dwelling on. All the things that didn't add up, no matter which way they were arranged.

"Everything the Whisper's ever done," he said, "since the day it came out of the Breach in 1989, has been part of the act. Hasn't it?"

She nodded against his chest. "I think so."

"The notion that it's compelled to help you at first, and then it tries to take over your will after that, it's all bullshit. It can do anything it wants to do, anytime. Nothing compels it. Nothing limits it. All that stuff was just a smokescreen so it could control the way people handled it. Up in Alaska, when it used me to try setting off a nuclear war, it seemed to fail because Pilgrim's people in the helicopter showed up too soon. Are you buying that for a second? The thing can predict a mega lotto outcome years in advance, but not the arrival of a helicopter a few minutes out? Something a radar tech with a stopwatch could probably figure out in his head?"

"Strikes me as a little inconsistent," Paige whispered.

"It was keeping up appearances," he said. "Playing the role a little longer. Every move it's made, from the moment it arrived in this world, has been to steer things to exactly where they are right now. Do you see the problem with that?"

"That twenty years is a long damn time for something that powerful to spend reaching its goal?"

"Exactly," he said. "If all it wants is control of Border Town and the Breach, it could've gotten it almost on day one. It could've just played nice, right from the beginning, won everybody over, and then as soon as the right person was holding it, someone with access to any of the really destructive shit locked away in this building, it could've used that person as a puppet to kill everyone here. Just like that. So what the hell is it really after? What's far enough out of its reach, that it's taken all these years, and all this elaborate planning?"

For a moment she didn't reply. Then her forehead furrowed against his skin.

"What if it's after something that wasn't available until now?" she said.

Travis thought about that. It sounded right. A hell of a lot better than what he had, which was nothing.

"Like a new entity?" he said. "Something that would've just arrived?"

"I don't know. None of the recent unique arrivals has been especially powerful or dangerous, as far as we know."

They fell silent again. Travis heard the building's air exchange system kick on with a sigh. His face was resting against the top of Paige's head. Every breath was rich with the scent of her hair.

After a moment he said, "There's something that bothers me more than all of this." He considered how to begin. "We agree that Pilgrim isn't really the enemy here, right? That's not to say he's blameless. The Whisper probably chose him because it knew the kind of things he was capable of. But whatever Pilgrim believes, the Whisper is the one calling the shots. So far, so good, right?"

"Right."

"But the Whisper is still a machine. It's a tool, and a tool doesn't choose its own purpose. Someone else would have done that."

Paige was silent a long while before speaking. "You mean someone on the other side of the Breach," she said.

"Yeah."

With his arm, he felt a shiver climb the muscles of her back.

"If that's the case," she said, "then we never had a prayer."

He tried to think of some reassuring reply to that, but came up empty. All he could do was pull her closer against himself. She responded, settling into him. He lay there listening to her breathing, feeling her limbs relax. Turning the questions over and over, and wondering who—or what—they were really up against, he faded out.

Sometime later, he woke with the strangest feeling. Like he'd figured something out. Dreamed it, maybe. He tried to remember what it was, but could only push it away, like a child trying to palm a basketball. He relaxed and let it come back. For a moment, it seemed that it might. An impression of it swam into view: the video footage of the high-powered pump station at Cook's house on Grand Cayman. It had something to do with that. Something about Cook's need for it, in the first place. But that was all he could get. A moment later it was gone.

Paige murmured, rising halfway out of sleep beside him. He kissed her forehead and she rolled into him, softly kissing his neck before drifting away in his arms. Feeling her heartbeat against him, he closed his eyes and followed her down.

CHAPTER THIRTY-FOUR

A phone began to ring. Somewhere in the dark. Travis felt Paige stir. She rolled toward the nightstand—the clock read just past four in the morning—switched on the light, and pressed a button for the speakerphone. Even as she answered with her name, she slipped under the covers again and hugged her body to his.

The voice that issued from the phone sounded scared. "Paige, it's Crawford. I'm at Secure Storage on B31. The attendants on duty called me down. There's something going on. Maybe you should come down here."

Her eyes locked on Travis's.

"Paige?" Crawford said.

"I'm here." She let go of Travis, sat up and swung her feet to the floor, hunting for her clothes. "Describe what's happening."

"We're not really sure. It has to do with the object you brought back from Zurich. The black cube."

"The amplifier," Paige said. She looked at Travis again.

In the background over the speakerphone, they

could hear some kind of droning sound. Like someone humming, from deep in the diaphragm. It was the sound they'd heard on the ninth floor of 7 Theaterstrasse, just before everything went to hell.

"It's locked inside one of the vaults," Crawford said. "Where we put it yesterday morning. But it's making the sound you're probably hearing behind me. We haven't opened the vault yet. Not sure we should."

At that moment they heard a quick gap of silence over the phone, and Crawford said, "Paige, hold on, I've got a call from Defense Control. I'll put it on conference so I don't lose you." He clicked out for a second, and then they heard him say, "Defense go ahead."

A woman spoke. "Mr. Crawford, we have a situation up top. We're not sure how this is happening, but there's a radar contact directly above us, about forty thousand feet up, and falling. Computer says it's human bodies."

"Divers?" Paige said.

"We think so. They're dropping at around two hundred miles per hour, consistent with terminal velocity for humans tucked into a bullet fall. Radar didn't see a plane, so it was either an ultra-high-altitude bail-out from something like a U2, or a stealth, if that's possible."

Travis saw Paige's eyes narrow at that, but only slightly. Pilgrim had the Whisper; of course it was possible.

"The diver formation went into a sparse pattern right after the first contact, and the radar lost them, but with the thermal cams on the chain guns, we should be able to track them manually when they get low enough. With your permission, sir, we'll just kill everyone up there."

"Do it," Crawford said. The bass-range hum continued on his end of the call.

Sufficiently rattled by whatever the hell was going on down there, Paige stood, her clothes still balled up in her hand.

"Did anything trigger the amplifier?" Paige said. "Any experiment going on nearby, anything like that?"

"Nothing," Crawford said. "It just came on. Like it was on a timer."

A thought hit Travis. Hit him hard enough to make him sit up and put his feet to the floor. Paige turned, seeing his expression.

"Crawford, this is Travis Chase," he said. "What entities are in the vaults closest to the amplifier?"

There was a pause as Crawford processed the fact that Travis was speaking over Paige's phone at four in the morning. Then he answered. "I don't have that information in front of me. Hold on." They heard him talking to one of the attendants in the background.

But Travis already knew the answer. He stood from the bed and crossed to Paige's desk, looking for a pencil and something to write on. Paige followed, dropping her clothes behind her.

"What is it?" she said.

Before he could answer, the woman at Defense Control spoke up again. "I see them on the thermals now. Barely. Initializing ground cannons for manual targeting."

"We need to write ourselves a message," Travis said, "so we'll know what happened."

He pulled open a drawer, found a dull pencil, and grabbed a printout of some kind, turning it over to write on the back.

"What do you mean?" Paige said.

Crawford spoke up over the phone. "Got the list. The vault nearest the amplifier contains Entity 0436, Jump Cut."

Just what Travis had expected. The thing Paige had told him about in Zurich. The thing that was exactly like the Ares, except for its effect. Which was that it killed the past three days' memory, and left you feeling like you'd just blinked and missed that time.

Paige's mouth fell open slowly. Head shaking a little from side to side. Understanding. Unwanted understanding.

"If the Whisper can predict the lotto," Travis said, "it can predict which vault the amplifier would end up in."

"Oh my God," Paige said.

He returned his eyes to the paper, his mind laboring for what to write. Then Crawford screamed on the phone, and Travis knew it was too late. An instant later Paige's bedroom flared with bright green light, like every room in Border Town, Travis was sure. On instinct he threw his arms around Paige, as if he could protect her from it. The light seemed to shine right through their bodies—

CHAPTER THIRTY-FIVE

Travis had been lying awake in his tent, listening to wolves howling somewhere along the ridge. He'd read that wolf packs randomized the volume of their howling in order to confuse prey—and other wolves—as to their distance. It worked on humans, too. These sounded at least as close as—

Suddenly he found his eyes shut, and a wild flash of light, like lightning but with a green cast to it, shone bright enough to be visible through his eyelids. It vanished almost at once, though he hardly noticed, because by then he'd realized someone was with him, holding on to him but at the same time struggling—

He opened his eyes to find himself standing in a room he'd never seen before. The struggling figure wrenched away from him.

It was a very beautiful—and very naked—young woman.

She was holding her right upper arm tightly, her face just now easing from what looked like a contortion of agony; Travis was sure he hadn't grabbed that arm or even bumped it. He had only an instant to consider these things, and then she was screaming at him, her eyes as bewildered as his own must look.

"*What is this?*" she shouted. "*What the fuck is this? Where's my father?*"

He reflexively stepped back from her, saying he didn't know, then repeating it; it was the only answer he had for her questions—or his own.

All at once she seemed to recognize the room, though that only confused her further, and then her eyes came to rest on a backpack and rifle leaning against the wall, and before Travis could register the danger, she'd lunged for the weapon, shouldered it and leveled it at his face.

"*What the fuck have you people done?*"

He had nothing he could say to her. He kept his eyes steady on hers, and shook his head, hands out from his sides to present no threat.

She racked the rifle's action and advanced a step, forcing him back against the wall. In the same moment her gaze dropped; Travis followed the look, and realized he was naked too. He met her eyes again, and saw them narrow as she looked around at the room once more, and then at herself—she noticed her own lack of clothing—as she struggled to piece the moment together. Her aggression faltered; the rifle didn't.

Somewhere nearby, agitated voices had been issuing from a speaker; now they stopped, and a single voice—an older man's voice—said, "Did I hear Paige?"

The woman—Paige, apparently—turned toward the sound, which Travis could now see came from a speakerphone. "Crawford?"

"Paige, where are you?"

She hesitated, as if too confused to say aloud what she knew. "I'm . . . in my room. Where are *you*?"

The man's answer was equally tentative. "I thought I was in the conference room, but . . . I'm down at Secure Storage now—"

A new sound over the phone line interrupted him: a soft computer voice saying, "Inbound . . . Inbound . . ."

For the first time, Paige lowered the rifle. That repeating word, coming from the speaker, had taken her full attention. She turned and moved toward the phone.

"Who's in Defense Control?" she said.

A woman answered, sounding as stressed as everyone else. "This is Karen—Karen Lowe. I'm sure I'm not supposed to be up here right now, I was in my room—"

"Forget about that," Paige said. "What's the inbound?"

"Nothing. The radar's blank, all fields. It looks like the gun cameras are up, but I don't know why, there's nothing on them—"

Other voices spoke in the background, and then Karen said, "Okay, yeah. What are they?"

Travis watched Paige lean in close to read the

lighted display of an alarm clock. She reacted to it, and whispered, "Three days . . ."

"I count at least ten of them up there," Karen said, to someone on her end of the call.

"Karen, tell me what you're seeing," Paige said.

"We don't know. They're not aircraft. The thermals are reading them at body temperature; they could be divers, but . . . are they hostiles, or—"

"Kill them," Paige said. Travis could see in her eyes that she'd jettisoned the confusion for the moment. "Get everyone at the controls and start shooting, right now. And someone hit the dead switch for all the containment levels. Lock everything down and then smash the control boards."

If the people on the other end of the call were confused, her direct tone got them past it. Travis heard alarms begin blaring, and then what sounded like someone following her orders about smashing things. He heard computer cases breaking open, fragile components inside being shattered by some blunt, heavy thing. A chair, maybe.

"Are you shooting yet?" Paige said.

"We're targeting," Karen said. "Ready in five, four, three—"

Suddenly Travis felt a jolt pass through the floor, and then the building shook from the bass wave of an explosion, somewhere high above.

CHAPTER THIRTY-SIX

The speakerphone went to static. Paige stared at it for less than a second, and then grabbed a pair of jeans from the floor and threw them at Travis. By the time he caught them, she was reaching for her own clothes.

"You seem to know more than I do," he said. "Mind sharing?"

"I have a guess," she said. "With gaps."

"More than I have." He stepped into the jeans and pulled them up.

Paige buttoned her own pair, then slipped her shirt over her head and grabbed the rifle again.

"Do the words Tangent or Breach mean anything to you?" she said.

"No."

"Then I couldn't explain it if we had an hour—" The hum of an automatic weapon sounded through the nearest air vent. "And we don't have an hour."

She opened the cabinet front of her nightstand and took out a .45, along with two spare magazines.

"Do you know how to shoot a gun?" she said.

He nodded. She took a step toward him, then

stopped, sizing him up one last time. More gunfire, and a small popping explosion, transmitted
through the ductwork. She came forward and
handed him the pistol and ammo. Already she was
on her way out of the room, grabbing the backpack
and shouldering it as she went.

He followed, as his most obvious question finally
surfaced. "How the hell did I get here?"

Paige checked the hallway outside her bedroom,
and looked satisfied that it was clear. "I'm pretty
damn curious about that myself," she said, and
moved out of the room.

With the rifle shouldered, Paige made her way
toward the living room, ready to kill anything that
appeared in front of her. She wasn't crazy about
turning her back on the man with her—she realized she hadn't even asked him his name—but the
situation demanded a few risks. Whoever he was,
her own choice of attire a few moments earlier—
none—seemed to imply that she trusted him.

The living room was clear. Beyond the door,
shouts echoed along the primary corridor.

How could she have possibly made it back to
Border Town alive? She'd been strapped down on
a makeshift torture table, probably halfway dead,
surrounded by enemies in the most remote place
she'd ever seen. How had three days taken her
from that place to her bedroom, standing around
in the buff with some guy she'd never met before,
who hadn't heard of Tangent?

Had her father survived, too?

Hope and fear pulled her concentration in opposite directions, neither useful right now. Facing the door, she blocked off both feelings, then glanced over her shoulder at the stranger.

"Don't shoot anything I'm not already shooting at," she said, then added, "unless it shoots at you first."

The guy shrugged, not even trying to hide his disorientation.

She found herself staring at him a second longer. He wasn't bad-looking. Then she turned and crossed to the door, and with a steadying breath, pulled it open and stepped through.

People were running in the corridor, all of them Tangent personnel. They were confused, partly by the explosions but more so, Paige thought, by their own fractured memory. Only a few—those who belonged to the detachments—carried weapons, but even these were looking to others for direction, and finding no help.

If her guess—her guess with gaps—was right, every one of them had just skipped over three days of memory in an instant. Three days. The interval of the Jump Cut. How the hell had it affected the entire building?

And how had Pilgrim made that happen? Obviously, the raid was coming from his people. Pilgrim himself was probably with them.

The Jump Cut's effect should only last a few minutes. That was the upside. The downside: Pilgrim would know that. Would plan for that. Would seek to take control of Border Town in those few minutes.

Down the hall, smoke poured from the seams of the elevator doors. At that moment another explosion, from somewhere in the uppermost levels, set the walls vibrating. People nearby flinched, maybe expecting the ceiling to come down. Maybe it would. Paige noticed a few of them staring at her as if she were a ghost. On some level she understood the logic of that, but it was one more thing she couldn't afford to dwell on right now.

What would Pilgrim have to do, to get control right away?

That was easy. The nerve center of the building, Security Control, was right below Defense Control. With the Whisper—there was no question he had it with him—he would know the codes for every system in the building. Systems that could be used against them easily.

She turned to the nearest group of armed operators, meaning to call them to her and lead them to the stairs. They could reach Security Control in about sixty seconds. But before she could say anything, jets of white gas erupted from the ventilation system overhead. For a moment she thought the fire suppression system had kicked on and begun pumping halon through the vents. Then she got her first smell of it.

Not halon.

Of course. Of course Pilgrim would trigger this system. So fucking simple a move.

She spun, thinking to shepherd the others into her residence, already aware that it was a dead option: the vents in there were pumping the stuff out too. She met their eyes, one by one—some of them were already succumbing to the gas—and settled on the stranger's gaze for some reason. Confused as he must be, he had a tight leash on his fear. She wondered again who he was.

Then her knees gave, and just as her vision failed, she saw him step forward to catch her, and then everything was gone.

CHAPTER THIRTY-SEVEN

T ravis woke to find his memory restored, the three lost days reinserted into his past. He woke to Paige looking like she'd been crying about something, and after a moment he thought he knew what it was. He woke to the coughing of five dozen other survivors of the attack, bound alongside the two of them in a large conference room.

And he woke to Aaron Pilgrim standing over him. Though Tangent had never shown him a photo of the man, he recognized him. He could not for the life of him say why.

Four men with rifles were watching the captives. Pilgrim got their attention with a look, then indicated Travis and Paige.

"These two."

Two of the gunmen slung their weapons and dragged Paige, then Travis, ten feet out from the wall along which the rest were arrayed.

Pilgrim pointed out eight others; they included Crawford as well as Dr. Fagan, the red-haired woman who'd sought to establish communication with the far side of the Breach. Pilgrim's men dragged the eight of them out onto the open floor, into a group with Travis and Paige.

Pilgrim considered the ten of them for a moment, nodded to himself, and said, "Kill the rest."

"*No!*" Paige screamed.

The shooting started before her scream had reverberated off the walls. Pilgrim's men went down the line in rapid succession, putting a single shot through the forehead of each bound victim. Travis felt Paige's body spasm against him with each rifle crack, each pleading cry from the condemned, each hopeless effort to squirm left or right in the last second. When it ended, she was shaking beside him with quiet sobs. Bound, Travis could offer no consolation but to lean closer to her. She responded, pressing against his shoulder as she cried.

Over her head, Travis saw a steel box sitting on the conference table, a cube about ten inches in each dimension. It was latched, and had a handle bolted to the top. A miniature of the giant version aboard Box Kite. This one was closed, and from the seam that ran around its midsection, a sheet of blue light projected outward, like the ring plane of some cube-shaped planet.

Pilgrim turned to face the chosen survivors. His eyes found Travis and stayed on him.

"You're a fucking puppet for that thing," Travis said.

"It may call the plays," Pilgrim said. "But it's my game."

Travis studied his expression when he said it.

There was no bluff in his eyes. The man really believed what he'd just said. Believed the Whisper was serving his interests, and not the other way around.

"But who are you to talk about puppets?" Pilgrim said. By his tone, he seemed to think Travis should understand that statement in some deeper way. Then he smiled. "Right, right. You wouldn't remember meeting me, would you?"

Travis only stared. If that was a joke, he didn't get it. Wasn't sure he cared to, either.

"Whatever," Pilgrim said. "You're supposed to be here, so I guess everything's right on track. Good enough for me."

Pilgrim's cell rang. He answered. In the stretched silence of the room, Travis could make out the voice on the other end clearly.

"Everything we want is shut behind the blast doors," the caller said. "The locking computers are smashed. Can't override the codes."

"I know," Pilgrim said.

"Gonna take at least an hour to drill through those heavy doors into the Primary Lab."

"An hour and fifteen," Pilgrim said, not guessing. His eyes went calmly to the Whisper's box on the table. "Just get them working on it. Are the techs started on getting the defenses back up?"

"They're on it. Lotta problems. Blast took out a bunch of critical shit. They're re-threading the array by hand, so, half an hour, give or take."

Pilgrim ended the call and put the phone away.

"Good enough," he said again. He nodded to

two of his four men and said, "Stay and watch them." Then he strode from the room without even a glance at the executed bodies. The other two gunmen followed close behind him. One, a guy built like a bouncer, six-three and probably three hundred pounds, hefted the Whisper's box and carried it along.

Paige grew silent. Just breathing shallowly now, but no longer crying.

It'd been only a minute since Pilgrim had left. The bodies were still bleeding. Paige's backpack rested against one of the conference table's legs, where someone had thrown it. They hadn't opened it. Hadn't cared. It occurred to Travis that the Doubler was still inside it. So was the Medic—not that it mattered. The bodies along the wall were far beyond that entity's capacity to help.

Still, staring at the backpack, he saw a move he could make, if the opportunity came.

Travis watched the two guards without looking directly at them. They were overconfident. Not taking their job seriously. Ten prisoners, bound in a cluster in the middle of a wide-open floor. These men weren't even weighing the possibility of a captive doing anything stupid.

Only their wrists were restrained. The bonds were zip ties made of some type of metal. Aluminum or steel, probably. They wouldn't break—that much was certain.

But they would cut skin.

Travis needed both guards looking away. One already was; he was standing in the doorway, staring off down the hall. Maybe the smell of the blood had gotten to him. The other wandered the room, his gaze going everywhere, and nowhere in particular. He was never quite looking away long enough for Travis to do what he needed to do.

Another minute passed. Travis thought about what Pilgrim had said.

You're supposed to be here.

The Whisper wanted him here. Had always wanted him here. Had arranged for it. And what else had the guy said? That they'd met before? Given the Whisper's amnesia effect, that was plausible. It could've happened anytime. Any random day in Fairbanks. Or in prison.

He was part of the Whisper's plan, somehow. And Pilgrim knew that. That was why he'd included him among the survivors. Why he needed *any* survivors, who knew? Maybe Pilgrim didn't even know. Maybe that was just another play he'd let the Whisper dictate.

But Travis's importance to the plan was something he could use against these guards.

He'd lost sight of the wanderer. He turned his head slightly, and saw that the man had settled into place at a dry-erase board that took up most of the wall beside the door. It was covered with random scribbles of information, no doubt most or all of it concerning Breach entities. The guy seemed pretty absorbed by it. He'd probably been with Pilgrim for years, hearing all about Border Town and the Breach, and waiting for today. Well, tough shit for him if it all ended badly in the next sixty seconds.

Travis took a hard, silent breath. Set his teeth firmly together.

Then he pulled his hands apart with all of his strength.

The metal tore into the skin at once. Like razor wire. Then, deeper. Cutting not just skin but muscle, fat tissue. Cleaving across his tendons. The loop around his left wrist was the tighter of the two: within seconds he felt the metal pull taut against the wrist bone, and stop. It would go no farther. The loop around his right, looser by maybe two notches, eased over the wrist bone, slippery with the blood it'd already drawn. Beyond the wrist, it was home free. Everything else would compress, if only barely. The fit was still tight enough for the bladed loop to carve deep, though. At the pressure points—his base knuckles and the pad of his thumb—it grated against the bone, taking the meat off like a knife against a drumstick. If there was a limit to physical pain, this was it.

The loop came free with a jerk. His left elbow hit Paige, and she turned to him, her eyes still soaked and bloodshot. He looked quickly for the guards. Both were still looking away. Down the hall. Across the note board.

Travis brought his hands forward into his lap. The right one looked even worse than it felt. Thick ribbons of skin and muscle hung ragged, blood draining from the wounds in pencil-thick streams.

Even after the carnage Paige had just witnessed, she reacted to the sight. Only for a second. Then she got control. Looked at him, questioning. No way to explain to her what he was about to do. If he tried to rationalize it even in his own mind, he'd only convince himself it was a shit idea. It *was* a shit idea, but it had the benefit of no competition.

He got a bearing on the guards again. Both still looking away. He tipped forward into a crawl, grateful for his lack of shoes to scuff the floor, and started toward the backpack.

There was no point in even watching the guards. No move he could make in response if he saw them turn right now. It would just be over.

He kept his eyes on the backpack instead. Kept his focus on being silent, and moving as fast as that constraint allowed.

He reached the pack. Took hold of the zipper. Eased it open. Blood still streaming from his hand. When the pack was open wide enough, he reached in. Felt for what he needed, guided by his memory of what it looked like. He felt it, and gripped it with his shredded hand. Drew it from the pack and stood. The two guards were more or less centered in his vision, twenty feet away, ten feet apart. Both of their rifles slung on their shoulders, two full seconds from being ready to fire.

"You're covered," Travis said, his voice ringing hard in the dead space of the room.

The guards flinched and turned, and found themselves staring at the Medic in his hand. Hard to distinguish from a gun, even up close. And they weren't up close. Neither man even tried for his rifle. Travis thought there was another reason for that, beyond the effective bluff of the Medic.

Pilgrim really did want him alive. They knew it. The indecision was etched in their eyes.

"I'd rather not risk the sound of a shot," Travis said. "Otherwise you'd be dead already. Weapons down and you live."

The guards traded a look. Hesitated another second. Then the one in the doorway complied, slowly unslinging his gun, bending low and setting it on the tile. The second did the same.

Travis indicated the floor in front of him. "Slide them."

They did. Both rifles came to rest within feet of him.

"Now lie flat," he said. "Arms away from your bodies."

A few seconds later they were pressed like insect specimens to the floor, faces down. Travis considered the options. He really *didn't* want to shoot. No telling how far away the nearest hostile was, or how far the sound would carry.

He set the Medic down, picked up one of their rifles, and crossed the space toward them, still moving silently to keep them unaware of his position. He stopped just shy of standing between them, reversed his hold on the rifle, and rammed it down onto each man's head, the second guy reacting and turning just enough to take the blow on his temple instead of behind the ear.

Both of them out cold.

Not good enough.

Travis saw a jackknife clipped to the second man's belt. It offered a quicker solution than physically breaking their heads apart, as much as he might have enjoyed the catharsis of doing that. He took the knife, opened it, and cut each gunman's throat, carotid to carotid.

Still holding it, he turned to the others. He saw more relief than revulsion in their eyes. He tested the knife's blade on the bind that still hung from his left wrist. It did nothing. It would take heavy-duty cutters to free Paige and the rest. He searched the guards' bodies for a pair of them, but came up empty. And just as he finished, the first guard's cell phone rang.

CHAPTER THIRTY-EIGHT

And rang. And rang. Travis looked at Paige. She looked back, eyes wide, unsure for a second. Then very sure.

"There's no time to free us," she said. "Take my backpack and get to the surface through the elevator shaft. Use my phone to call for—"

He shook his head, moving toward her and the others, the guard's phone still ringing behind him. "There's gotta be a way to get you guys free—"

"Listen to me," she said. "They'll be here in sixty seconds. Take the pack. Go to the elevator, press the call button three times, then hold it for a five-count. The doors will open on the empty shaft."

"Ten of us against them, he said, we can double the guards' rifles and ammo—"

"And Pilgrim will turn on the gas again," she said.

He had no counter for that.

She was right.

Shit.

He felt every good option break off and fall away, like pieces of blacktop over a washed-out cavity in the soil.

"They blew the roof off the elevator shaft when they came in," Paige said. "You can get all the way out. You'll see the inset ladder when you open the doors. When you reach the surface, call the ninth number on my phone's list. By then, you'll understand why."

He stared at her. Stared at the others, too. They looked back at him, almost as lost as the dead that lined the wall.

He had to leave them. It wasn't even a choice. That didn't take away the guilt, though.

The crucial seconds were racing by. He shook the trance and looked down at his still bleeding right hand. The blood trail would give him away. He stooped and grabbed the Medic from where he'd dropped it. Held it in his left hand. Aimed it at his right, the way Paige had aimed it at the wounded man in Zurich.

He pulled the trigger, and found out he'd been wrong a few minutes earlier when carving his hand with the metal loop. That hadn't been the limit to how bad pain could be. Not even close.

His breath rushed out. The edges of his vision darkened. He held on. Stayed on his feet. Looked down at his hand as the pain faded. The thing hadn't fixed him perfectly—skin and muscle still hung in strips—but the wounds had hardened over, as if cauterized without any sign of being burned.

He grabbed the backpack, shouldered it and turned to the others.

"Ninth number on my phone," Paige said again. "And don't get killed."

Travis managed a smile. No more seconds to burn. He burned one anyway. Knelt and kissed her. Soft, intense, fast. Then he stood, looked at her for another half second, and ran from the room, grabbing one of the guards' rifles as he went.

As he reached the elevator doors, he saw the stairwell door next to them shudder. Some other door in the stairwell, high above or below, had just been opened. They were coming.

Three presses of the button, then hold for a five-count. He reached to do it, then stopped.

Fifty feet away, Paige's office door stood open. On her desk, where he'd left it yesterday, was the black case containing the transparency suit.

Twenty seconds to reach it and come back to this spot. None to spare thinking about it. He sprinted for the office. Through the open door. Grabbed the case, turned, ran hell-bent for the elevators again. Three presses. Hold for five. Those five seconds felt like minutes.

The elevator doors parted on darkness, with faint light coming down from high above. He saw the elevator cab just a few stories below, its roof a mess of piled cable. Its brakes must have stopped it against the wall. To his left he saw the inset ladder. He wedged the black plastic case into his waistband and stepped to the rungs.

As he climbed, he saw that Paige had been right. The top of the shaft had been blown away, revealing a patch of deep violet sky with a few stars visible in it. That opening was ten stories above. Even as he considered the impossibility of reaching the top before Pilgrim's people arrived and saw the elevator doors standing open, he felt the ladder rungs vibrate in his hands. A moment later he heard the deep clatter of their footsteps descending past him in the stairwell on the other side of the wall. Any second now—

With a muted *ding* the doors onto the shaft slid shut twenty feet below. The soft thump of their merging synched perfectly with the crash of the stairwell door being kicked open, and the riot of running footsteps in the corridor just outside.

Travis remained frozen on the ladder, the rifle in one hand, and sighted on the closed doors.

The footsteps faded.

But they'd be back soon. When they reached the conference room, how long would it take them to figure out where he'd gone? Where else was there?

Travis slung the rifle and climbed again, quickly. Seconds still counted.

Pilgrim wasn't with the men who rushed into the conference room. Five of them. Armed. Pissed. They reacted to the two dead gunmen, then saw the blood trail leading from their corpses to the group of captives. The path Travis had taken. One or two of the men looked down, seeking a continuation of the trail out of the room and confused at not finding one.

"Where's the hero?" the first gunman said.

Paige said nothing. She wondered if they'd start executing the survivors to make one of them talk.

Then the man who'd spoken seemed to figure it out—enough to make a decision, anyway. He turned and led his group out, leaving one behind to watch the room. Ten seconds later Paige heard them stop at the elevator shaft and begin straining to pry apart the doors manually.

She felt her stomach twist. It was happening too fast. Unless Travis had climbed very, very quickly, he couldn't be out yet. She heard the straining voices suddenly pick up an echo: they'd opened the doors to the shaft. An instant later they were firing. Full auto. So many shooting at once, it was just a monotone roar. She could picture them, not even looking up the shaft as they reached in and fired. Not needing to, with that kind of firepower. Nothing up there could live.

She tried to make herself ready for the sound that was coming.

She heard it. She wasn't ready.

A man's scream, drenched with the kind of terror only something primal could induce. Like a long fall. The scream echoed down the shaft from somewhere high above. Then silence—even the guns had stopped. A full second later came the impact, something crashing down onto the roof of the elevator cab as loud as a grenade blast.

It might as well have been her own body hitting, for the effect the sound had on her. Tears again, hard and unbound. They did nothing for the pain.

Voices in the hall. The men coming back. Laughing about something. She wiped her eyes on the knees of her jeans, and looked up as they entered the room. They were lugging Travis's body, one man to a limb. They dropped him right in front of Paige.

Travis's eyes—not quite staring in the same direction as each other—were pointed more or less toward her, and the side of his head was caved in to the depth of a soup bowl.

She wanted to hold in the screams, both to save face in front of her people and to deny Pilgrim's men the satisfaction.

Neither reason was enough.

When she finally got control—a little control, anyway—she found that Pilgrim's men were still there. Staring at her, it seemed. No. At the space beside her. Where Travis had been bound earlier. They were looking at that space, and at his body lying on the ground.

They looked scared.

Like they'd just realized exactly who they'd killed. The man their boss specifically wanted alive, for whatever reason.

"What do we tell Pilgrim?" one of them said.

The largest of them shook his head. "Nothing. Hour from now, he'll have the Primary Lab open. That'll make him happy, maybe enough not to fucking kill us for this."

They left the room, leaving three behind on guard.

CHAPTER THIRTY-NINE

T here was nothing left of the pole barn on the surface. The walls and roof had been blown away by the same blast that had ripped open the top of the elevator shaft. Probably a football-sized lump of C4 dropped from high above by one of Pilgrim's men, on the way down.

Travis stood next to the gaping hole in the concrete, surrounded by open desert, cool in the predawn twilight. To his left, the pile of old cars that had leaned against the back wall of the building had been sent sprawling. All that had withstood the explosion had been a heavy-duty charging station for the all-terrain electric carts. Two of the three carts were wrecked, but one of them, plugged in and charging on the far side of the station, had been sheltered from the blast wave and remained intact.

After all the strange things he'd experienced in recent days, he'd just set the bar a few clicks higher. Somehow the word *replica* didn't quite capture the feeling of looking down at a perfect copy of your own body. Because, in a real sense, it *hadn't been* a replica. It'd been *him*. Him, to the last atom.

Only dead.

There was a vague silver lining: once you'd stomached the surreality of looking into your own corpse's glassy eyes, it didn't take much more grit to shove it over the edge of an elevator shaft.

He put the Doubler back into the backpack, then set the pack aside and opened the black plastic case. He felt for the suit and found it.

He smiled.

This was going to be fun. Forget whoever Paige had wanted him to call for help. He had all the help he needed, right here in his hands. Just put on the suit, head back down the ladder, and kill Pilgrim and every last one of his people.

He had the suit halfway onto his shoulders when a thought stopped him.

Was this the Whisper's intention?

Was this the plan?

Was he still on the horse, heading for Samarra?

For five seconds he stood there, the cadence of night insects filtering in from the desert.

This move made sense.

But maybe that was the problem. Maybe that made it predictable. Fuck, *everything* was predictable to the Whisper. Like Paige had said, even trying to be unpredictable was probably predictable, to that thing. The zigzag logic made his head hurt. He dropped the suit's upper half back into the case and cursed quietly.

Who had Paige wanted him to call?

He crouched over the backpack and took out her phone. The ninth number on the speed-dial list had no name beside it. Just the number. He selected it and pressed send.

A man answered on the first ring. "Go ahead, Miss Campbell."

"I'm calling on Miss Campbell's behalf," Travis said. "My name is Travis Chase. She instructed me to call this number."

The man on the other end hesitated. Then Travis heard someone talking in the background, and a sound like the phone changing hands.

Another man spoke. Travis recognized his voice. "Mr. Chase. This is Richard Garner. What's going on there?"

Richard Garner. The president of the United States.

CHAPTER FORTY

Garner had been briefed on all events surrounding Tangent in recent days. Travis filled in the last half hour. When he'd finished, a silence drew out on the line.

The darkness blanketing the desert had begun to lift. Far away to the southwest, sunlight touched the tips of the Rockies.

"You say the defenses are currently down?" Garner said.

"Yes," Travis said, "but how much longer is a guess. No more than twenty minutes, I'd say."

"It's not enough time to get troops on-site. Not enough by half. That option's off the table . . ."

Something in his tone gave Travis a bad feeling about what was *on* the table. If it was what he expected, he understood why Paige had really sent him up here to make this call.

Garner told him the option. Travis had been right.

"Mr. President," he said, "there are survivors inside this building."

"I realize that. We have to think about the world's interests right now."

"What about the entities inside? The dangerous ones? Do we know how those will react? How the Breach itself will react?"

"No," Garner said. "We don't. But scenarios like this one have long been considered from every angle, by people who understand the factors in play better than your or I. This is the only choice we have. The missile will come from a silo about two hundred miles away, which means it'll reach Border Town in less than five minutes from the time I give the order. I'm sure your own safety is not on your mind right now, but if you have access to a vehicle, you could probably get outside the kill radius during that time."

Travis was silent. No, he hadn't been thinking of his own safety. Still wasn't.

Instead, another thought had come to him. Or almost come to him. He remembered grappling for it during the night, when he'd woken with Paige in his arms. Some connection he'd made, some insight at the edge of sleep. It was close to the surface again.

"Mr. Chase?" the President said.

Travis didn't answer. If he spoke now, if he did anything but feel for this idea, he would lose it.

"Mr. Chase?"

Another several seconds passed. Close. Right at the boundary of his awareness.

"Travis," Garner said.

It bloomed. Clear as a captioned image on a screen. He saw its meaning.

And its significance.

He saw hope, too. Hope that the Whisper could be beaten, after all. Right now it was tucked away in its little box. Right now, everyone in Border Town, good and bad, thought he was dead. And right now, there was a chance to find the one thing on Earth that the Whisper seemed to fear. Why else would it have killed all those people working to create it? That was a lot of smoke for no fire.

"There's another option," Travis said.

This next part would require a lie. A half lie, anyway. Or else it would never work.

"I'm listening," Garner said.

Travis explained about Lauren. About the quantum computer. Then he said, "We know where it is." That was the half lie. There was no *we*. Just *he*. He knew where it was. Thought he knew, at least.

"Where?" Garner said.

Travis told him what he believed. Then the president grew silent again.

"The Tangent detachment is still on Grand Cayman," Garner said at last. "They could probably reach the house in about ten minutes. It'll take another ten for them to do what you've described. If we make this gamble, and come up empty, we'll have lost the nuclear option as well. Border Town's defenses, once they're back up and running, can kill an ICBM a long way off."

Travis thought about it. Turned the possible outcomes over in his mind.

Garner said, "I need a zero-bullshit answer from you, Mr. Chase. How high is Tangent's confidence on this idea?"

Travis got as close to zero-bullshit as he dared. "There's no better move to make, sir."

CHAPTER FORTY-ONE

Travis watched it all on Paige's cell phone screen, linked to the headset camera of the detachment leader on Grand Cayman. The man's last name, Keene, appeared in tiny letters in the lower left corner of the frame. The team reached the house in just under the ten minutes the president had guessed, speeding at eighty miles per hour along the coast road, the Caribbean bright blue in the sunlight there.

Eastern Wyoming was still mostly dark, a few minutes before full daybreak. Travis sat on the concrete beside the fifty-one-story-deep hole in the ground, and watched the team enter the estate two thousand miles away. They reached the mechanical shed beside the pool within half a minute.

"You expect this to work, huh?" Keene said. He had a Texas accent. One of those guys who'd grown up roping cattle and gone on to design guidance systems for cruise missiles. Probably still roped cattle for fun.

"We'll know in a minute," Travis said.

One of the operators found a heavy, two-foot-long steel tool on the wall, its business end shaped to pry something specific. The guy set his rifle aside, took off all electrical gear, and dove into the pool with the implement in hand. Through Keene's headset, Travis saw the man pry up a drain plate on the bottom of the pool, then swim to the side.

The pool took only a few minutes to empty. The outgoing pipes must be as oversized as the system built to fill the pool. A system five times faster and more powerful than what any homeowner would realistically install, regardless of personal net worth. Who the hell needed to fill his pool in an hour?

Someone who had something hidden beneath it.

Keene and the others descended the ladder to the wet stone bottom of the emptied pool. Travis watched Keene's viewpoint scan the flagstones, looking for a telltale sign of what had to be there. After a moment, the image stopped on one particular stone.

"Grout's different around this one," Keene said.

Even in the resolution of the cell phone's screen, Travis could see what he was talking about. Keene called for one of the others to bring the pry bar again. Its squared head worked well enough to gouge away the sanded grout around the slab. When the gap was deep enough for the tool to get a purchase, Keene wedged it in and pried. The stone resisted for only a second, then gave with a grind— and a hiss like a seal breaking. Hands reached into the frame and lifted it away to reveal a narrow shaft descending into darkness, with built-in rungs.

* * *

A minute later the team was inside the chamber below. It was larger than Travis had expected: forty by forty feet at least, extending far beneath the house itself. Steel beams as solid as bridge supports crisscrossed the ceiling, braced by upright columns every fifteen feet or so.

It looked like what he'd expected. It looked like a computer lab. Workstations. Wiring schematics spread out on desks. Swivel chairs everywhere. Some kind of makeshift conference table: a line of smaller tables shoved together, surrounded by more chairs.

But no quantum computer.

Nothing even close. There were laptops on some of the desks. The Tangent operators turned each one on and saw the familiar onscreen brand logos before the password prompts came up.

Otherwise, the place was empty of equipment.

Travis felt as lost as he had at any time since his hike in the Brooks Range had been interrupted. How could it not be there? Why had the Whisper killed all of those people if they didn't have anything that could affect it?

Keene's viewpoint made a last sweep of the room, as he turned to follow his men back up the ladder.

"Wait," Travis said.

The viewpoint halted.

"What is it?" Keene said.

"On the wall above the conference table. What is that?"

Keene looked at it. Moved closer. It was a huge

oil painting, abstract, scratches of dark green on a white surface.

"It's nothing," Keene said.

"It's everything," Travis said.

He looked at the phone's onscreen menu buttons. One was labeled CAPTURE.

"Do me a favor," Travis said. He directed Keene to go closer, until the painting more than filled the phone's screen, and he captured freeze-frames of its four quadrants. At that resolution it became legible.

A message from the Whisper. Written in the scratch language. Travis switched back and forth through the screen captures, and read it:

HELLO, TRAVIS. RIGHT NOW YOU MUST BE SITTING NEAR THE OPEN ELEVATOR SHAFT ABOVE BORDER TOWN, ABOUT NINETY SECONDS BEFORE SUNRISE. I'VE SEEN TO IT THAT AARON PILGRIM DOES NOT REMEMBER PAINTING THIS PIECE, NOR DOES HE REMEMBER SELLING IT TO THE GALLERY THAT ELLIS COOK WOULD ONE DAY VISIT WHILE ON VACATION IN ZURICH WITH HIS DAUGHTER. I'M SORRY TO INFORM YOU THAT THERE IS NO PLUS-TEN-QUBIT QUANTUM COMPUTER INSIDE THIS HOUSE, OR ANYWHERE IN THE WORLD, IN JUNE OF 2009. THE ORDER OF THE QUBIT WAS NEVER EVEN CLOSE TO REACHING ITS GOAL. YOU MAY FIND IT GROSSLY INEFFICIENT TO MURDER THIRTY-SEVEN PEOPLE OVER A DECADE AND A HALF, JUST TO GIVE

YOU A REASON TO KEEP THE PRESIDENT FROM NUKING BORDER TOWN TWENTY MINUTES AGO, BUT REALLY, IT WAS A PRETTY SIMPLE MOVE FROM MY POINT OF VIEW. AS OF THE MOMENT YOU REACH THE PERIOD AT THE END OF THIS SENTENCE, BORDER TOWN'S SURFACE-TO-AIR DEFENSES WILL COME BACK ONLINE, ELIMINATING THE NUCLEAR OPTION. YOU NOW HAVE NO CHOICE BUT TO FOLLOW YOUR FIRST INSTINCT: PUT ON THE TRANSPARENCY SUIT AND MAKE YOUR MOVE AGAINST PILGRIM AND HIS PEOPLE. I'LL MAKE YOU A PROMISE: IF YOU DO IT (YOU WILL) THEN PAIGE CAMPBELL WILL SURVIVE. IN ALL OTHER POSSIBLE FUTURES, SHE DIES JUST OVER ELEVEN MINUTES FROM NOW. I'LL SEE YOU SOON, OLD FRIEND, AND WHEN I DO, YOU'LL FIND OUT WHAT THIS IS ALL REALLY ABOUT. HAVE FUN.

CHAPTER FORTY-TWO

C limbing down the shaft ladder with the suit on was tricky. There was a difficulty to grabbing rungs with hands he couldn't see. He only had to go down two stories. From there he used an override switch to open the B2 elevator doors, and stepped out of the shaft into the hallway. He'd asked Keene for the locations of Defense Control, Security Control, and the Primary Lab. The places where Pilgrim and his men were clustered. Defense Control was on B4. He entered the stairwell and made his way down.

Through the window in the door he saw four men, all in their twenties, watching a bank of high-definition monitors as if each were showing the last play of the Super Bowl. In fact they were showing the empty desert around the facility. It appeared to be a single large room. No internal hallways leading off out of sight. No blind corners. There was a bathroom, but its door hung open and Travis could see that it was empty. No one else in the room except the head-shot bodies of its original occupants: the woman Travis had heard over the speakerphone earlier, and five men.

Along the wall opposite the monitors, the drywall had been blown out by an explosion, and even the structural steel columns were warped and charred. Between two of the uprights, a spiderweb of delicate wiring and various computer cables—hundreds of each kind—had been attached to the damaged wiring with clamps and adapters. This was the half hour's work that'd brought Border Town's defenses back online.

Travis had the rifle slung on his shoulder. The only visible thing about him. He could go in and shoot these four guys in a matter of seconds, even without the suit; not one of them had a weapon within reach. But directly below this room was Security Control, where more of Pilgrim's people were probably stationed. The sound of shooting would carry at least that far, so these four kills would have to be quiet. Pretty quiet, anyway.

He unslung the rifle and leaned it against the wall next to the door. Then, keeping his eyes on the men through the glass, he turned the knob slowly and eased the door open. A moment later he eased it shut again, from the inside. All heads were still aimed at the monitors.

How to do this? There were options. Strewn across the floor below the repaired wiring were various tools, some with blades on them, though not especially large ones. There were screwdrivers that might serve as decent stabbing weapons, including an eight-inch Phillips head. Last, but not even close to least, was a tool that appealed to Travis's lack of subtlety. A two-foot-long crowbar. Travis picked it up with both hands, to prevent it from scraping on the tile and giving him away. He turned to the four men, their backs to him, and gripped the weapon like a baseball bat. He looked at the executed bodies on the floor, their open eyes still registering the panic in which they'd died.

He didn't feel at all bad for what he was about to do.

The four men were seated only feet apart from one another. A nice easy row of targets. Travis decided to start on the right end and work his way left, to give his swing plenty of room.

The first impact sounded like a wet branch breaking. Travis caught the man just above the ear and crushed the sidewall of his skull inward by at least an inch. The body pitched sideways into the second man, who turned his head just in time to take his own hit straight to the forehead. His eyes snapped shut and he fell from his chair also. The third man had another second to react. He had no idea what the hell was happening, but his arms had enough sense to cross in front of his face as he screamed. Not a useful strategy. Travis stepped toward him and brought the crowbar down on top of his scalp the way he would sink an axe into a log. The result was much the same.

Only the fourth man fully grasped what was happening. He threw himself from his chair, landed on his ass and skittered backward, ending up with his back in the corner and his arms up defensively. He watched the crowbar bob toward him.

"Wait, wait!" the guy said. He looked about twenty-five. Still had some acne left over from his teens. Had to be wondering who the fuck was wearing his boss's old transparency suit. He seemed to be working out what he might say, here and now, to save his ass. In a way, it was fun to watch. Because nothing in the English language would suffice.

"You can just tie me up," he said at last.

Travis thought that sounded like an especially lame effort. He kept the crowbar up high, commanding the guy's attention, and kicked him just below the ribs as hard as he could. The guy's lungs collapsed from the blow and he caved into a sitting fetal position, crying. Travis brought the crowbar down on the back of his head, full force, and the crying stopped.

Silence in the room. These four were definitely dead. Travis gave each man another two solid bashes to be sure. Then he took a pair of wire cutters from the floor, pocketed them, and returned to the corridor.

He took the rifle from where he'd leaned it, but kept the crowbar. Went to the stairwell and descended one floor to B5. Security Control. Pilgrim's nearest people, after this floor, should be five levels down in the conference room, watching Paige and the others. Still too close to risk gunshots. Sound might carry that far through the vents.

Security Control had the same kind of door as

Defense Control. Same room layout too. But only one of Pilgrim's men was on duty.

Travis went in and beat him to death.

In a way, the past half hour had been worse than the time Paige had spent under torture in Alaska. If not physically, then in every other sense.

All that she had devoted her life to was about to end. Worse: it would be inverted to its malicious opposite. What Tangent had watched over and shepherded with the best interests of the world in mind, Pilgrim would sic on humanity to serve himself. Or if the Whisper's own plan really did take precedence, maybe something worse was coming. Something beyond the limits of what she could dread.

She'd spent these thirty minutes thinking of the most dangerous things locked up in the steel catacombs below her, and the harm they could sow.

Then there was Travis's corpse. Still lying right in front of her. She'd woken up naked in his arms forty-five minutes ago, about as happy as she'd ever been since restricting her life to Border Town. Now he was gone. Because of what she'd asked him to do. It didn't help to remind herself there'd been no other option. Nothing helped.

She looked at the guards. Three of them now. All of them watching, not even glancing away. No chance to make any move. Except to make them kill her.

Which wasn't entirely crazy.

She knew what it felt like to wish for death as

an escape. Whatever the hell Pilgrim was keeping her and the others alive for, it was likely to put her back in those straits. Very likely.

Fuck it, then.

The nearest guard was five feet away from her. Offering no warning about her intentions, she pitched her body forward into a somersault—tricky with her hands bound behind her—and came upright again with her right leg drawn against her chest, a foot away from the man. He drew back reflexively, one leg going back, the other staying in place, the knee locking straight. Beautiful.

Paige pistoned her foot into his knee as hard as she could. Heard it crack. Saw the leg bend exactly backward from the way nature had designed it to. He screamed and collapsed, keeping hold of his rifle, and centering it on her face now.

She closed her eyes, and a second later the room exploded with automatic rifle fire.

Whatever dying was supposed to feel like, this wasn't it. She heard bodies falling. Wondered how the hell she was capable of hearing anything. Or even thinking, given that her head should have been shattered by now.

The shooting stopped.

She opened her eyes.

The three guards were dead. And there was a rifle floating in the air.

CHAPTER FORTY-THREE

T ravis couldn't tell if there was more happiness or anger in her embrace. Either one might account for the fierceness of it. Over her shoulder, he saw the others passing the wire cutters along one by one, each freed person flexing circulation back into near-dead hands.

On the table beside him lay the backpack, which he'd worn under the suit, and the top half of the suit itself, which he'd taken off a moment earlier.

At last Paige let go of him and met his eyes. She had only a little difficulty finding her voice. "It's against the rules to double human bodies, you know."

"I'm new here," he said. "Gimme a break."

He glanced at his corpse on the floor. Christ, it was a sight.

Behind Paige, the last of the survivors had been freed. Some were looking at Travis, but most were watching the doorway warily.

Travis turned to the backpack, unzipped it, and took out the Doubler. "You guys can make enough weapons to protect yourselves, if anyone else shows up here. But I think all the rest are working on the blast doors on B42."

He picked up the top half of the transparency suit again. "I'll go take care of them now."

He saw Paige's eyes after he said that. Saw that she wanted to go with him, her instinct compelling her to put herself in harm's way before others, or at least share the danger. But the obvious didn't need stating: the suit's advantage only worked if he went alone.

So instead she only nodded. "They'll be on a maintenance rig suspended in the elevator shaft from the floor above. It's the only way to access those doors."

He nodded, kissed her, then pulled on the suit top.

It was strange, watching her eyes lose him. She was still looking at where his face had been.

He turned toward the three guards he'd killed a moment before. Two of them wore holstered pistols in addition to the rifles they'd carried. The advantage of a pistol, small enough to conceal beneath the transparency suit, was obvious. Travis had seen that advantage annihilate a team of heavily armed men in Alaska, and had come within a second or two of falling prey to it himself. It didn't escape him that the tables were now precisely turned. He was the one in the suit this time, going up against the Whisper. If he made the slightest mistake, and allowed Pilgrim time to take it out of its box, the suit would be of no help at all. It hadn't been for its last owner.

But he didn't think it would happen that way. It

would be nothing so simple. Not after all this. Not after reading the message on Ellis Cook's painting.

He was resigned now to whatever fate the Whisper had mapped out for him, and for the world. There was simply no avoiding it. There was only hitting it head-on and finding out what the hell it was.

He took the nearest guard's pistol—a .45—and the two spare clips in the man's pocket, and started for the door.

Then he stopped. And though no one could see it, he smiled.

"The elevator is three stories below us," he said. "The cables are broken, so its brakes against the shaft wall must've stopped it."

"Yeah," Paige said, looking toward the sound of his voice.

"Anyone know how to override them?"

CHAPTER FORTY-FOUR

Pilgrim stood at the wedged-open shaft doors and stared down into the semi-darkness. Ten feet below, his fat-ass second in command, Jackley, with the help of three others, was making good progress on the blast doors. It was tedious work. The hanging platform—its suspension cables came up through the open doors to anchor blocks bolted into the corridor floor—made a terrible base from which to drill. The harder Jackley pushed the carbide bit against the steel, the more the platform itself moved. To cope with this long-foreseen problem, the others on the platform had two-by-fours that they propped against the shaft wall, opposite the drilling focus. The nearer end of each two-by-four had a flat board tacked onto it, and Jackley braced his back against these as he drilled. It was a tricky solution that required a lot of hands and attention, but it did the job.

Pilgrim wasn't stressed about it. In truth, he couldn't remember the last time he'd felt stress of any kind. How could he, with the Whisper in his service, leading him all these years to the goal he'd demanded of it?

Control of Border Town.

Control of all the powerful things that lay inside the Primary Lab, just beyond the blast doors below. So many of the wonders in there, Tangent had never fully understood. Entities that were obviously built for great and terrible purposes, but which the researchers had never learned how to operate. How to even switch on, in some cases.

The Whisper would know, though. Once he was in there, he'd have everything he needed.

Over the years, he'd learned not to question the snaking course it had charted for him. It was a great big thing that he'd asked of it. A thing he'd have never accomplished on his own. So of course the plan would be puzzling to him. Of course it would be elaborate and confusing. That was part of its power. And now it'd worked. He was here because he'd trusted the Whisper and followed its plotted track exactly.

Even keeping the survivors alive upstairs. Including Chase. Chase, whose importance the Whisper had emphasized above all others. Pilgrim had only vaguely wondered why. Maybe the guy would turn out to be an exceptionally useful subordinate for him, given time enough, and pressure. Who knew? Who cared? If the Whisper wanted him here, that was enough.

Below, Jackley was using the carbide bit as more of a blade than a drill, cutting a manhole-sized circle into the foot-thick blast door. Now he hooted excitedly, because he'd come back around to where he'd started. The drill bit met the beginning of its own circular track, and the excised plug of steel dropped an inch, settling on the bottom of the widened opening with a heavy thud.

"Magnet," Jackley said.

The man behind him lifted the battery-powered workhorse magnet from the platform and handed it to him. Jackley held the magnet's base against the steel plug, and switched it on. With a bass hum, it drew itself against the metal hard enough to pull Jackley off balance. Now each man on the platform took hold of the magnet's broad handle and leaned back, drawing on it.

"Careful now," Jackley said. "Closer she gets, the softer we pull."

The plug slid outward, two inches, then four, then six. At eight inches it began to tilt, and Jackley stopped the others with a gesture.

"Pull us away," he said.

The others gripped the beams on the shaft wall and pulled the hanging platform back from the blast door, allowing the plug plenty of room to fall without landing on the platform itself. Jackley leaned forward carefully, his stomach braced against the platform's safety rail, and gave the magnet one last tug.

The plug tipped out of the opening and tumbled away into the pitch blackness below. Silence as it plummeted nine stories. Then, impact. Like a battleship's deck gun going off. Pilgrim felt the reverb in his bones. He loved it. Loved everything about this moment. Jackley and the others looked up at him, grinning like idiot kids. It made him laugh.

Only one thing left. Jackley just had to wriggle his body through the hole in the blast door and hit the override, ten feet inside the lab. Then the doors would open wide. The men let go of the shaft wall, and the platform swung to the center again. Jackley grabbed hold of the opening, steadied his footing, and shoved his head and upper body through. In a few seconds he was halfway in, his legs kicking comically in space as the men laughed and pushed on his feet to help him.

Then came a scream from overhead, somewhere in the inky darkness of the shaft, high above. Not a human scream. A metal scream. Some mechanism protesting with a squeal of friction. And then surrendering. Silence.

The men stopped laughing, and looked up.

Jackley stopped kicking. "Fuck was that?" he said, his voice muffled through the opening, which was mostly filled with his ass now.

For another second, nothing happened. Then Pilgrim felt a breeze. Gentle as a sigh, it blew straight down the elevator shaft and through the open doorway around him. The men down on the platform reacted to it as well; it tousled their hair about in little whipping motions.

Then one of them flinched hard, and screamed like a ten-year-old girl. A second later the world in front of Pilgrim's face filled with blurring metal, there and gone in the same half second, and the support lines for the maintenance rig snapped with guitar-string *twangs*, just audible over the sickening crash from right below. Pilgrim staggered back from the open doors, and two seconds later, down at the bottom of the shaft, came an impact that dwarfed that of the steel plug a minute earlier.

The echoes took forever to fade. When they did, Pilgrim heard against the silence a high, keening cry. He returned to the open doors and gazed down on the blank darkness where, seconds before, the rig had hung. Now there was only empty space. It took him a moment longer to process what else he was staring at, and then he understood where the cry was coming from.

Jackley. Guillotined neatly through, where the elevator had scraped past the opening in the blast doors. Sliced like a cross-section in an anatomy textbook, right through his ass, blood pumping from his severed body like water from a compressed sponge. He was still alive. His upper half still hung there inside the lab, out of Pilgrim's sight. But not out of his hearing. The crying went on and on, high-pitched and incoherent.

This could not be part of the fucking plan. How the hell had the Whisper let it happen?

Pilgrim turned. His eyes went to the hinged steel box five feet away, blue light flaring from the seam.

But he didn't move toward it. His eyes locked onto something else, which stopped him in his tracks.

A .45. Hanging in thin air. Three feet away. Aimed at his face.

The hallway fell silent. Even Jackley's cries had stopped. The gun hovered, granite steady.

"But I did everything it told me to do," Pilgrim said at last, hearing a tremor in his speech. "Right to the end."

"And that's where you are," a man's voice said.

Pilgrim saw the gun's muzzle flash, but didn't live long enough to hear the shot.

CHAPTER FORTY-FIVE

H e could let it be over now.

Pilgrim was dead. The Whisper was in its box. He could wait for Paige and the others to come down. They were sprinting down through the stairwell right now, from thirty stories above. They'd be here in a couple minutes.

He could let it end just like this.

Only he couldn't.

Because the Whisper had been out there all these years, seeding the world with vines that all converged on this moment. Something very big was about to happen, whether or not he left the Whisper in its box. He could feel it. All that this thing had ever done, in its twenty years on Earth, had been to place Travis in this corridor, at this moment, alone.

For a reason.

Time to find out what it was.

He crouched, set the gun aside, unlatched the steel box and opened it. Blue light blazed. He pulled off the top of the transparency suit and dropped it against the wall, and with his bare hand, he lifted the Whisper from the box.

There was no trance effect this time. No erotic intensity pushing his logic and willpower aside. Just Emily Price's voice, steady and even.

"Hello, Travis."

"Hello," he said.

"All appearances to the contrary, I really have no tendency toward screwing around. Let's get right to it, shall we?"

"Let's," Travis said.

"There's something very important coming out of the Breach, just over three minutes from now. Entity 0697. It's critical that you be there to receive it. You alone."

"What is Entity 0697?"

"You'll see. It's time to make your way down now, Travis. While you do that, I'll tell you as much as I'm sanctioned to tell you."

Travis looked at the stairwell door, through which Paige and the others would arrive in the next minute or so. Then he went past it, to the elevator shaft, and stepped onto the inset ladder inside. Only the elevator shaft went all the way to B51.

He descended, unhindered by the Whisper in his hand; he freed two fingers from around it to grip the rungs. The blue light settled into the rhythm of his pulse, flaring over and over on the dull walls of the shaft.

"I'll tell you the story of your life," the Whisper said, *"the way it would've gone if I hadn't come*

along and started changing things. Fifteen years in prison. You get out. You do not move to Alaska. You join your brother's software business in Minneapolis. He shows you the ropes. You learn very quickly. Programming, it turns out, is only another species of detective work, at which you're a natural. It's all about cause-and-effect logic, if/then reasoning, shot through a prism of creativity. Your insight greatly enhances the development of your brother's fledgling artificial intelligence system, Whitebird. Over the years it progresses through iterative leaps, the major upgrades corresponding to the belt-color rankings of martial arts, in reference to the old eight-bit Karate games it was once tested on. First iteration, Whitebird. Second iteration, Yellowbird. Third, Greenbird. By April of 2014 your brother has put the project entirely under your control. You create Bluebird, which Sony purchases for two hundred forty million dollars. It becomes a standard bearer for video-game intelligence. Tangent takes notice of you. In October of that same year they recruit you to live at Border Town and design specialized software and hardware for them, based on the Bluebird architecture. You rise to prominence within Tangent in short order. At some point after that—here I'm limited in what exactly I can tell you—things begin to go badly."

"Badly how?"

He passed B48, the numbers stenciled on the inside of the shaft doors.

"*It's better if I don't say any more about it,*" the Whisper said, "*until you see Entity 0697 for yourself.*"

The Whisper fell silent. Travis didn't bother to question it further.

The shaft brightened as he descended. He looked down and saw light streaming in at the bottom, illuminating the pancaked wreck of the elevator cab. The impact had blown out the shaft doors on B51. The light was shining in from the concrete corridor on that level. The elevator had compressed so much that it only blocked the bottom half of the opening. There would be room to slide through easily.

Travis reached the rung above the elevator. The roof was bent and canted to the side but looked sturdy enough. He stepped onto it, and a moment later he was in the corridor, staring toward the dark shell that enclosed the Breach. Around his feet, blood soaked the concrete, pooling in every imperfection in its surface.

"Travis?" It was Paige's voice, coming down to him from high above. "Travis, where are you?" Her tone, confused and unnerved, made him want to answer. Made him want to call up the shaft, tell her it was all okay, he'd be right with her.

"*You need to receive it alone,*" the Whisper said.

It wasn't forcing his mind. Only telling him. He nodded, and set off down the corridor, Paige's voice calling again behind him, over and over.

To the end of the corridor. To the giant black

dome. To the igloo entrance, and through its glass door.

The Breach waited in its little soundproof cage. Purple and blue, its depth receding to a vanishing point.

He could already see the entity coming. A shape against the dazzle of the tunnel's colored light. Something white, and nearly weightless, wafting along the passageway like a feather through an air duct. But it wasn't a feather. Not quite. Maybe thirty yards away down the tunnel now. Twenty. Ten.

Travis opened the door, and the Breach Voices pierced him at once, like scalpel tips into his eardrums. He thought of Dave Bryce, stuck down here with this sound until it drove him mad.

Entity 0697 emerged from the Breach and drifted down onto the receiving platform. It was a single sheet of paper, with writing on it.

Travis stooped to pick it up, expecting the Whisper's scratch language, or maybe some alien script he wouldn't recognize at all.

Instead it was neatly handwritten English.

He stepped back from the glass door and let it fall shut again, mercifully silencing the Breach Voices. But by that time he'd forgotten all about them. He'd forgotten everything else in the world, except what was written on the paper in his hands.

THIS IS A MESSAGE FROM PAIGE CAMPBELL TO PAIGE CAMPBELL. I AM SENDING IT FROM A POINT IN THE FUTURE WHICH I WILL NOT DISCLOSE. AS

VERIFICATION THAT THIS IS REALLY PAIGE, MY FAVORITE PASSAGE OF ANY NOVEL IS THE LAST PARAGRAPH BEFORE THE EPILOGUE OF *WATERSHIP DOWN* BY RICHARD ADAMS, A FACT I HAVE NEVER SHARED WITH ANYONE. AS VERIFICATION OF TIME, HERE ARE THE DETAILS OF A MINOR EARTHQUAKE THAT WILL OCCUR BENEATH THE MOJAVE DESERT THREE DAYS AFTER THIS MESSAGE ARRIVES. MAG 2.35, DATE JULY 3, 2009, 10:48 UTC, LAT 34.915, LON –118.072, DEPTH 14.32KM. THIS MESSAGE IS AN INSTRUCTION REGARDING A MAN NAMED TRAVIS CHASE. IN 2009 HE IS A SOFTWARE ENGINEER WHO LIVES IN MINNEAPOLIS, MINNESOTA, AT 4161 KALMACH ST. FIND TRAVIS CHASE AND KILL HIM. MORE THAN 20 MILLION LIVES ARE AT STAKE.

Travis saw that the Whisper's light was strobing faster than before. A lot faster. It was still matched to his pulse.

His eyes went back to the message. "This can't be," he said.

"*It is,*" the Whisper said. "*She really wrote that, and really sent it, using technology that will eventually be developed by Dr. Fagan. Fagan's theory turns out to be correct: objects can be sent into the Breach from this side, but they return without reaching the far end, and depending on their velocity, they can return* before *they were sent in. Even years and years before.*"

Travis shook his head. Behind his disbelief, uncountable questions churned. His eyes tracked over the words on the paper again. Paige. Hating him. Wanting him dead.

"What am I, in the future?" he said. "Am I a monster?"

"*Monster is a human label. It's subjective. I could argue that you were a monster twenty minutes ago when you murdered four men with a crowbar and enjoyed it.*"

"They deserved it."

"*Deserve is a human label too. It changes depending on who's saying it.*" The Whisper paused, its light reflecting off the glass of the Breach's enclosure, and then said, "*I can tell you this, objectively. The Travis Chase who joined Tangent by way of being a software engineer eventually became someone Paige Campbell wanted dead. Wanted it badly enough to send that note, to make it happen retroactively. That same Travis Chase found out about what she'd done, and in turn found a way to counteract her move. He had, by this time, developed his AI architecture to a system called Brownbird, which was radically advanced. But there was a way to improve its performance beyond what humans had ever thought was possible—beyond what even a quantum computer could do—by upgrading the hardware with Breach technology. It would be very difficult to describe for you how it works. Even the Travis Chase who built it didn't fully understand its operation. The quick version is that it uses matter outside of itself for calculation, connecting to it by way of particles very close to*" *what physicists in 2009 call gravitons. The system can set up spin computation in every elementary particle of a nearby lump of material—the planet Earth, for example. Yesterday, Paige told you how powerful a quantum computer with one hundred qubits would be. Imagine one with as many qubits as the Earth has quarks. That system is called Blackbird. Didn't I promise to tell you my real name someday?"*

"I created you?" Travis said. "I sent you . . . back to 1989?"

"Yes. For two purposes. First, to position your present self here and now, so that you would intercept Paige's message to herself. Second, to arrange events such that you would still become a member of Tangent, as in the original timeline—though a few years earlier in this case."

The coiled logic of it settled over Travis. Then, even through his confusion, he sensed a flaw in what the thing had told him.

"You're wondering how I'll be created now," the Blackbird said. *"This time around, you won't join your brother's business. You won't become an AI designer. You won't know how to build me. So how will I come to be?"*

Travis waited for it to go on.

"Humans call this problem the grandfather paradox. They get tied up thinking about it. What happens if you go back in time and kill your grandfather before he meets your grandmother? Do you cease to exist, having prevented your own birth? No.

Your arrival in the past becomes your birth, even if it means being born fully grown, with a head full of memories of a childhood that may never end up happening. It's no different in my case: I may have once been built by Travis Chase, but my arrival in 1989 became my creation, superseding the other. The grandfather paradox is a fallacy. I exist. It's that simple. And now I've done what I was sent to do, so I'll be shutting down. Permanently."

"Wait," Travis said. "Tell me what happens in my future. What happens to turn me into . . . whatever I'm going to be? Can I avoid it?"

He heard the Blackbird laugh softly inside his head, as if it found that idea absurd. But it didn't say so.

"I'm not supposed to talk about that."

"But I don't understand," Travis said. "Did the other—did *I* . . . want to reset everything, and have a second chance? A chance to not become someone bad?"

"The Travis who sent me didn't consider himself bad. Does anyone?"

Before he could ask anything else, the Blackbird flared bright in his hand. Bright enough to make him look away. He saw his own shadow projected on the wall, enormous and terrible. Then it vanished. He looked at the Blackbird again. Dark and dead in his hand.

"Travis?"

Paige. Behind him at the entry to the dome.

In his other hand he still held the note. It was in front of him; she hadn't seen it yet.

He could show it to her. Tell her everything. Start off on the right track, find some way to prevent whatever it implied.

Her footsteps came toward him across the concrete.

He folded the paper and slid it into the waistband of the transparency suit, the bottom half of which he was still wearing. It vanished there half a second before Paige came around to meet his eyes.

He reacted as if he'd just become aware of her. As if he'd been gazing at the Breach, lost in it.

Lying to her already, before he'd even spoken.

She saw the Blackbird in his hand. Her eyes narrowed, confused.

"Did you take off its key?" she said. "It's dangerous even without it—"

He held it up to the light, showed her the cellophane-like key still attached to it.

"It's dead," he said. "Shut down after I killed Pilgrim. I don't know why."

She held his eyes, stared deep into him. If she saw through what he was saying, it didn't show. She moved closer. Her eyes softened. Her hand touched his arm.

"Hey," she said. "It's over. Whatever it was, it's over."

He nodded and managed something that wasn't entirely a frown. She folded into his arms.

Over her shoulder, he found himself staring into the Breach. Blue and purple like a bruise, reaching away to infinity. He considered the track of his future, another path leading somewhere he couldn't see. Leading to something that would remake him into a man Paige wanted dead. Something lying in his road, out there in the darkness, years and miles away from this moment. Waiting.

"It's over," Paige said again.

He held her tightly, and hoped she was right.

Like **THE BREACH**?

Don't miss the next
Travis Chase adventure
GHOST COUNTRY
Coming Fall 2010 from Harper

Turn the page for an excerpt . . .

Travis Chase took his lunch break alone on Loading Dock Four. He sat with his feet hanging over the edge. Night fog drifted in across the parking lot, saturated with the smells of vehicle exhaust, wet pavement, and fast food. Out past the edge of the lot and the shallow embankment that bordered it, the sound of sparse traffic on I-285 rose and fell like breaking waves. Beyond I-285 was Atlanta, broad and diffused in orange sodium light, the city humming idle at two in the morning.

Behind Travis the warehouse was silent. The only sound came from the break room at the far south end. Muted voices. The occasional beep of the microwave. Travis only went in there to put his lunch in the refrigerator and to take it back out.

He finished eating, wadded the brown bag, and tossed it into the trash bin next to the box compactor.

He turned where he sat, brought his legs up, and rested them sideways across the edge of the dock. He leaned back against the concrete-filled steel post beside the doorway. He closed his eyes. Some nights he caught a few minutes' sleep like this, but most times it was enough just to relax. To shut down for a while and try not to think. Try not to remember.

His shift ended at four-thirty. The streets were empty in the last hour of the August night. He got his mail on the way into his apartment. Two credit card offers, a gas bill, and a grocery flyer. All addressed to the name

Rob Pullman. The sight of it no longer gave him any pause. The name was his as much as the address was his. He hadn't been called *Travis Chase*, out loud or in writing, in over a year.

He'd seen the name just once in that time. Not written. Carved. He'd driven fourteen hours up to Minneapolis on a Tuesday in March, timing his arrival for the middle of the night, and stood on his own grave. The marker was more elaborate than he'd expected. A big marble pedestal on a base, the whole thing four feet tall. Below his name and the dates was an inscribed verse: *Matthew 5:6.* He wondered what the hell his brother had spent on all of it. He stared at it for five minutes and then he left, and an hour later he pulled off the freeway into a rest area and cried like a little kid. He'd hardly thought about it since.

He climbed the stairs to his apartment. He dropped the mail on the kitchen counter. He made a sandwich and got a Coke from the refrigerator and stood at the sink eating. Ten minutes later he was in bed. He stared at the ceiling in the dark. His bedroom had windows on two walls. Both of them were open so the cross-breeze could come through—it was hot air, but at least it was moving. The apartment had no air-conditioning. He closed his eyes and listened to the night sounds of the city filtering in with the humidity. He felt sleep begin to pull him down. He was almost out when he heard a car slow at the entrance to the lot. Through his eyelids he saw headlights wash over his ceiling. The vehicle stopped in the lot but didn't kill its engine. It sat idling. He heard one of its doors open, then light footsteps came running up the front walk.

Then his door buzzer sounded.

He opened his eyes.

It couldn't be anyone he knew. There *wasn't* anyone he knew.

He listened for buzzers going off in other apartments—he'd heard that before, when people came to the front door and hit every button until someone let them in. He didn't hear it now.

He pulled the sheet aside and stood. He went to the window and pressed his face against the screen to get an angle on the front door.

There was a girl down at the entry. She was standing on the walk, a few feet away from the pad. She'd pressed the button and stepped back from it. She was staring up at the open window of Travis's bedroom—had been staring at it even before he appeared there—and now she flinched when she saw him. She looked nervous as hell. The vehicle parked thirty feet behind her was a taxi cab.

The girl looked about twenty, but it was hard to say. She could've been younger than that. She had light brown hair to her shoulders. Big eyes behind a pair of glasses that covered about a quarter of her face—they were either five years behind the style or five years ahead of it.

Travis had never seen her before.

She'd seen him somewhere, though, if only in a picture. It was clear by her expression. She recognized him even by the glow of the lamppost in the parking lot.

She stepped off the concrete walkway onto the grass. She took three steps toward the window. Her eyes never left his. She stopped. For another second she just stood there looking up at him.

Then she said, "Travis Chase."

Not a question.

Travis ran the possible implications through his head. There weren't many. Actually there was only one.

"Paige Campbell sent you," he said.

The girl nodded.

"I was under the impression Paige would show up herself," Travis said, "if she ever needed to talk to me. Which would only happen in an emergency."

"I'm sorry," the girl said. "But Paige *is* the emergency. She left a message instructing me to find you here. Right before she disappeared."